DOn't DRaG THiS OuT

Emery Lee

EMERY LEE

ISBN: 978-1-967512-03-4

First Edition:

10 9 8 7 6 5 4 3 2 1

Author's Note

Over the past four years, I've been asked many times if I'd write a sequel to *Meet Cute Diary* or *Café Con Lychee*, but my answer has always been the same—I don't have any story left to tell! But the more the question came up, the more I kept coming back to this story I had pitched as a joke to my group chat about two older brothers falling in love in the most ambitious crossover of our lifetime. It's hard to sell traditional publishing on sequels—often even harder to sell them on spinoffs or crossovers—so I never planned for that book to become a real thing.

Then I shared the idea with my readers to a huge outpouring of support, and we managed to get the entire book crowdfunded, and now it's here, my silly little exploration of what happens when worlds collide and two hopeless older brothers fall in love at a drag show.

While this story is cute and humorous, just like *Meet Cute Diary* and *Café Con Lychee*, it does touch on some more serious topics such as toxic relationships, mental health, queerphobia and queerphobic slurs, racism, and ableism. If any of these topics become too uncomfortable for you, I highly encourage you to set this book aside to return to at a later date or not at all.

And, finally, I would like to thank my readers, those of you who've been around since day one and those of you just coming onboard today. This book truly only exists because of readers' dedication to seeing more queer books on shelves and their passion and love for the stories I tell, and I could not be more grateful for that. I hope this story helps to provide some closure for those of you seeking more after *Meet Cute Diary* and *Café Con Lychee*, and for those of you coming onboard for the first time, I hope you find something within these pages that you want to carry with you, wherever you end up next.

Some marks, once made, never really wash away, and Brian was learning that lesson a few too many times this summer.

"Would bleach work?" he asked, holding up his shirt to showcase the little wine smear just below the breast pocket.

Pearl's eyes shot wide from where she sat on his bed, business pants and heels still on from work. "On *satin*?" she squealed. "I swear, you straight guys are hopeless."

Brian rolled his eyes as he cast the shirt aside. It was one of only three nice shirts he owned, a gift from his father before he set off for New York to start his internship. Brian wasn't the type to attach sentimental value to a scrap of fabric and a swatch of buttons, but he had to admit that he'd put a whole lot of faith into the garment, and watching it flutter to the disheveled carpet of their two-bedroom apartment was making some of that faith fall, too.

Pearl stepped up next to him, eyeing his pathetic closet with a pitying look. "Aren't you late?"

"Yes! Which is why I need something to wear!"

"You're meeting up with your *girlfriend*. Wear whatever."

But that was a sentiment reserved for people like Pearl, who'd been dating the same guy since he'd staged a flash mob promposal to ask her out junior year of high school. For people like Brian, who'd traveled across the country to spend the summer with the love of his life and prove that he really was the perfect boyfriend for her despite their many, many differences, the nonchalance of "who cares?" wasn't really on the table. Especially not when, after only three weeks in the city, Anna had insisted Brian come over to meet her parents.

"I have to make an impression, Pearl! It's not every day you find a girl you want to build your whole future with."

He waited for the standard Pearl follow-up questions, already pulling up all the reasons he was sure that Anna really was perfect for him—how good she was with the kids when she'd visited Brian at work at the summer camp, the way she'd also grown up in a city but still wanted to settle somewhere quieter, her ability to talk 80s rock with his dad for a solid hour straight—but instead, Pearl's eyes locked on something in his closet. She leaned forward, pulling out the gray blazer he'd worn to his internship interview. "How about this?"

He'd considered i, before the pressure had really sunk in. But since he'd moved to New York and gotten that free gym membership with his job, he'd put on a few pounds of muscle that made the blazer a little tight. It wasn't exactly the type of thing he'd wear to impress his girlfriend's wealthy parents.

Then he glanced at the wall clock above his twin bed.

Okay, the blazer it was.

Even on the warmest days, the steeliness of the Manhattan skyscrapers made Brian feel small. Comparable, perhaps, to the mountains of Denver, but even coated in a perpetual layer of snow, the distant peaks felt warmer—the difference between a natural piece of earth tall enough to humble a person versus a man-made structure meant to keep certain people humble.

When he'd lived in Florida, he'd associated wealth with beachfront mansions, private yacht parties, and a penchant for golf clubs, but New York's upper elite were a different sort of wealthy—penthouses on the highest floors, luxury cars with nowhere to drive, and sterile lobbies lined with security guards to remind people like Brian that even if the doors opened long enough for them to enter, they were only ever visiting.

He texted Anna that he was outside as he began his trek down the long, marble-floored hallway. Everything about the place felt too expensive, like if he even touched a doorbell, he might shatter it and spend the rest of his life paying it off.

As he reached the dark apartment door, it swung open. A white woman stood in the doorway, both familiar and not, the spitting image of Anna, but showcasing a few more years on her face and several thousand dollars more in her finely pressed pantsuit and gold earrings. Her hair was pulled back in an elegant bun with dark ringlets cascading along the sides of her face. The lines surrounding her mouth and eyes looked more like fine sketch work than wrinkles, each one elegantly carved to add to her poise rather than steal from her youth.

But as she glanced at him, her icy gaze froze him in place.

Then, she looked past him, scanning the hallway with a feverish desperation. When her eyes finally returned to him, resignation settled along the lines of her face.

"Hi. Um, good evening," he said, rushing to hide the embarrassment he felt as her eyes roved along his too-tight blazer. "Um, I'm Brian. And you must be Mrs. Hastings."

She flashed him a grimace but offered no confirmation that he'd arrived in the right place until she stepped back into the loft and called out, "Darling, your...boyfriend is here."

Doing his best to keep his face from reacting to her words, he followed her over the threshold, quickly scanning the entryway for somewhere to put his shoes but finding none.

If the two-two, barely five hundred square foot space Brian rented with Pearl and her boyfriend, Dustin, could be labeled "an apartment," it felt deceptive to use the same term here. The vaulted ceilings and wall-length windows made the massive, open floor plan feel even larger, and as Anna scurried down the hallway dressed in a bright green cocktail dress, the red-brick walls rose like tidal waves around her.

"Brian!" she squealed, racing up to him and throwing her

arms around him. The familiar warmth of her embrace melted some of the frost still clinging to his muscles.

When she pulled away from him, a stray strand of her dark hair fell from her ponytail, and he tucked it behind her ear. The elegant slope of her nose, the sprinkle of freckles along her forehead, and the strawberry scent of her perfume were all comfortingly familiar. Standing there with her, the apartment started to feel more familiar, too—the red brick and city skyline through the windows that served as the backdrop for her Instagram icon, the stack of throw pillows on the white suede couch laid out exactly the same as the stack she'd left in Brian's dorm back in Denver, and the collection of plants she'd lined the window sills with, several of which he remembered from her own Colorado apartment.

"I'm glad you're here," she said, sliding her hand into his.

Anna led him over to the couch, but he eyed it warily. It was a bit too white to sit on—none of the pet furs and crumbs he was used to from his friends' couches or the protective coverings his grandmother was so in love with.

With a gentle tug to his wrist, Anna sat, pulling him down with her. A moment later, her mom brought a tray of tea over, pouring the reddish blend into three cups. Anna took the first, but Brian hesitated before grabbing the second. He didn't want to think about what kind of irremovable stain he might leave behind if he jumped in too eagerly.

"Your father will be right out," Mrs. Hastings said curtly, turning her face toward the kitchen like just the sight of Brian and Anna holding hands was too much for her to stomach.

A door opened down the hall, shoes pattering down the hallway until a man stepped out. He was of average height and broad-shouldered, hair thinning at the top, but the eye more eagerly drawn to the bold mustache above his lip.

Brian flashed the man a smile, but the look returned to him left a pit in his stomach.

Mrs. Hastings interrupted the cold stare-off, clearing her throat before saying, "This is Anna's boyfriend, dear."

"Ah, I see," the man said, his voice gruff as he crossed the room and sat down next to his wife.

The room fell quiet. Brian reached for a teacup, but the tea was bitter in a way no sugar could sweeten.

Anna all but chugged her own cup before setting it back down on the tray. "More tea?"

Before Brian could say he was pretty sure he'd had more than enough, Anna pulled him to his feet, gently leading him toward the open dining room, where a coffee cart lay in wait for them, a porcelain kettle perched atop it like a white flag.

Anna cleared her throat just as her mother had a few moments prior, dropping her voice low as she said, "I'm sorry. For the awkwardness."

Brian waited for her to say something else, but she just froze, eyes locked onto the kettle like her life depended on it.

When he'd agreed to meet Anna's parents, there'd been some apprehension about sitting down with two people who earned more in a year than he'd probably earn in a lifetime, but he'd also known it was inevitable. He and Anna had been together for a year, and while his internship was in Manhattan, he'd only agreed to spend a summer in New York because he knew she'd be there with her family. And since Anna had met Brian's brother, Noah, the last time he'd visited Denver and joined Brian a few times during his family video calls, it was about time he spent some time with her parents.

But while he'd worried about impressing them, he hadn't prepared himself for them to turn their noses up at just the sight of him.

"At least I'm not just imagining it," he said because he wasn't sure what else to say. "So, what now?"

"It's probably better that you just go."

Even whispered, the words echoed awkwardly off the expensive marble and minimalist stainless steel. "*Excuse me?*" Brian said, a sharpness to his tone that he hadn't meant to put there. "You're just telling me to leave?"

"I mean, what else do you want me to tell you?" Anna

snapped. "It's not like tea and small talk is going to fix this."

Which was irrefutable, but was it really asking too much for her to defend his honor in the slightest? He'd come all this way just to make her happy, and yet she was acting like he'd stormed in and spat on her mother's ten-thousand-dollar rug.

"So what is *this* exactly?" Brian shot back.

Anna turned to face him, her mouth drawing downward in a frown. It was strange to think that just that morning he'd been kissing those same lips with reckless abandon, thinking about how perfectly the two of them fit together.

"I don't know what you want from me, Brian," she said. "I can't help that my parents are the way that they are."

"Racist?" Brian said, letting the unspoken words rise to the surface. "Did you not tell them I wasn't white?"

"I told them you were Hispanic, which you are!" Anna said.

Brian spluttered. "*Hispanic*? Jeez, why not just say we're Spaniards to make it easier? The whiter the better, right?"

Anna rolled her eyes. "Oh my God, you're being such a diva. My parents aren't racist. They were probably just surprised when they saw you, but you've made everything so awkward, and now of course things are going to be weird."

Brian paused, mouth gaping. "Wait, you're blaming *me* for this?"

"I wasn't blaming anyone until you started blaming *me*."

It was only as the room fell quiet that Brian realized how distinctly *not* quiet they'd gotten. How much had her parents overheard? Did it matter? What was the point of standing here trying to explain racism to this white girl and her parents who couldn't even look him in the eye?

"Look, I think we've both said more than enough," Anna said. "So, you should just go."

Which was probably the best thing she'd said all day. "Fine."

"I'll walk you to the door."

"Don't bother," he said. "I don't think we have anything left to say to each other."

Despite never traveling by foot until his time on campus, Brian didn't hate the New York City commute. It served as a great opportunity to get some alone time in, even when surrounded by two million random strangers. With everyone doing their own thing together, it was all actually rather calming.

The terrifying part was taking the trains—schedules, transfers, random people performing with an open guitar case and desperately trying not to meet their eyes because you didn't have any cash on you and didn't want to hurt their feelings when they were actually really good at their craft. Navigating it all was a learning curve that Brian wasn't sure he'd ever fully acclimate to, and considering he was from a city where people stood out in the street soliciting money or selling car bobbleheads and mangoes they stole out of their neighbors' yards, he could only imagine how overwhelming a place like this would be for a small-towner.

Still, the city wasn't without its upsides. With an apartment and a summer job located a few intersections from each other, he wouldn't have to worry about taking the trains anymore now that he and Anna were over. It'd just be three months of getting drunk at home, watching Netflix, and only turning up for the handful of work events he was expected to attend. An overall relaxing summer, even if he was guaranteed a lecture from Noah the next time they saw each other for wasting three months in the Big Apple.

It was a small price to pay for some peace and quiet. Fighting through the crowds in Times Square, clinging to Anna's hand so they wouldn't get separated, trying to focus on the smell of Anna's perfume to ignore the creeping odor of horse shit as they traversed Central Park—he hadn't minded it all before, but it was the Anna part of the equation that made it all worthwhile. Big cities were never really his thing, and the biggest, smelliest city with its too bright lights and too many tourists and never-ending traffic jams was probably better off with one less person roaming its streets.

Stepping out onto the sidewalk after clearing the subway

stairs, Brian looked down at his phone to see a text from Pearl saying, *Grab oat milk on your way home, please?*

On his list of things he could actually stomach about New York, bodegas were pretty high, so he didn't mind stopping at the one a block from his apartment to grab Pearl's oat milk. The place had felt pretty cozy to him ever since Anna asked to pop in there, telling him all about the bodega she used to hang out in with some middle school friends and painting the messy little shop in secondhand memories. As he pushed the door open, even the fat cat in the corner reminded him of Anna crouching down to try to scratch its head the last time she and Brian had come through.

Brian quickly shuffled into the tiny shop, bypassing the old lady counting cans one aisle over as he headed toward the oat milk. The trek was becoming a bit familiar since he'd stopped in for Pearl a few times since moving in, but he wasn't sure how to feel about the muscle memory now.

Once upon a time, he'd really thought his summer in New York would be less about navigating the whatever-letter trains and more about setting down roots. Maybe not *in* New York, per se, but *with* Anna. She was the big deciding factor in choosing to take an internship with an LGBTQ+ nonprofit's PR & Marketing team despite "building queer community and connecting queer youth with necessary resources" not being anywhere on his list of special skills. That wasn't to say that he didn't feel some sort of passion for the queer community— especially with his brother being trans—but it wasn't the type of job that really paid the bills, and it certainly wasn't a gig he could see himself getting a full-time job in post-graduation. It was just a job he could enjoy that gave him all the time in the world to spend with Anna as they went about planning their new lives together.

So what the fuck was he supposed to do now?

He stared at the long line of oat milk in front of him, quickly grabbing one off the shelf. It was a simple, menial task, but he could focus on it for now. Just buy the oat milk. Just get home. Just keep putting one foot in front of the other until some direction started calling out to him again.

Brian shot a quick smile at the cat in the corner before checking out and walking the block back to his apartment. Even if his name wasn't technically on the lease, it was easier to refer to the two-bedroom, one bath with the bad paint job and rusted dead bolt as "his" apartment. In the past three weeks, he'd developed a fondness for the place, even if he almost always had to take the stairs up to the third floor since the elevator was typically broken. The fuzzy feelings probably said more about Pearl and Dustin as roommates than the eighteenth century building itself.

Locking the door behind him, he cut through the tiny living room crowded with two mismatched couches and Dustin's art supplies. The equally cramped kitchen boasted old, cracked tile, permanent sauce stains, and one petite Pearl perched on the counter, a lopsided coffee mug in hand. "Oh, you're back early."

"Uh, yeah," Brian said, prying the fridge open long enough to shove the oat milk where it always went along the door. "Things went south pretty fast."

"Oh?" Pearl raised an eyebrow as she lifted the mug to her lips again.

The lopsided ceramic looked like the kind of thing Brian associated with preschool arts and crafts, but when he'd asked Pearl about it, she'd insisted it was simply avant garde, a gift from Dustin for their first anniversary, which must have meant something given they were still together five years later, while Brian was single once again.

He winced. "Let's just say, I think I'm back on the dating market."

"Aw, shit, I'm sorry," she said. "You wanna talk about it? I give great relationship advice."

"Easy for you to say when you've only ever been with one person."

"Okay, but that doesn't mean I'm not great at helping

others," she said. "Why do you think I work for a nonprofit?"

It might take a special kind of person to put all their life's energy into helping other people with a promise of low pay, weak benefits, and pretty frequent mistreatment, but that didn't mean Pearl was capable of fixing the disaster that was Brian's love life. It wasn't just that he'd dated a lot of girls. It was also that the relationships always ended badly, dating back to his first college girlfriend, who'd turned out to be a transphobe. And then there was the one from a few months later who'd turned out to be an anti-vaxxer.

And now, eight girls later, there was Anna.

It would require a specialist to figure out how he kept falling for people only to realize they were nightmares in disguise, but his afternoon with Anna's parents had just confirmed for him that he didn't have the money to afford one.

"How do you find someone you vibe with who isn't a secret asshole?" Brian asked.

Pearl smirked. "Date a bi guy. They're the sweetest."

"Noted."

With a laugh, she scooted off the edge of the counter. "You know what your problem is?"

"Bad luck?"

"You fall in love too fast," she said. "You just nose-dive into the honeymoon stage, and then you miss all the red flags and fall head over heels for the person you think you're with instead of the person you're actually with."

"We've lived together for three weeks, and you know all this about me, do you?"

Pearl shrugged. "I see it all the time."

Where, exactly, an administrative assistant for a queer youth community outreach organization was "seeing" this specific brand of relationship disaster was a question Brian didn't care to ask.

Before arriving in New York, he'd met Pearl through a company Discord group just after he'd signed onto his internship, and that had pretty much changed everything. She'd taken the reigns and dragged him along, inviting him to spend the summer shacking up with her and Dustin for minimal rent payments, and he'd eagerly accepted because he'd been raised never to turn down a good deal.

And despite Pearl being more forward, combative, and impulsive than Brian could ever imagine being, he'd found they had quite a bit in common. Her third-gen Filipina heritage vibed with his Asian American side, and her food tastes and appreciation for indie music made him feel right at home.

"You going to the show tonight?" Pearl asked, drawing Brian's attention to the Dinner and Drag Show he'd spent the last two weeks assisting with.

"Do I have a choice?"

Technically, events were optional, but Brian's supervisor was insistent he go to everything, since it would "help him really get a feel for these things." He wasn't sure how to tell her that he didn't see himself working in events after his internship ended, so he just went along with it.

He groaned, running a hand through his hair. "I forgot I told everyone that Anna was coming. Now what?"

"Tell them you broke up."

"I don't want them in my personal business."

Pearl shrugged. "Then tell them she got sick? You're missing the point."

"Which is?"

"It's a dinner and *cabaret* show?" Pearl said, raising her eyebrows. "Bruh, you just dropped the one thing holding you back from getting wasted and having a good time. You're twenty-one. Live a little. Enjoy the view!"

Brian just rolled his eyes. "It's a *drag* show."

"So?"

"*So?*" Brian said. "So, I'm straight and recovering from a bad breakup. How is this gonna solve anything?"

"Oh, honey, you *need* to get out more." Pearl draped an arm around his shoulders. "Besides, you know how important this event is if we're gonna secure future funding. Don't you want the thirteen-to-twenty-four-year-old queer New Yorkers to have somewhere to turn to in their time of need?"

Brian rolled his eyes. "Guilting me is not the way to do it."

But he also didn't know how to refute that argument without dismissing the value of their whole organization, so he decided to just let her have this one.

2

Just like the perfect fabric cut and stitched to a flawless fit could imbue its wearer with unmatched power, awkward lumps and makeup stains always left Thomas feeling absolutely helpless.

It was a lesson he'd learned from a young age, plopped in front of the TV watching Sailor Moon reruns. If one gaudy brooch could turn Usagi from a weeping mess into the all-powerful Neo Queen Serenity, the right costume could surely take Thomas from an awkward nerd into…well, something he could be proud of. It was why he'd first started cosplaying, putting countless dollars and hours into dressing up like whatever character he'd hoped seeing in the mirror might hit him with a rush of dopamine.

"You know, makeup, by any other name, has historically transcended cultures and gender," Thomas said, the pre-performance jitters careening him straight into info-dump territory. "Makeup could mark a great leader, be used for masking purposes—"

Kris didn't even look up at him as he said, "So what, pray tell, is the historical significance of glitter liner? You know, other than fabulosity?"

Thomas rolled his eyes, slipping his last palette into his makeup bag. God, his makeup bag. Just the fact that he'd actually spent his hard-earned money on one was probably enough to give his grandmother an aneurysm.

There were still a few hours until the show—another half hour before they needed to head out from the little studio apartment Thomas was renting from the Korean couple that lived downstairs—but Thomas was already nervous rambling. He'd invited Kris over in the hopes that having a friend to chat with before the show might calm his nerves a little, but Kris's presence was making things worse.

"You wanna grab a late lunch before we head over?" Kris asked.

But Thomas was sick to his stomach as it was. "Um, better not. Don't want your clothes to be too tight."

"Bitch, please, could not be me, but I respect your abundance of caution."

Thomas resisted the urge to roll his eyes.

There was a fine line between confident and cocky, and Kris often barreled completely through it before running another couple miles straight into "egotistical douche." Thomas knew his opinion was a little bit biased since he'd bounced from admiration to a deep-seeded, unearned jealousy toward Kris ever since they'd been introduced by a mutual friend two years before, but it didn't dampen the feelings that swelled up in him about three-fourths of the time when Kris spoke.

It also didn't help that Kris was exactly one of those white twinks that the queer community glorified to no end and straight society deemed the epitome of true gayness. It was like he'd been carefully carved by the drag gods to make him the ultimate canvas for deconstructing toxic masculinity while never once having to question white beauty standards. Thomas's insecurity aside, though, Kris was the one friend who'd taken Thomas's side when he'd been unceremoniously cast out of his previous circle. The powerful cocktail of gratitude, envy, and intimidation proved to be just enough to hold their friendship together like hot glue.

After all, no matter how powerful the tiny skirts, fake titties, and thousand pounds of makeup could make you feel, all it took was one bitter bitch to remind you that it was still all just playing dress up.

But bitterness was contagious, and Thomas was doing his best not to catch it. It was why he'd moved out to New York in the first place—a new city, a new start, and a new drag community. Well, except Kris, who was both his one familiar lifeline and his one unfortunate reminder of how much it hurt to spend three years climbing the drag ladder only to be unceremoniously kicked off a middle rung.

Thomas stepped over to his costume trunk, carefully tucking the edges of a half-finished cape into the body of it before closing the top.

Unlike cosplay, drag wasn't as simple as tossing together a costume and posing for a couple of pictures with someone dressed as his fictional lover. It was a whole counterculture—a community of people with something to prove and even more to say, a deconstruction of restrictive gender norms and an exploration of self on a public stage. Suddenly, donning the perfect costume wasn't just an ego boost and power play—it was a responsibility.

The shoes he stepped up onto that stage in weren't just about matching some character's aesthetic. They were about telling a story to his community, laying himself out as a statement in billowing fabric and fishnets and glitter liner, and honoring the people who'd lived and died fighting for his right to wear them.

Drag was all about freedom and self-exploration and a bunch of other things that had gotten lost in all the torn seams and regret. Ever since the falling out, he hadn't even been able to bring himself to do another show until tonight, constantly putting it off, saying he was still working out his next look or waiting for inspiration to strike. He'd been too afraid to admit that getting shunted from the community back home had been enough to convince him that no amount of intricate costuming and makeup could ever cover up the fact that he just didn't belong there.

Since coming to New York, he'd set all the pieces in place to reinvent himself—a new apartment, a new job, a new drag persona that was a little more him and a little less "my college friends helped me pick this out." He wasn't in Vermont anymore. He wasn't bound by whatever rules he'd let govern his life for the last twenty-two years. He could finally try to piece together enough confidence and charisma to build something that wouldn't fall apart at the first misstep.

It was time for him to step into a skin that fit just a little bit better.

The trip from Queens to Manhattan was an easy trip by train, but given their trunks of clothes and wigs and makeup bags, wading through the turnstiles and out to the platform made Thomas's skin crawl. In the time he'd spent in the city, he'd gotten pretty used to the roaring noises, industrial smells, and inconsistent lighting of navigating the stations, and but while drag was liberating at bars or conventions, even the thin layer of makeup he had on as they boarded the train felt like a neon beacon, inviting every passerby to scrutinize him until he died of mortification.

Not that anybody ever did. This was New York City. But even though he'd been there for just over a month, he couldn't shake his roots. Not just the way he always felt like he was drawing eyes back home by being Asian in a white-majority state, but the specific terror of knowing any person on the street could be one of his parents' customers, ready to report back seeing their oldest son in drag. Even being in New York, he had no way of knowing if any random stranger might be friends with some of his mom's family that lived in the area. Then again, running into one specific individual in Times Square was like trying to hunt down your lesbian friend at a Home Depot.

"Enough with the deep thought," Kris said, jabbing Thomas in the shoulder. "You're driving me crazier than I already am."

Kris didn't even glance in Thomas's direction, a compact mirror open in his palm as he carefully applied rhinestones around his eyes. There was an inherent lack of self-preservation involved in applying glue and gems to one's face in a New York subway car, one that Thomas wasn't sure if he should respect or fear. Probably both.

"So now I'm not allowed to be nervous?" Thomas said.

"Oh, honey, no. *Nervous* is normal. You look like—well, I'm gonna need you to do a one-eighty if you're half as sick as you look like you are."

Thomas rolled his eyes but turned his face away anyway. He wasn't about to throw up on the elderly woman crocheting in the seat next to him, but Kris's flippant tone was still grating. It was easy to be condescending about someone else's nerves when you already knew you were guaranteed success.

The whirring whine of the train speeding down the track served as another reminder that Thomas was completely out of his element. Vermont traffic was practically nonexistent, and driving down the open roads with the green mountain backdrop felt like dozing to lo-fi compared to the cacophony of honking horns and squealing tires that served as the standard rush hour soundtrack out here. The dull roar of chatter and footsteps through the train car permeated by the occasional ping or announcement that was too muffled for Thomas to make out only made his blood pressure skyrocket.

When they finally reached their stop, Thomas carefully navigated the exiting crowd and the small anthill of people already surrounding the doors. His eyes darted desperately around the teeming platform like a priest in a sex shop before Kris finally cut past him, latching onto his wrist and dragging him along.

Out on the street, people skittered along the sidewalk in a traffic flow that was one part comfort with the city and two parts dictated by a force of nature. The seamless ebb and flow of people rippled like the tides, bodies spilling past one another fluidly, another always following behind to take the place of the last.

Like he'd been molded from the city itself, Kris easily slipped into the cosmic pull of the city's inhabitants despite the fact that he'd only lived there a month longer than Thomas. Tugging Thomas along like a small child at an amusement park, he sidestepped a sewer drain to keep his heels from slipping into the holes before slipping past a pile of trash laid out on the street.

The hotel awning loomed ahead in a bold hunter green, and Thomas fixed his eyes on it. As they stepped over the threshold into the lobby, he let a rush of air flow out of him.

Large and filled with a low rumble of chatter and rolling luggage, the lobby stood in weird contrast to the city street. Everything felt too clean, too bright, golden hues over white floors and cream walls. Before Thomas could stumble around like a lost chick, Kris led him over to the front desk, giving a quick introduction and asking where they could meet the LGBTQ Center program coordinator.

"How are you so good at this?" Thomas asked as they stepped away from the front desk, mild annoyance lacing his tone.

Kris just flashed him a smile. "You would be too if you stopped dragging your feet about everything."

"What's *that* supposed to mean?"

Before Thomas could insist on an answer, a member of the LGBTQ center stepped out to greet them. She had a friendly smile despite her thick, stern eyebrows. The rainbow "Staff" shirt she wore felt even more ridiculously bright in the overwhelming light of the lobby, but at least Thomas could focus on the little black and white nametag resting on her chest.

"Hi, I'm Ella, she/her/hers," she said, extending her hand out to Kris. "I'm the events and talent coordinator. We spoke via email."

"It's nice to meet you," Kris said. "I'm Kris, pronoun indifferent. This is Thomas, my friend I was telling you about."

He dropped his voice low and said, "She's new."

Thomas jabbed Kris in the shoulder, quickly turning to Ella and saying, "Thomas. He/she/they, all fine."

Ella smiled. "It's great to meet you both. I'll take you backstage so you can get ready."

She motioned them forward, quickly crossing the lobby and bypassing a pair of double doors that Ella vaguely gestured at without stopping. "This is where the ballroom is, but we'll head in the back way to get you to the dressing rooms. Tonight's event is in partnership with the university geek club, and it's eighteen plus, so feel free to do whatever makes you comfortable, get a little risqué, show a little skin…"

Kris smiled. "Oh, sweetheart, you don't have to tell me twice."

Thomas just turned his face away so Ella wouldn't catch sight of the blush rising in his cheeks.

"I'm sure you'll both be amazing," Ella said as they stepped down a long hallway toward a side door. "We do a lot of outreach events in partnership with the local high schools and universities, but this is our first drag show. We actually polled a lot of our usual attendees, and most of them said they'd never seen a drag show before, so you'll be their first! Leave 'em with a good impression."

She pulled open the side door, and they entered the ballroom. A wide swath of tables sprawled out in front of the stage, and they quickly took the four steps up onto it, stepping around a room divider that led to an open doorway. As they entered the hallway beyond, the lighting in the space changed— bright overhead lights against an industrial backdrop. To their left stretched a line of all gender bathrooms and to the right, a collection of vanities, some already occupied by a few other queens, music playing as they brushed their wigs and fitted their eyelashes.

The first show Thomas had ever done was back in Vermont at his university, only two other queens involved, no pay, and a bunch of loud, college students caught up in a haze of beer.

Maybe that should have turned him off from it altogether, but he'd jumped into it whole-heartedly after that, even if his schedule was tight between school and work and squeezing in time with his family.

After leaving his old drag life in the ashes of his university friend group, the idea of doing another show particularly targeted at college students, and even more specifically tied to geekdom, wasn't something he could resist. It had felt like the perfect opportunity to step back into all the things that had drawn him to drag in the first place in a relatively safe environment.

But it was only now, standing in the dressing room, that it really hit him just how exposed his costume left him.

"Let us know if you need anything," Ella said. "Oh, and break a leg!"

"Merci beaucoup," Kris said as Ella rushed out of the dressing area. "I love doing the little shows where people actually appreciate you, you know?"

But Thomas was too busy clutching his trunk for dear life to pay attention to anything Kris was saying.

Just standing in that dressing room, he already felt the smallest he had since he'd first gotten ousted from the drag community in Vermont. Surrounded by New York City drag queens—the kind with tons of money and experience who probably had stage credits like Broadway or Drag Race rather than the local queer bar with a max capacity of sixty people— the voice in the back of his head told him he was a liar for even trying. These other queens were the real deal. They could step out onto that stage as anyone they wanted, and it'd be undeniably believable. He'd stumble out after them like a kid who'd gone digging through his mother's make up only to end up sloppier than Jared Leto's Joker.

"Relax, will you?" Kris said, stepping over to one of the vanities. "It's literally not that serious."

"Um, I'm gonna go to the bathroom," Thomas said, quickly escaping to one of the all gender rooms and slipping inside.

It'd been a while since he'd felt uncomfortable changing in front of other people, but he pushed the awkwardness aside as he pulled out his costume—a gray leotard coupled with fishnets and character gloves. God, was he really about to go out there and make a fool of himself?

He shook his head, digging his fingers into the buttons of his shirt. The slight quiver to his hands as he unfastened each button and the clamminess already forming in his palms were just distractions he wouldn't waste time on. Once he stepped into costume, the rest would slip into place like his favorite pair of shorts, just like it always had when he used to do cosplay and back when he'd first started doing drag.

Under the glaring, overhead light, this was his magical girl transformation. Nerdy, awkward Thomas could be sucked into the void or wherever else it was the main character always went behind all the flourishing sparkles and upbeat music.

He was Mia Sake—powerful, beautiful, and radiating confidence.

Once he was dressed, he stepped out of the bathroom, quickly dropping his makeup bag in front of one of the open vanity mirrors. Even while he knew most of the people getting ready around him, Kris was the only one he didn't feel like he was intruding on, so he opted to sit next to him.

Kris whistled. "That's a lotta skin for you, isn't it, baby?"

Thomas flipped him off, but he couldn't help the blush rising in his face. Nothing a little foundation couldn't cover.

"Oh, honey, don't be nervous," Day said as they flashed him a smile from over Kris's shoulder. Thomas knew them from work, but they didn't talk much beyond Day passing Thomas their coffee order. Their rich, dark cheekbones had already been highlighted to the heavens and back, but they twirled the brush in their hand as they reached for their highlighter palette. "First time?"

Thomas laughed awkwardly. "Not exactly."

"Bitch has been on hiatus for a little too long," Kris said.

Thomas shot him a look, but he figured Kris was pretty much invincible now. He'd only finished the makeup portion of his Princess Belle look, but he already looked like royalty, just like he always did. He pulled out a shredded corset, and Thomas just eyed it warily.

"*Bitch*, what the fuck is that?" Day turned to Kris with the highest raised brow Thomas had ever witnessed.

Kris just flashed them a radiant smile. "I mean, what else would you expect after a night with The Beast?"

Day turned back to where Thomas was laying his character claws out on the vanity, eyebrow still raised. Thomas just flushed, staring down at the floor.

"Totally unrelated," Thomas mumbled.

Kris laughed, but Thomas just floundered around in his makeup bag looking for his foundation. It was very Kris to get a nice little chuckle at his expense.

"Look, there's nothing wrong with feeling a little choked up before a show," Day said. "It just means you've got something to say, and you've got even more reason to be here."

The words felt a little undeserved coming from the mouth of a queen dressed like Storm, only with twice the skin and no visible electricity. But Thomas felt his stomach settle a bit as he uttered a soft, "Thank you."

"Any time.

3

There wasn't anything inherently wrong with showing up to a work event without someone on his arm, and under ordinary circumstances, Brian might even consider it liberating.

But these were not ordinary circumstances.

While Pearl had headed back to her room after their conversation for some time to chill and get ready for the show, Brian had headed to the liquor cabinet. He needed a shot. Just something to take the edge off while he battled with himself over whether or not to fake the flu to get out of leaving the apartment.

Then Ella sent a photo to the work group chat of her and her girlfriend looking like teenagers at their first concert, some of the drag queens posed behind them, and Brian realized there was no way he was getting through the night sober, regardless of where he spent it.

Just after seven, Pearl basically pried Brian off the couch to say that Dustin was waiting for them downstairs, and they should get a move on if they didn't want to be late. By that point, Brian had worked most of the way through Pearl's rum reserves, so he stumbled to his feet, barely aware of whether he'd actually agreed to go or if Pearl had made the decision for him.

The trip to the hotel had been a blur of busy streets and passing crowds interspersed with just the occasional familiarity—the little taco truck Anna had fallen in love with at first bite, the intersection where they'd met up when Brian first got to town, and the bar Anna had dragged him to as celebration of his first completed day at his internship. Now he was standing out on the street, arm feeling too light without Anna's weight leaning against him, wondering how well he could hold onto said internship now that he was showing up to an event already plastered.

"I can't go in there," he snapped as Pearl pushed him toward the door.

"Sure you can," she said. "No one'll notice."

The show was being held at a four-star hotel in Koreatown, and while Brian had spent countless hours there as his team had gotten everything in place, showing up there after hours with the lingering taste of rum on his lips felt like the worst possible plan.

"Losing my girlfriend and my internship all in one day is not a great score to have," Brian said.

Pearl laughed. "What are they gonna do? Fire you? You're off the clock, and you barely get paid anyway."

"Dustin, do something!"

But Dustin just followed a few feet behind them as Pearl shoved Brian into the lobby.

"I don't know what you want me say," Dustin said. "I can't change Pearl's mind once she's set on something."

"Bruh, you're whipped."

Pearl grinned. "Now move it!"

The state of the hall should've been a source of pride for Brian, the countless hours and hard work he and his team had put into it evident the moment he entered with Pearl and Dustin. While the stage was provided by the venue, the sprawling sea of round tables adorned in colorful tablecloths so that the horde of them together cast an illusion of the pride flag, the specialty lighting that cast a savory tone over the space while they waited for the performances to start, and the smell of the catering drifting in from the kitchen were all carefully selected by the event planning team. Even decisions like where to order the cutlery from had plagued his mind for the past few weeks as everything was strung together. And now, here it all was, the culmination of their labor laid out for everyone to appreciate.

But Brian could appreciate it least of all.

A sea of faces filled the tables, the low buzz of chatter joining in with the soft drone of the music hovering around them. Most of the crowd was unfamiliar to him, but he ducked his face anyway, trying not to draw the attention of anyone who might put in a bad word about his terrible condition.

"Oh, good, they haven't started yet," Pearl half-shouted as she looked around the room for somewhere to sit. "You think Ella's around here somewhere?"

"I tell you I don't want to be seen, and your first instinct is to sit with my supervisor?" Brian snapped.

Pearl waved him off with a laugh. "Whatever, she's cool. Oh, there she is!"

Brian only hesitated for a moment before swallowing his pride and following Pearl and Dustin through the crowd.

Ella sat at a near-empty table, only a purse and a drink keeping her company a seat over.

"This place looks great," Pearl said as she invited herself to sit down. Dustin and Brian followed suit, leaving the seat next to Ella open.

Looking up from her phone, Ella flashed Pearl a smile even as exhaustion weighed down the corners of her brown eyes. "Thanks. Things were kind of messy during the rehearsal, so hopefully that's all straightened out."

"Oh? How so?" Pearl asked.

"Let's just say, it's hard to find good lighting help these days."

"With our budget?" Pearl said. "We're lucky we're not sitting in the dark."

Pearl and Ella laughed, but Brian couldn't bring himself to give their small talk much attention. Just keeping his body moving in normal motions was becoming a full-time job.

Ella looked over at him, flashing him a grin. "I didn't think you'd show."

Brian blinked, trying to screw his face into a look of alertness. "I—wait, why?"

She shrugged. "Straight guys aren't usually into drag."

Considering he'd given that exact excuse to Pearl earlier, he didn't really have any right to disagree with her comment, but he reached for his napkin and grumbled, "You know, my brother is trans."

"Yeah, you've said," Ella said with a short chuckle. "Well, I'm glad you could make it anyway, given how much we're banking on tonight to do some heavy lifting. Meg just stepped out for a smoke break. I told her she should get away from all the hairspray before she accidentally lights someone up."

Brian had never met Meg, but Ella had mentioned her a few times before. Plus, Ella's phone background was the same photo of her and Meg that she kept on her desk. While they didn't have the high school sweethearts schtick Pearl and Dustin boasted, they had been together almost a decade now, which would surprise no one who laid eyes on the two of them together. Even in photos, they fit like a custom frame—the matching shades of brown to their hair and the mirrored smiles when they looked at each other, the way Meg's small stature left her perfectly fitted under Ella's arm, and the way said arm folded perfectly into the round curves of Meg's waist. They were sweet in a way that was only soiled by the bitterness Brian felt at being the fifth wheel.

"Speaking of which," Ella said, the words shooting through Brian's head like squealing breaks just before a car crash, "is what's her face on the way?"

"Oh, Anna?" Pearl suggested.

"*Pearl*," Brian snapped.

She rolled her eyes. "Better to just not ask."

Ella spared him a pitying look, but he turned toward the stage in his best attempt at ignoring it. While the alcohol had taken some of the edge off his grief, it came back to him now why he'd sought out the bottle in the first place.

That pitying look.

God, he hated it.

Because of course Ella would feel sorry for him when the love of her life was just outside on her smoke break. Of course, Dustin and Pearl would think him tragic given their perfect six-year relationship. Everyone around him had found their soulmate so easily, and here he was, debating whether or not he should step out of the room to call Anna and beg her to give him a second chance. As bad as things had been with her family, were they really worse than the curse of being single among a swarm of happy couples?

A woman stepped out on stage looking uncomfortable in a messy bun and a dark green dress that lumped awkwardly around her like it was just a size too small. It was almost cruel to have a volunteer embarrass herself ahead of a bunch of glamorous drag queens, but she smiled out at the audience like she wanted to reassure everyone that she wasn't being held against her will.

"Thank you all for coming out tonight and supporting a great cause," the volunteer said. "Just a reminder that while your admission fees support our organization, all tips go to our queens, so definitely considering opening up your wallets if you see something you like." She laughed awkwardly, the crowd staring back silently. "Um, okay, so without further ado, here are your hosts for tonight's show—Miss Lana Del Reina and Brandy Wine."

The volunteer skittered off the stage as two queens stepped out to replace her, and the crowd erupted in cheers.

"Well don't you all look lively tonight!"

"They always do until you get talking."

A laugh rippled through the crowd as warmth settled in the air, like a gentle embrace of familiarity as the queens introduced themselves. As a visitor both to New York and the world of drag, Brian wasn't sure how many of the locals knew them from other shows, but the crowd was already smitten, hanging onto every line of banter batted between the two of them.

But Brian's attention was already starting to wander.

Not that they didn't look impressive with their wigs swirled up like cotton candy and elaborate makeup straight out of an art gallery, but as Meg slipped back into her seat at the table and Ella took a quick second to introduce her to everyone, a wave of claustrophobia washed over him. The lights, the music, the queer jokes he probably shouldn't even be allowed to laugh at without it being considered a hate crime—it all came crashing down around him like a hurricane. By the time the first performer stepped out, launching into a lip sync of "Fabulous" from *High School Musical 2*, all the colors on stage were starting to bleed and blur together. He needed to get out of there.

"Oh, bro, are you gonna hurl?" Pearl whispered at him. "Cause you should step outside for that."

He rolled his eyes. "I'll be right back."

"Grab a mint on your way back!"

Brian pushed Pearl's comment aside and bee-lined for the door. The hotel blurred by in a rush of color as he cut through the lobby and then found himself back on the street.

The Manhattan evening air was still something foreign, so much more humid than when he'd been in Colorado for school but still cooler than the Miami nights he'd grown up with. Coupled with the lights and the people and the vague smell of trash and piss and vehicle exhaust that lined every crevice and alleyway, it lacked the sort of grounding comfort fresh air was supposed to bring.

He leaned against the hotel wall, staring up at the starless sky. He missed Denver, the mountainous landscape and clear, empty nights at the edge of the city. Even growing up in Miami, he'd never understood the concept of being surrounded by so many people but feeling so alone until he got to New York. Loneliness wasn't just a feeling here. It was a living, breathing soul that shadowed him like an unshakeable companion.

In the time he'd spent with Anna, the loneliness had felt more like a shadow. Just the right amount of light, and it would retreat. At just the right angle, he could almost pretend it'd never existed at all. But now, the memory of their time together haunted him. Was there anywhere he could go in this city that wouldn't hold the ghost of her scent or the lingering taste of her mouth against his lips?

Slipping his phone out of his pocket, he stared at the blank screen, a bubble of disappointment settling in his chest. No amount of denial could hide the fact that there had been a part of him, no matter how conflicted that part might be, that had hoped Anna would call.

He glanced up, half-hoping she'd be standing just a few feet away, bathed in the city's lights, arms crossed the way they always were when she felt a little out of her element as she tried to muster up the perfect apology. It was the sort of hopeless idealism he'd expect from Noah, but then, maybe idealism was just the crutch of the desperate, and maybe that was just what Brian was.

Against his better judgment, he hit the call button, placing the phone to his ear while he waited through the ringing.

I'm unable to answer your call right now…

Groaning, he hung up, reflexively reaching for Noah's contact instead.

It felt almost degrading to have to call his little brother for advice. Maybe that was where some of the desperation stemmed from. Here he was in New York City of all places, and he couldn't even string together a fun Friday night while his younger brother had managed to curate the perfect life for himself. Humiliating.

After a few rings, Noah's voice cut through the other end with, "What?"

"You don't have to be rude," Brian said.

Noah laughed, accompanying the sound of shuffling coming through the phone. "It's a Friday, and I have plans, so what could you possibly want, brother?"

"*Plans?*" Brian said. "Since when do you have plans?"

"Since Devin's here."

Oh, right.

It wasn't that Brian had a problem with Devin. Actually, Brian rather liked em. E was a pretty chill person, nice if not a little awkward, though it seemed like maybe e'd shaken off some of that once e'd started college.

But the last thing Brian's fragile ego needed right now was a reminder that his little brother was heading out on a date while he was still single. Noah and Devin had been together for two years now, a picture-perfect fairytale couple like Noah had always dreamed of. Even living on opposite sides of the third largest state, they were constantly calling or video chatting or roadtripping to see each other, and sometime in the spring, Noah had mentioned that they were roping Noah's best friend, Becca, in to launch some sort of queer youth writing program or something. At this rate, they'd be shopping for wedding venues, and Brian would still be waist deep in Tinder profiles.

Brian sighed. "You know what? Never mind."

"Are you okay?" Noah asked, the usual snarky edge to his voice disappearing for a moment.

But Brian wasn't interested in getting that pitying tone from Noah. It was bad enough getting it from Ella. "Just bored. Forget it. Have fun on your date."

"How are you *bored* in Manhattan? You—"

Brian groaned, ending the call. He had to admit, there was something weirdly empowering about hanging up mid-sentence. Now he understood why Noah did it.

And maybe Noah was right. Maybe there was something to be said about how sorry it was to be bored in Manhattan, a city so vibrant and full of life and vigor that people would pay an arm and a leg just to spend a weekend there. And maybe it was even worse that Brian was at a cabaret show with friends, and he still couldn't bring himself to have a good time.

But how the hell was he supposed to enjoy a city this big

when all it could do was remind him of just how alone he was?

The alcoholic stupor that'd clung to him since he'd left his apartment had already waned, so Brian stopped at the hotel bar before heading back to the show.

Besides the occasional beer at the occasional party, he pretty much stuck to water, so as he bypassed the one other patron sitting at the end of the neon-lit hotel bar, took a seat on one of the chipped leather stools, and slapped his card and ID down in front of him, he decided to keep things simple. A rum and coke. Quick to down, and then he could head back to the show and convince himself to have the time of his life.

Only the first drink went down a little too easy, so he ordered a second before finishing that one, too, and ordering a third to take with him. He ignored the knowing smirk the bartender shot his way as he stumbled away from the bar.

There was a point in time when the booze stopped feeling warm as it slid down his throat, where the dulled edge of his problems drifted into fuzziness and white noise. He wasn't sure at what point his drifting down the hallway started to feel more like floating, but he was grateful that he'd navigated the venue enough times while planning the event to rely on muscle memory to guide him.

He pushed the door open, awkwardly scanning the tables in search of Pearl and Dustin. The room was a little unsteady under the bright wash of blue light, and he realized he had no idea where he'd left them. They could be just about any of the shadowed faces in the crowd for all his mind could make out.

He took a few steps forward, scanning to his right, and then another few before scanning to his left. The bright blue light filling the room felt like a flashlight shined directly into his eyes, and weird, atmospheric music floated around him like he was about to get spirited away into some animated feature.

If luck were on his side, he'd wake up and realize he'd passed out on the couch after a few too many drinks, the blue glow and whimsical tunes just the TV he'd forgotten to shut off spilling into his dream world.

Instead, he felt a tap on his shoulder.

Turning around, his eyes landed on the most beautiful woman he'd ever seen—dark eyes surrounded by a flurry of thick, dark lashes, cheekbones sharper than any mountain in Denver, and cherry red lips turned upward in a cheeky grin. Her whole face practically glowed, like she was an angel with a halo of light surrounding her.

Except, in place of a hand, it was a gray claw that moved away from his shoulder.

Along the top of her head, a pair of gray, pointed ears peeked out through dark strands of hair. Whiskers like ink traced her cheeks, and triangular patches of gray fur wove across her chest.

"My, Totoro, you've changed," Brian mumbled.

She giggled, her exuberantly long lashes brushing her cheeks as she blinked. "Do you mind, sweetheart? You're kind of in the way. That is, unless you wanna ride my kitty."

Brian spluttered, warmth rising in his face. "Ride—what?"

Her voice was painfully teasing as she said, "I have a bus to catch," and gently turned his face with her claw, pointing him toward a large screen where the massive, cartoon cat bus from *My Neighbor Totoro* stared back at him with a look so condescending, he could only imagine it was mocking him, too.

A chorus of laughter broke out through the crowd, flipping a switch in Brian's brain.

She wasn't glowing. She was standing directly in the spotlight.

Right. The drag show.

Which she was a part of.

And he, most certainly, was not supposed to be.

"I—"

"No, no, it's okay. Allow me," she said.

She pressed him back against the stage, sliding along past him to squeeze between him and the table just next to her. The fluff of her tail and the netting of her fishnets brushed across

Brian's waist and against his arm as she wiggled through the tight space. His breath hitched in his throat as he pieced the scene together—here he was, pressed against the wall by a sexy Totoro.

A *very* sexy Totoro.

And he'd just touched more of her than was probably appropriate, regardless of what kind of show this was.

Laughter and cheers tore through the crowd, but Brian's whole face caught fire—and not from the alcohol.

"I—sorry," he said.

She dropped him a quick wink. "No worries."

She was on the move again, but before Brian could think, he was racing through the crowd, stumbling over his own feet as he searched for the nearest door and spilled back out into the hall again, his heart thudding in his chest.

He told himself it was just the adrenaline of being caught under the spotlight that had his blood pressure skyrocketing. That was all.

His phone vibrated, and he fumbled it out of his pocket, looking down at the screen as Anna's name filled it. He stared at the name for a moment as he struggled to remember who she was and why he'd called her earlier.

All the feelings rushed back over him—the conflicting love and disgust and anger and humiliation. Even through the drunken haze and blurred thoughts, her name sent a dull ache thudding through his chest. All the empty promises. All the bending over backwards to save something long since dead. All the hopes that would never amount to anything. He couldn't make sense of them now—not this plastered—and he wasn't even sure if he wanted to.

Turning his phone on silent, he headed back out to the city street.

4

Applause at her back, Thomas floated backstage like drifting away on a cloud. She couldn't remember the last time she'd felt that invigorated. And while her whole performance had been a sort of out of body experience, that last bit especially had left her feeling uniquely powerful. Relying on improv usually sent her spiraling into a ball of anxiety, but somehow, she'd managed to bat that drunk guy between her claws like a cat jostling its favorite toy, and the audience ate it up. The wave of applause was so big that only the blindingly bright light of the dressing room could drag her back down to earth.

She followed the sound of low voices and laughter as they washed around her.

"Yeah, but that slut will sleep with literally anyone."

"You heard that hick accent. She'd probably sleep with her own cousin."

"Well, we knew she wasn't right in the head. That's for damn sure."

Thomas turned the corner to find a group of four queens gathered together around the otherwise abandoned vanities. She immediately recognized Felix—one of her bosses at the tech startup—but the other three took a moment to place. Two of them were also temporary hires at Thomas's job—Lola and

Damien, she was pretty sure—but the last one she didn't recognize. Probably not someone who ran in any of her other social circles. Yet, despite these three leaving very few marks on Thomas's memory, the tone of their conversation felt like a shard of glass jabbed between her ribs.

Gossip was a poison, and as long as you were on the side dealing the doses, it kept you feeling as powerful as a tidal wave of applause could, but Thomas remembered what it felt like to have the vial wrenched from her hands a little too well. Now just the mere mention of it was enough to churn her stomach, like her body remembered all too well the pain her mind had done its best to forget.

"Who're you talking about?" she asked, her voice low.

She and confrontation went together like suede and polyester, but she couldn't just stand by waiting for the dressing room air to be overrun by toxins. She couldn't even imagine how she'd feel if people were back here talking shit about her just as she struggled to get her confidence back.

Lola flashed her a smile, waving her off and saying, "Oh, no one. You did amazing, by the way!"

"Thanks," she said, but the word fell flat into the space between them.

She tried to box them out as she stepped over to her stuff, but she could still see them out of the corner of her eye as they ducked their heads together to continue their conversation.

"Hey, Mia."

Thomas turned to find Day walking up behind her, already pulling some of the pins out of their wig. "Um, hey."

"Do you wanna go for drinks with a few friends later?" they asked.

Day had the sort of welcoming and warm energy that, coupled with the sincerity of their tone, was almost enough to convince Thomas that she wouldn't just be a nuisance if she tagged along. This was obviously just the sort of polite invite a coworker extended to keep from causing any drama at the company water cooler, but Thomas had to turn her face away to ignore Day's wide, brown eyes or she'd forget that.

"Oh, um, that would be nice," Thomas said, fumbling around for a polite excuse, "but I came with Kris, so I should check with her."

"Oh, cool. Well, she already said she would come, so—"

Thomas's eyes shot wide. "Did she now?"

Day laughed. "It'll be great to have y'all. I'll text Kris the location."

Thomas forced a smile before turning back to the vanity.

She'd only really planned on coming back to the dressing room long enough to get out of her claws and then catch the tail end of Kris's performance, but even the cheers tearing through the undertones of *Beauty and the Beast* had little impact on her overall excitement for the show. It was so like Kris to agree to plans without even checking with Thomas first, and so unlike Thomas to have the energy to jump from one social activity to another. It was already a lot just to be in the show at all.

And then there was that guy who'd stumbled in during her performance. He was obviously just some drunk college guy who'd wandered in through a wrong door, but Thomas had to admit that he was cute, cute enough that regular Thomas would never have had the guts to so much as talk to him.

And yet, Mia-Thomas had rubbed her ass all over him.

The audience may have loved it, but now that the costume was coming off, Thomas felt vaguely ill about the whole thing.

She shook her head, quickly chasing any rogue thoughts out. She needed to focus on her next steps. As powerful as she felt in a good pair of heels, she wasn't about to go strutting through Manhattan in full drag, and if she got cleaned up fast enough, she could even spare a few moments of peace in isolation, even if that meant hiding in a bathroom stall until Kris was ready to leave.

"Super rude of you to just agree to plans without telling me."

"Bitch, if you want to go home at nine-thirty on a Friday

night, you shouldn't've befriended so many fire signs."

Thomas rolled her eyes as she and Kris made their way down Broadway.

It was still kind of amazing how lively the city was at nine thirty. No one was heading home, closing shop, or turning out the lights. If anything, the street was just getting brighter as everyone headed out for the evening.

"I didn't say I was going home," Thomas grumbled. "I just wish you'd asked."

Kris shot her a look, the piercing blue of her eyes tearing straight into Thomas's soul. "You're young, you're hot, you got your groove back. What more do you need?"

Not only did Kris have eyes sharp enough to cut glass, but Thomas suspected the term "if looks could kill" was coined specifically for her.

"You're so uptight, I swear," Kris said. "We gotta get you laid."

"I'm good."

"Oh really?" Kris said with a lilting tone that set Thomas on edge.

"What?"

"Who was that guy from earlier?"

Thomas shrugged. "Someone else's gay awakening just waiting to happen, I'm sure."

"You didn't know him?"

"Should I have?"

"Please. He seems like exactly the type you need. Tall, hot, and not a lot going on upstairs. The perfect plaything."

"Yeah, no thanks." But Thomas knew there was only one way to get Kris off of a topic once she'd latched onto it, so she said, "So how long did it take you to make that ball gown just to rip it off mid-show?"

Kris laughed. "Believe it or not, it actually wasn't that long. I already had the base, so—"

And with the conversation turned to Kris, Thomas figured she could just sit back and enjoy the night air while Kris drawled on about herself for a while.

When Day had said "a few friends," Thomas had presumed the definition of "a few" to mean the customary "three," or even "maybe four." However, when they reached the bar and grabbed their drinks—filtering past the crowd dancing to the loud thrum of music and heading for the patio—Thomas quickly found herself at a table with Kris, Day, Felix, and six complete strangers who were all at various stages of wasted.

"So happy you two could make it!" Day said as they joined the table.

Much like Thomas, Day had stripped off most of their drag makeup, tossing the wig and costume in favor of a plain black t-shirt and a pair of dark jeans. With their shaved hair and a single gold ring in their ear, they'd somehow mastered the androgynous look while still exuding a whirlwind of both masculine and feminine energy.

"I'll never pass up an opportunity to drink," Kris said, and Thomas could pretty much vouch for that.

Thomas quickly tossed back a shot, but she wished she'd grabbed something a little more hands-on. There were way too many people around for her comfort, too many voices bleeding into the muffled music leaking out of the bar. At least if she had a cup to fiddle with, she might not feel so *watched*.

She turned toward the twinkling patio lights that hung overhead like the bar hoped they could make up for the Big Apple's starless skies. Despite the thrum of the music bouncing through her seat, the patio lay almost startlingly quiet compared to the dance floor below, which meant Thomas could at least decompress a little. But it also meant she'd probably be forced to make at least a little small talk.

"It was a fun show, huh?" Day said. "I love the college crowds. They're always interesting."

"If only they paid more," Kris said.

"Oh, they do if you get the right side of town."

Felix draped an arm around Day's shoulders like it was just

a natural reflex as he said, "I did a show near Columbia once. *They* paid in several ways."

Day just rolled their eyes before pushing Felix's arm off. "I don't think Kris does coke." Then Day paused for a moment, an eyebrow slowly rising. "Or *do* you?"

"Bitch, I'm not doing anything harder than NyQuil unless you want me trying to blow your stepdad's ficus again."

They all laughed, but the easy conversation between them grated on Thomas's ears. It was the same at the office. Kris had helped Thomas get the job, explaining that Day was launching a tech startup under their stepdad's company, and they wanted some fresh minds to help test run their first app and bounce ideas off of. When Kris first brought it up, it sounded like a fun little escape from Vermont. It was only once Thomas actually arrived in New York that she realized how cutthroat the project really was. It was just supposed to be a queer networking app, but suddenly, she had a whole floor of temporary hires competing with her for a long-term position, and the only thing she had going for her was that Kris was her friend.

But Kris was obviously better friends with Day and Felix, and with the three of them running the show and bringing in their own recruits, Thomas doubted being friends with Kris would mean much come the end of the summer. That was, assuming Kris even cared to keep her around that long. Considering how fast Kris had dropped all his college friends the second he left Vermont, Thomas wasn't naive enough to believe there was something special between them keeping their friendship from falling apart.

Thomas jumped to her feet, awkwardly glancing around before saying, "I'm gonna grab another drink."

Kris raised an eyebrow at her, mouthing, "*You good?*" Thomas just offered a quick, almost imperceptible nod before scurrying off to the bar.

A part of her was grateful that Kris had adopted a habit of checking in with her to make sure she was okay, but right now, she was pretty sure it just made her look bad in front of her coworkers. It wasn't like Thomas had no basic gauge of social etiquette, but she couldn't just sit still at that table. At least not while she was this sober.

And really, she was a stone, cast out over an open lake and left to sink to the bottom. Even if she managed to settle among a new group of rocks, that didn't mean she was actually supposed to be there. They may not have noticed it during her performance tonight, but eventually they'd realize she was just a Vermont outcast stumbling around trying to fit in where she didn't belong.

Maybe the guy at the show earlier had the right idea. Maybe it was better to just get drunk and let the tides pull her. Maybe being out of place didn't feel so bad when you were too wasted to realize the space you were occupying was never yours to begin with.

5

"Brian, what the *fuck*?"

Brian's brain rattled around like the swirling insides of a snow globe. Only as his eyes blinked back against the sunlight spilling into the room did he realize that the room wasn't actually being tossed around like something a small child had picked up at a souvenir shop. The reverberating pounding was the sound of Pearl's fist smashing against the wooden door as his head bounced along with the beat.

He grumbled, reaching for his phone and checking the time. Just past eight.

And he had five missed calls from Anna.

His sheets were knotted around his legs, but he kicked them back as he sat up, letting his forehead rest against the cool, bare wall for a minute as he pieced the night before back together.

"Gimme a sec!" he called out.

Even after Pearl stopped knocking, the room felt unsteady, and his brain continued to throb. He tossed himself out of bed only to stumble into the nightstand. Maybe all of this was just the universe's way of scolding him for leaving the show early to go to a bar by himself.

"If you're not out in five minutes, I'm kicking the door down!"

Brian threw the door open to find Pearl standing on the other side, eyebrows raised. "Morning," he grumbled, stepping past her and heading for the bathroom.

Pearl laughed. "You okay?"

"Egh."

Pearl laughed again, a spike of pain shooting through his head.

The bathroom door closed just a little too loudly as he leaned awkwardly over the sink. The room swayed underneath him, so he put all his focus into taking each mundane task one by one. Turn on the faucet. Rinse his face. Grab his toothbrush.

But he wasn't sure how he was gonna deal with Anna. God, why the fuck had he called her?

With a towel-dried face and a mouth tasting of mint, he walked out of the bathroom to find Pearl pouring two cups of coffee.

"What happened to you last night?" she asked.

He shrugged, accepting one of the mugs from her. "The show was a little much, so I just went to a bar."

"Jeez, drinking alone? You could've just drank with us."

"Yeah, about that. I couldn't actually find the table."

"You know, for someone who's pretty smart, you're not very bright," Pearl said, slapping his arm. "You could've just texted me."

Brian raised the mug to his lips, half burying his face behind the glossy white surface. "Seemed like a hassle."

"Ah, so instead you decided to jump into the middle of the show? You're lucky that queen was a good sport. She could've shamed the hell out of you, but instead you just got the VIP treatment."

Right. The queen.

The one dressed as sexy Totoro.

As far as oxymorons went, that sounded like a pretty ambitious one, and Brian told himself that if he'd been even halfway sober, he would *not* have been nearly so turned on by an animated bunny-type character reimagined with boobs and fishnets.

But there was also a memory surfacing in his head as he stood in the kitchen, one he was pretty sure had never happened in real life.

One involving nails and tongues and about two-thirds of that sexy Totoro costume in shreds on the floor.

God, that was one hell of a dream.

"Brian?" Pearl said, waving a hand in front of his face. "You good?"

"Huh?"

"I was just saying that you have to stop running from your problems." She finished off her coffee before reaching over to pour herself another cup. "If you're really this broken up about Anna, maybe you should call her. Or just get back out on the dating scene. But I don't think bailing on your friends and embarrassing yourself in front of your boss is the solution you're going for."

"This is all your fault. I told you I didn't want to go."

"My fault?" Pearl snapped. "I was just trying to help you have a good time because you were all broken up. You could've really enjoyed yourself if you hadn't kept fighting it."

Brian forced down the first instinct that told him to fight *that* and tell her how wrong she was. Even if there was a part of her that was wrong, there was also a part of her that was right, much in the way that Pearl so often was. If he hadn't rushed out of the show to call Anna and reopen that can of worms, maybe he could've had a good time, gone out afterwards with the team, and stumbled into the perfect rebound girl at some bar instead of waking up to a hangover and a million missed calls.

But then, if he hadn't stepped out, he wouldn't have stepped in just in time to run into that queen.

But that hadn't amounted to anything more than an awkward shimmy and some tail action, no matter what his dreams were telling him.

"And I don't even know her name," he mumbled.

"Whose name?" Pearl asked.

Brian looked up to find her staring back at him inquisitively. Quickly ducking his head, he raised his mug to cover half of his face. "Nobody. Nothing. Don't worry about it."

Pearl eyed him suspiciously. "Did you meet someone last night?"

"It's not like that. Um, Anna called me while I was sleeping, so I'm gonna go call her back. Maybe we can straighten things out."

Pearl nodded, but the arch to her brow told him she wasn't quite letting go of the conversation. "Yeah, okay. Let me know how it goes."

"Will do," Brian said, quickly ducking back toward his room before she could change her mind about letting him leave.

Pacing a room the size of a shoe closet wasn't exactly a workout, but a few feet could easily turn into a mile as Brian spent the next twenty minutes running from his problems.

He'd all but worn a hole into the deteriorating carpet when he got a text from Pearl saying, *I'm heading out. Talk later!* Which was both a relief, since he wasn't sure he'd be ready to face her any time soon, and a call out reminding him he'd wasted twenty minutes but still hadn't called Anna back.

And it wasn't because he didn't miss her or even that he didn't want to smooth things over. Ironically enough, it had more to do with what Pearl had said.

You miss all the red flags and fall head over heels for the person you think you're with instead of the person you're actually with.

There was certainly an argument to be made about Pearl needing to mind her own business since they hadn't even known each other that long.

But there was also a voice in the back of his head shouting that she was right. Maybe he was always ignoring the bad in favor of falling in love with the idea of the person. Did he only miss Anna because he'd convinced himself to look past the red flags and pretend she was something she wasn't?

And then there was the part of his brain that kept asking

what Noah would do in a situation like this. He would probably drop Anna faster than he'd dropped his old wardrobe the second he decided to transition, not only because he was more confident and decisive than Brian, but also because he could never look past someone he disagreed with politically.

And, in a way, it made sense. Why try to make things work with someone who could never understand things that were so integral to your existence? But isn't that exactly what every successful long-term couple was doing? Finding a way to "make it work?" If he didn't settle, wasn't he all but guaranteed to end up alone?

God, dating sucked.

He plopped down on his bed again, staring at his phone screen like the answer would magically pop up in front of him. Then a call came through, lighting up his screen. But it wasn't Anna. It was Ella.

"Hello?"

"Hey, Brian," Ella said, a little rise to the end of her words like she was barely holding herself back from something. "Hope you're okay after last night. Party a little too hard?"

Brian winced. "Yeah, I guess so."

Ella laughed. "Nothing wrong with celebrating the completion of an event well done. Anyway, I know you're technically off today, but I was wondering if you might want to come help out."

"Why would I want to do that?"

"Well, Carla called out, so we're a person short," she said. "But don't worry. It's not cleanup duty or anything. Marty decided last minute to do a promotional video before we put the recording up on the website, so some of the queens are coming back for a short shoot. You'd just be an extra pair of hands in case we need anything."

But Brian's mind was already racing with clipped images of stockings and skin and snippets of a dream he most definitely should not be recalling while on the phone with his boss.

Some of the queens are coming back for a short shoot.

What were the odds that she'd be with them? Not that low. How many performers even *were* there last night? It was definitely a much higher chance than stumbling into her again somewhere out in the city.

But then, was there really anything to get out of finding her again? If he couldn't make things work with Anna, what hope did he have with this random stranger?

"Brian?"

"Um, sure, yeah, I'll be there in an hour."

He needed to stop overthinking things. Because it didn't really matter what the odds were.

When you asked the universe to intervene, and it offered you a door, you didn't have a choice but to use it.

6

If there was a single thing Thomas hated about makeup, it was the way it lingered.

It was worse than a hangover—the cakey feeling of his skin no matter how many wipes he used to try to scrub it all off, the way the lines of his lips were always just a little too pink afterwards.

And while he was the type of person who couldn't even wear sunscreen without feeling weighed down by it, the worst part about the makeup stains was the betrayal of having your skin broadcast your sins like a neon sign. On mornings like today, when he desperately needed to wash yesterday's events down the proverbial drain, the weight of lipstick remains on his skin might as well have been a flaming pride flag stapled to his chin.

It was just a quick, two-hour lunch in Chinatown before his parents flew back to Vermont. But he knew better than to assume any event with his parents could ever be that easy.

Ever since he'd begun exploring his gender and sexuality, the already sensitive dance of engaging with his parents had become more like rollerblading over a field of landmines. They'd already been thrown for a loop when his younger brother, Theo, had come out a few years prior, and Theo was, indisputably, a much more straight-friendly kind of gay than Thomas could ever be. It wasn't Theo's fault that he leaned more Neil Patrick Harris while Thomas leaned more Billy Porter, but it also didn't serve as encouragement for Thomas to open up to their parents about his "alternative lifestyle."

Sometimes, the rant his grandmother went on before cutting them out of the family still replayed in his head—calling Theo an embarrassment, telling their mother that she failed as a parent, that the whole family would be ruined because she'd raised such a shameful son. It wasn't the first time she'd said some vile things about Theo, but the vitriol in her tone still struck Thomas like a stab to the ribs when he least expected it. He'd done his best to shield Theo from the worst of it, but he couldn't protect his own mind from the constant chorus of, *now imagine if she saw you in a dress.*

Boarding the train to Manhattan, Thomas did his best to push those thoughts from his mind. His parents were just in town as part of their "scouting the competition" mantra, which was really just an excuse for them to try as many new restaurants as they could. If there was any mercy in the world, they'd be too invested in comparing menu fonts and judging the shop's soy sauce to even notice that there was still some glitter around his left eye that he'd fought like hell to get off.

The doors slid closed, and he headed over to one of a handful of vacant seats, trying not to think too much about how even on a Saturday without all the commuting workers, the train cars were never empty. As loud and overwhelming as the city could be, he was pretty sure he'd rather stay than return to Vermont at the end of the summer. It wasn't just the painful sterility of living in such a white, suburban neighborhood, but the fact that any "stealth" he'd had before moving west was long gone now. If trying to contort himself back into a shape that could get by in his family for a few hours was this hard, he couldn't even imagine trying to reshape himself for Vermont.

He pulled out his phone, despite the fact that he almost never had signal underground. The act of locking and unlocking his screen just gave him something to focus on as he avoided a deep spiral into doomsday territory.

Once he cleared the train, he kept his head down as he darted toward Chinatown. Despite the sidewalks being a little less crowded than usual, it felt like everyone was closing in around him. He put his focus into keeping his breathing steady even as his heart rate increased with every step.

"Wow, don't you look miserable!"

The familiar voice shocked Thomas out of his deep-thinking. Theo stood a few feet away, waiting just past the crosswalk with a dorky grin on his face. The relief Thomas felt at seeing him was quickly overshadowed by the awkwardness as his eyes landed on Theo's boyfriend, Gabriel, standing next to him. Once upon a time, Gabriel's family was public enemy number one, and Theo would've willingly ridden a cheap metal tube down to the bottom of the ocean before spending ten minutes with the guy, but now, to Thomas's disappointment, they were almost never apart.

"I see nobody ever clipped that tongue of yours," Thomas bit back. "They should work on that."

"Good to see you, too," Theo said.

A feeling of warmth settled over Thomas as he stepped onto the sidewalk and looked at the line of restaurants. Despite the distinctly New York style architecture and layout, the red lanterns and Chinese text felt almost as familial as seeing his brother. The smell of hotpot and dim sum and the melody of Mandarin tones buzzing through the passing crowds grounded him for a moment. This was definitely his favorite part of New York.

When Thomas's mom had called to let him know they'd be in town, she'd also mentioned that Theo would be taking care of the shop, but obviously that plan had been thrown out. With the shop being a joint venture between their family and Gabriel's family, letting the Morenos take over for a weekend might seem like a reasonable course of action, but Thomas had his suspicions that his parents still didn't fully trust them to handle things on their own, even if they'd worked together for a couple of years.

But then, if Theo was here, too, maybe that meant things had changed.

"Theo. Gabriel."

"Uh, you can call me Gabi," Gabriel said, a line Thomas was certain he'd heard before, but he still elected to ignore him. There was just something supremely off-putting about addressing his brother's boyfriend who he barely knew by a nickname, and the last thing he wanted to do was accidentally imply they were friendlier than they were.

"Anyway," Thomas said, "where are the parents? And what are you guys doing here? I thought they were coming alone."

"You thought we'd just miss out on the free food?" Theo said. "Not in a million years."

"Thomas!"

He turned, catching sight of his parents as they made their way over to them. His mother had never been a very tall woman, but given Theo had shot up a few inches over the past couple of years, she looked even smaller as she joined them. Then she bypassed Theo entirely, stepping up to Thomas and pulling him into a hug. Ordinarily, a hug meant he should be asking whose funeral they needed to prep for, but she'd gotten a bit more physically affectionate over the last few years, which Thomas could only assume was partially Theo's fault.

"Hi, Mom," Thomas said, carefully pulling away. "You look lovely. Hope everything's going well at home."

"Yes, it's good," she said, waving him off, "but it'll be better when you come home."

He just offered her a sweet smile in place of dropping the news that he would hopefully not be doing that.

"It's good to see you, Thomas," his dad said, squeezing his shoulder. "How's the city treating you? Find a girlfriend yet?"

Kris's voice surfaced in the back of his mind saying, *Not a girlfriend, but maybe a new boo thang,* and Thomas's face instantly heated in mortification.

"Okay, okay, screw the pleasantries," Theo said. "I'm hungry. Can we eat now?"

"Theo!" their mom snapped.

But their dad just laughed, motioning them away from the crosswalk and toward the restaurant.

Thomas turned to Theo, mouthing a quick, "*Thank you*," and Theo just flashed him a grin.

"So how's your new job?" Theo asked, a diabolical smirk spreading across his face as he pulled his wooden chopsticks apart. "Sounds like a *drag*."

Thomas kicked him under the table. "It's great, actually. I really can't complain."

It was so like Theo to try to get a rise out of him in a bustling hotpot restaurant surrounded by their parents and a hundred strangers, but given he was the only person in the family who knew about Thomas's hobby—and had managed to keep that secret for a few years—Thomas let him get away with it.

The booth they'd set up shop in extended further than the typical New York haunt would allow, but Thomas figured that was why their dad picked the place. They'd barely gotten their menus before he and their mom were already rattling off a list of appetizers they wanted brought out, and now the table was so overcrowded, Thomas was rushing to get plates stacked and ready to take away before the waiter could bring out their main courses.

"You make computers, right?" his mom asked. "I ran into your old teacher at the store, and she asked about you, so I told her you make computers."

Thomas winced, taking an empty plate out of her hand and adding it to the stack. "You know what? That's fine. Just tell them I make computers."

He'd already given the "it's a software company, and I'm really just there to help look for bugs with the app" spiel a few times, so it hardly seemed worth the fuss to try again.

"If you get bored, you should come back and work for the shop," his dad said, and Thomas just nodded along in what he hoped was a convincing act. "We're launching a new line of drinks next month. It was all Gabi's idea."

Thomas froze.

"I—well, it wasn't *all* my idea," Gabriel said, his brown cheeks darkening. The guy was like Rudolph with how easily his face lit up. "I mean, Theo and I were talking about changing things up a bit, and it just came to me."

"Please don't call me your muse," Theo said, smiling almost giddily at Gabriel. "That's corny even for you."

Gabriel flashed Theo the most enamored smile Thomas had ever seen, and suddenly, even the rice cake was starting to taste bitter.

"Sounds like a blast," Thomas muttered. "Unfortunately, I'm very busy, so I probably won't be by the shop for a while."

Silence slammed into the table, but Thomas did his best to ignore it as he focused on his dish stack like it required expert precision to manage.

A few moments passed in silence before he decided that he needed a better distraction. "I, um, I'm gonna go to the bathroom before the food comes out," he said, rising from the table.

"Thomas," his mom said, her eyes narrowed with alarming severity, "you better not try to pay the check."

Theo stood, too. "I'll go with him to make sure he doesn't."

"Good boy, Theo!" their dad said.

Thomas rolled his eyes, but his feet were already on the move, dragging him through the slew of restaurant tables as he rushed toward the glass doors.

He only realized Theo had fallen into step beside him when he said, "You know, if you're gonna run for the hills, you could at least be subtle about it."

"I just need some air."

Throwing the door open, Thomas burst out onto the sidewalk like breaking through the surface of an overbearing sea. The rancid smell of gasoline clinging to the afternoon air struck him like a slap to the face compared to the savory smell inside the restaurant, but the sunlight felt nice. Less suffocating.

Theo followed a step behind him, but when Thomas turned to face him, it was to find a glare leveled in his direction. "So, any particular reason you just freaked out and stormed off?"

Thomas raised an eyebrow. "Any particular reason you had to follow me?"

"Because causing a scene is my thing, not yours."

A couple of years before, Thomas would've easily agreed with that, but cheeky comments aside, the line between Theo's kind of thing and Thomas's kind of thing hadn't been so clear in a while. Even going to New York had always been more of a Theo thing. He'd always talked about wanting to run away to the big city, getting away for college or whatever, while Thomas always thought he'd stay with the family, happy to keep things moving smoothly at home.

Until he wasn't.

"So how's the drag thing going?" Theo asked. "You never really give any updates."

"You never ask."

"Well, I'm asking now," Theo said. "I mean, it's not like you're around a whole lot."

Which wasn't entirely Thomas's fault considering they also never really spoke on the phone or texted. If Theo really wanted to know what was going on in Thomas's life, he could be the one to reach out first.

But a voice in Thomas's head said that was the only reason they got along anymore—the novelty of never really talking.

"Drag is...fine," Thomas said. But he hated how empty it felt, so he added, "Good, actually. I had a show last night, and it was fun."

It still felt a little hollow, but he didn't want to go into the details of the show. There weren't any real secrets between them, but he still wasn't ready to dive into how he'd hyper-sexualized their favorite childhood cartoons.

"Well, I'm glad," Theo said. "You ever gonna tell Mom and Dad about it?"

Thomas laughed. "Probably not. I'll tell them I'm queer eventually, but I don't think they can handle drag."

"Yeah, that's fair. So, are you seeing anyone?"

Thomas raised an eyebrow. "Dad, is that you?"

"Oh, come on! I had to ask after you dodged the question before. I mean, obviously you don't have a girlfriend, but—"

"I'm not seeing anyone," Thomas said. "I'd tell you if I was."

"Okay, good. I know it's weird talking about this kind of shit with Mom and Dad, but you can talk to me, you know?"

It was a lot more complicated than Theo made it sound, but Thomas just nodded anyway. "Yeah, I know. I take it everything's good with you, too?"

"Yeah, for the most part. I'm thinking about taking a semester off from school. Just working in the shop with Gabi."

"Wait, why?" Thomas said, his pitch just a little too high to seem casual. "School's important."

"Mom, is that you?"

"I'm serious! I know college is exhausting, but if you take a break, you may not want to go back. It's better to just get it over with."

"Well, if I don't want to go back, maybe I won't," Theo said. "I mean, Gabi's not doing a degree at all. Does it really matter?"

"You really want to be tied to that shop your whole life? What happened to Theo the adventurer who wanted to move to New York or London or anywhere that wasn't Vermont?"

Theo shrugged. "I have a decent job, all my friends, and a perfect boyfriend right in Vermont. Why would I want to leave?"

"I'm glad you're happy, but you shouldn't lose sight of your dreams," Thomas said. "You'll regret it if your relationship doesn't last forever."

"Wow, *subtle*," Theo snapped.

"I—what?"

"If you have a problem with Gabi, just say it."

Thomas blinked back at him in shock. "I-I don't have a problem."

Theo just rolled his eyes, shoving his hands into his pockets as he physically turned away from Thomas. "Sure you don't. Like I haven't noticed the way you act every time you see him. Calling him *Gabriel*."

"That's his name, isn't it?"

"Yes, it's his name, but he's told you to call him Gabi! That's what everyone calls him except you because you can't stand to be around him."

"I never said that. Besides, you used to hate him, didn't you?"

Theo just scoffed. "He's not the enemy's son anymore! He hasn't been for a long time! And in case you hadn't noticed, he's my boyfriend, and I *love* him!"

Thomas flinched at the words, and Theo's brows knitted into a glare, any civility between them evaporating into the summer heat.

Theo turned back toward the restaurant, and Thomas's hand shot out, grabbing him by the wrist. "Theo, wait."

Theo paused for a moment before letting out a huff. "Let go of me."

Thomas pulled his hand back, his chest heavy. "I'm sorry, okay? I'm *really* sorry. It's not him. It's me. I just—I'm sorry."

Theo turned back to look at him, and by some miracle, he almost didn't look mad. But the anger clearly hadn't gone up in thin air because a heavy tension coated his words as he said, "I love him. I'd really appreciate it if you could at least try to love him, too."

"I am trying," Thomas said. "I swear. I just—I don't really know him."

"Then *get* to know him!" Theo shouted. "And maybe start by not pushing him away and acting like you're disgusted by his name."

"I—yeah, I will. I'm sorry."

Theo rolled his eyes, not hesitating even a moment before heading back into the restaurant.

When Brian arrived in the hotel lobby, the place was so quiet compared to the night before that he almost didn't recognize it. He texted Ella to let her know he was there, and a minute later, Pearl showed up, a clipboard in hand.

"Ella have you running the show today?" Brian asked.

Pearl just rolled her eyes. "Please, I'm always running things. I just don't usually get the credit."

"Well, it seems like everything's quieted down, at least," Brian said.

"Oh yeah? For who? I'm still swamped, considering this was our biggest event yet."

"Yeah, I know," Brian said, all the days Ella'd cornered him after his lunch break to lecture him about how important this event would be for their funding resurfacing in his mind. "It seems like it went well, though?"

"I mean, I think so, but it's not my opinion that counts," Pearl said. "I mean, the commentary on Instagram last night seemed pretty positive, so I'll count that as a win. The real question will be how the Board perceives it, but we won't know until we get all the numbers tallied, and then—"

"So, where am I needed?" Brian asked before Pearl could launch into Ella's signature "this organization can't function without funding and what will the community do without us? Do you know how hard it is to find programs like this?" rant.

While the organization itself had been founded by local community members, once it grew in scale, they started relying heavily on corporate donors, which meant that even if they weren't looking to turn a profit themselves, growth was still important. Bigger events, better press, more marketing opportunities—if they couldn't prove some sort of ROI to their corporate overlords, they wouldn't have the funds to keep running at all, including paying their staff and interns, which Ella really loved to remind him about.

"Right, right," Pearl said. "The queens are in the hall, so if you could just make sure they have everything they need, that would be great."

"Will do," Brian said, already heading to the door.

With the tables pushed into corners of the room and the neon lights replaced with bright tungsten, it was easy to separate the events of the night before from the work environment of today. Any remaining humiliation washed off Brian's shoulders. The stage still held mostly the same layout, except for the three director's chairs that were now set out near the center, a drag queen sitting in each one.

But none of them were the one he was looking for.

"Oh, Brian, hey!"

The girl trotting his way with the short cropped blonde hair and sprinkle of freckles across her nose waved at him as she came to a stop. A name tag on her jacket read, *Zoey, she/her/hers.* Matching her name to her Discord profile, he pieced together that she was the assistant to the video director, which meant she was also probably in charge of the shoot.

"Hi." Brian flashed her a smile. "Ella called me to help out. Do you need anything?"

"I actually need to go grab another lens from my car, but I'm parked a block over. Do you mind keeping them entertained while I'm gone?"

"Um, yeah, sure."

As Zoey scurried away, Brian fixed his best customer service face into place and then headed toward the stage, hoping none of his disappointment would show.

The three queens turned to him as he approached, but he only recognized the one in the middle as Lana Del Reina, the host from the night before. Princess Belle from Beauty and the Beast sat to her left and Storm from X-Men sat to her right. Actually, Princess Belle was eyeing him curiously, leaning forward as she tapped one glittering pink fingernail against her cheek.

"Um, hi," Brian said. "My name's Brian Ramirez, and I'm a marketing intern. If you need anything, I'd be happy to take care of it."

"Oh?" Storm said, eyeing him once over.

Belle clapped her hands together before jabbing a manicured finger in Storm's direction. "Back off, I saw him first."

Storm raised an eyebrow, the white contacts making the expression just a little off-putting. "Bitch, what are you on about?"

Belle just turned back to Brian, flashing him a smile. "You were at the show last night, weren't you, sugar?"

Brian spluttered. "I—yeah, I was. How did you—"

"Oh, don't be silly. I saw you with Mia."

"Oh, so *Mia* saw him first," Storm said, "yet here you are being all possessive."

"*Semantics.*"

"Wait, Mia?" Brian said, his mouth going dry.

Lana just giggled. "You got that close and personal with her, and you didn't even know her name."

Brian winced.

But Belle just said, "Mia Sake? The sexy Totoro? She's hard to forget."

"Very," Brian said before the logical part of his brain could tell him to keep his mouth shut.

Lana smirked. "Ooh, someone's got a crush!"

"I—what? No, I-I just—"

"Aw, how cute," Storm said. "He's too flustered to speak."

It only dawned on him then that, somehow, he'd managed to be humiliated in that exact same spot for a second day in a row.

These queens were obviously just teasing him, so it was probably unreasonable to have this much warmth rising in his face. What did it matter if he'd thought Mia was cute? Literally anyone would. At the end of the day, it didn't mean anything since she was just a drag persona.

Belle leaned toward him, offering him her hand. "Call me Kris."

Brian returned the handshake, careful not to scratch himself on her over-sized acrylics. "Uh, Brian."

"You already said that, sweetness," Lana said.

"Um, right."

"Anyway," Kris said, grinning knowingly at him, "you wanna talk to Mia? We're having drinks later. You should come by."

The breath rushed out of him, and his legs felt weak. "I—can I?" he said, struggling to find enough air to put any volume behind his voice. "I don't want to make it weird."

"Not weird at all," Kris said, waving him off. "It's just gonna be us and a bunch of friends. I'm sure she'd be happy to see you. Let me give you my number."

She reached into her bra, drawing out a little white business card and passing it to him. The design was simple, the words *Agenda Social* written across the top, followed by *Kris Westwick*, IT underneath. "We'll be at the karaoke bar across the street tonight at eight. Just text me when you're outside, and I'll send her down to you."

"I—thank you."

"Oh, sure thing," Kris said with a dismissive wave, but she kept her eye on him even after Zoey returned with her lens and opted to continue the shoot, so he had to wonder if maybe she was just as invested in seeing where this went as he was.

"So did you talk to her?"

Brian's stomach dropped the second Pearl's words came through his phone. "Talk to who?"

"Anna, dipshit," Pearl snapped, and Brian had to fight back the urge to let out a sigh of relief.

No one else in the busy deli was paying him any mind, but he still felt painfully watched as he said, "Oh, um, no, I didn't."

Once the queens had finished their shoot and were free to go, Ella had sent Brian off to grab lunch so they could look over and discuss some of the numbers from the night before. In the grand scheme of things, it was really only the Board's final opinions that mattered, and they weren't supposed to be making any big decisions about whether or not the nonprofit would be allowed to keep running until the end of the summer, but he knew Ella was stressed, so if a couple sandwiches and some chatter would help bring her back to baseline, he could manage that.

"Seriously?" Pearl said. "You couldn't find time for a five-minute conversation? You're just supposed to be a gofer."

"It's not that important."

Pearl spluttered. "It's not? You seemed pretty broken up about it yesterday."

"But that was yesterday. This is today."

The line fell quiet, and Brian awkwardly turned his attention toward scrutinizing the menu hung above the counter as if Ella hadn't told him exactly what to order down to the "mayo on the side, make sure you salt the fries." When Pearl had called to check if he'd left work yet, he'd considered not answering for this very reason. Escaping Pearl's judgment was like tax evasion, except even the IRS let you self-report before jumping to conclusions. And with his head already scrambled due to the whole Mia thing, he definitely wasn't in the best place to prove his competence to his overbearing roommate.

"Boy, what are you on about?" Pearl said.

"Um, sorry, I have to go," Brian said. "Gotta order lunch."

"Yeah, okay, but whatever's going on with you, you're gonna have to answer for it eventually."

Pearl hung up, and Brian tucked his phone away. Just like he could always count on the sound of angry drivers to keep him awake at night, he could always count on Pearl reading into things in exactly the way that would make him most uncomfortable.

But assuming things went well tonight, at least he'd have something to tell her when she hounded him with follow-up questions over breakfast. Not that he could concretely pin down what "well" would even mean in this context.

After all, he was a straight guy chasing a drag queen he'd met while drunk at a work event.

Realistically, this whole adventure probably wouldn't amount to much. He'd probably get more out of bringing Ella the wrong sandwich than he'd actually get out of meeting this Mia tonight.

But considering she'd been running through his head all day, he figured he owed it to himself to at least try.

8

The sound of the door slamming shut behind Thomas was almost cathartic as he threw himself onto the sofa. The moment he'd told himself it was "just lunch" and "not a big deal," a voice in the back of his head had told him he was being more naive than the time he'd started talking to a self-proclaimed "weeb," thinking they might not be a fetishist, but he'd silenced it all the same.

And now, instead of seeing his family off, he'd basically just pushed them away.

He knotted his fingers in the fluffy blue throw pillow he'd bought on a whim, squeezing tight enough to ground himself. The logical part of his brain told him that his parents wouldn't disown him since he hadn't actually snuck off to pay the check, but when it came to Theo, he just didn't have that kind of certainty.

Even just a few years before, they'd been perpetually at each other's throats, so Thomas may have made a fatal mistake in letting himself get too comfortable. He should've known better than to believe that people would actually stick around forever.

The smooth fibers at his fingertips finally settled him enough that he could let go of them and reach for his phone, but the notification on his screen just unsettled him all over again—a missed call from Kris.

Not only was Kris near terminally allergic to phone calls, but of the three times Kris had actually called him over texting him, two had been the result of psychotic episodes, and the third was to yell at him for borrowing a pair of heels and stretching them out. All things considered, Thomas was pretty sure he wasn't in the right headspace to handle either of those scenarios.

But if the call held some connection to work, the last thing Thomas needed was to put it off just to find out he was getting fired and needed to go home to the family he'd just made hate him. So Thomas clicked the button, leaning back against the couch cushions to brace himself.

"Hey, bitch! How was breakfast with the fam?" Kris said, the dull drone of Penn Station surrounding him.

"It was lunch."

"Whatever, you know what I mean."

"If you're thinking about fleeing the country again—"

"Oh my God, relax, I'm fine," Kris said. "Well, actually, I might be manic because I'm so horny right now, I almost hit on a ginger."

Thomas sighed deeply. "I didn't need to know that."

"Don't be so uptight! Anyway, I just wanted to make sure we're still on for drinks later."

"You called just to ask that?"

"I can't just want to check on you?"

Thomas rolled his eyes. "Well, in that case, I don't know if I'm in the mood—"

"Well, go hit up a therapist then head over. You have to be there. There's someone who's very excited to see you."

Thomas's chest tightened as he asked, "Someone like…?"

"You remember that guy from the show last night? The one you said was, and I quote, 'someone's sexy gay awakening just waiting to happen'?"

"I definitely did not say 'sexy.'"

"So, it wasn't an exact quote. Sue me. The point is, that boy was moping around the venue like a lost puppy looking for you."

"Is that also a poorly transcribed quote? Cause I'm not really in the mood for a game of telephone."

"Well, he didn't say that *exactly*, but you could see it on his face. Boy's got it *bad*." The eagerness in Kris's voice made Thomas clutch the throw pillow again. "I told him to meet us tonight, so you'll see what I mean."

"I—you told him where to *find* me?"

"Relax, love, I sent him a block over so you can ghost him if you don't wanna show," Kris said. Then his voice took on the sort of serious tone that was about as rare as their phone calls as he said, "You've been single an awfully long time."

"It hasn't been that long," shot out reflexively, but Thomas knew how weak a defense it was.

Spending the last year working through school, emotional trauma, and a lot of self-loathing made his last relationship feel entirely outside of time. That was, if he could really call it a relationship, since it'd been spurred entirely by guilt and dissolved just as emptily. But the situation with Michelle was exactly why he had no interest in wading into the dating pool, especially not when he was still learning how to stay afloat on his own.

"You should've gone into counseling," Kris said. "Maybe helping others would make you realize just how full of bullshit you are."

Thomas rolled his eyes again, even if Kris couldn't see him.

"Anyway, I gotta go," Kris said. "If you want me to tell the guy to take a hike, I will, but I think it'd do you some good to just give him a chance. Just sleep with him and see where it goes."

"Yeah, I'm not gonna do that, but I'll think about meeting up with him."

"Perf, we love to see it! Okay, see you tonight, boo!"

Thomas sighed, ending the call and letting the phone slide out of his hand onto the thinning carpet.

There was a chance—no matter how resistant Thomas was

to the idea—that Kris had been right about him having been single for a while, but the memories tugging at his mind didn't deserve to be revisited. They were the type with claws—and not in the sexy way. Any time he let his mind stray back toward Michelle, he was always drawn back into the pit. The *descent*. Spiraling back into that feeling of being dragged underground with no means to dig himself back out.

The last time he'd gone looking for love, he'd ended up broken, and she'd ended up brokenhearted. Throwing himself into that kind of miserable flurry willingly was a level of self-destructive he'd promised himself he would never be again. Add to that the complexities of trying to explain to anyone that he was seeing someone he'd met while playing the role of sexy Totoro, and the prospect of trying to launch into a new relationship felt too miserable to dwell on for long.

But he had to admit that there was a sort of allure to meeting up with someone who'd only ever known him as Mia. Like, maybe the grave he was so afraid of being drawn into was more like a cocoon, helping him melt away the skin he'd never felt fully comfortable in to metamorphose into something radiant. It was almost too optimistic of a vision for Thomas to entertain, but Kris was always pushing him to step out of his comfort zone, so maybe, just this once, he should just shut up and trust him.

9

One of the first lessons his mother had taught him was the "don't talk to strangers" spiel, so Brian had to wonder where exactly he'd found the courage to meet up with one outside of a Manhattan bar. Yet, as he bypassed a few questionable puddles that may have been water but carried an equal likelihood of being piss, any life lessons he should've carried with him left him in favor of his dream from the other night. As messy as it was to chase the tail of a sex dream, he couldn't go the rest of his life not knowing if it could've been something more.

The neon sign above the bar Kris had directed him to shone brightly in his eyes as he finally came to a stop. The streets of Koreatown roared with life as always—people spilling out of karaoke bars and Korean BBQ joints and boba shops. Anna was a pretty picky eater, and her biggest weakness had always been spicy food, so they hadn't spent a lot of time in Koreatown, leaving his current environment feeling a little strange. Not totally unfamiliar, thanks to his internship, but lacking something that the rest of the city seemed alive with.

He pushed the thought away as he leaned against the bar wall and pulled out his phone to text Kris. His thumb hovered over the send button as Mia's face crept up behind his eyes. Was he really about to do this?

But as he looked up at the busy street, taking in the sight of so many couples and families and friend groups, the loneliness he'd felt since he and Anna had split grew heavier than the smell of gas and exhaust in the air.

So he hit send.

Would he even get a response?

Was this whole thing just an elaborate set up with cameras waiting nearby to broadcast to some TikTok audience?

Fiddling with his phone but not opening any apps, the sinking feeling in his stomach grew. Being humiliated for social media would be tough to live down but not impossible. The bigger fear gnawing at his insides was that maybe he'd gotten his hopes up for nothing—maybe Mia wasn't even real.

Not only would that mean that he'd spent an entire day fantasizing about someone who could only ever exist in his dreams, but also that the entire foundation of those dreams had been altered for nothing. Because while he'd spent the last few hours trying to remember what things had been like with Anna—trying to replay the good moments so he could get wrapped up in her again—he realized that he couldn't. It was like the mere existence of Mia had been enough to completely erase what made Anna special from his mind. Where he'd thought Anna's mark would be laid down in permanent ink, Mia had washed it away in a moment without so much as a scar left behind.

Because how could he ever be excited about girls like Anna when there were girls like Mia?

Assuming Mia even was a girl.

No, he wasn't going to think like that. He'd been drawn to her as a drag queen—the quintessential embodiment of femininity—because he was attracted to women. He just had to hope that the version of her he'd been dreaming about was actually the real deal.

He'd all but forgotten the phone in his hand until it lit up again with Kris's response—*She's on her way. Good luck!*

Shit.

He slipped his phone back into his pocket, freeing his hands up long enough to carefully rub his clammy palms against his pants. Everything about this night was foreign territory, even the nervousness. The last time he'd felt so out of his league with a girl was when he'd started dating Maggie, his college girlfriend from a few years back, and if that relationship was any indication of what he had in store for him with Mia, he'd be better off turning tail and racing home.

But before he could cut his losses and flee, a voice cut through all the other noise filling the night air. "Brian?"

The sound of his name cut right through his spiraling. No, the sound of that *voice*. It had the same tonal quality as the voice from the other night, though a bit less theatrical.

And coming down the street toward him was someone who felt both extremely familiar and completely new at the same time—long legs, high cheekbones, those deep, dark eyes. Even with Mia in just plain jeans and a flannel button up over a plain black shirt, Brian could still make out all the features that had left him enraptured at the show, like the stage magic wasn't actually where the magic had come from at all.

"Um, hi," he said, his voice sounding awkward even to his own ears.

But somehow, those awkward words elicited the single brightest smile he'd ever seen.

Fuck.

"Um, not that I'm complaining, but how did you know my name?" Brian asked.

"Oh, Kris told me. You know, about everything. I didn't realize you were looking for me."

"I—it's not that I was looking for you, I was just—"

But when he dug through his mental index for a way to say, *I've just been thinking about you nonstop and needed to know if you were actually real* in a non-creepy way, he drew up blank.

"Um, so what should I call you?" Brian said.

"Oh, right. My name's—well, actually, why don't you just call me Mia?"

"Is that your real name?"

Mia laughed. "No, not at all, but—well, I hope it's not weird, but I've kind of been dancing around the idea of changing my name for a while, so I thought maybe I'd try out a new one with you. If you don't mind."

Brian smiled. "I don't mind. Mia it is. Pronouns?"

Mia's eyes widened. "They/she generally," Mia said. "He is fine sometimes, too."

"Okay, got it. Um, I use he/him."

Mia laughed. "Sorry, it's just not every day you meet someone who actually asks about pronouns without being a dick about it."

"My brother's trans," Brian rushed to explain, "and I work with this queer organization. I-I'm an ally."

That last part slipped out entirely on its own. The first part pretty much covered it, but Brian also didn't want to give off the wrong impression and end up appropriating queerness or something. But he *also* didn't want to give the impression that he was uncomfortable around queer people because he definitely wasn't.

Mia eyed him with a raised brow, a slow smile creeping across their face as they said, "An ally, huh?"

"I-yeah, why?"

But Mia seemed totally disinterested in helping resolve the bubble of embarrassment that had built in Brian's chest, opting to just wave him off instead. "You know what? Never mind. Do you wanna grab a drink?"

Brian pushed the uncertainty down, instead focusing on the way the streetlights left shimmers in Mia's hair. "Yeah, I'd love to."

Mia turned on their heel, flying down the sidewalk fast enough that Brian's couple seconds' hesitation was enough to nearly leave him in the dust. He took off at a light trot, falling into step beside them as they neared the intersection and turned right.

"Are you from New York?" Brian asked.

"No, why?"

"You just walk like you really know where you're going."

Mia laughed. "Pretty ironic considering I don't know anything."

"What does that mean?"

When Mia turned to look at him again, Brian stumbled, quickly rushing to regain his footing before he could eat the pavement. Mia's eyes were the deepest shade of brown he'd ever seen, and the moment he was swept up into them, he might as well have lost touch with the ground. Here he was, falling endlessly in a gaze so deep and dark, he might as well plummet straight into the night sky.

Then he was drawn back down to the city street as Mia said, "Oh, nothing. I just feel a little directionless sometimes." Then they blushed, turning their face away long enough to free Brian from his trance. "And sometimes I say things I'm probably better off keeping to myself."

A smile tugged at the corner of Brian's mouth. "I get that."

It was actually a little reassuring. If someone as enrapturing as Mia felt a little out of their element, he couldn't feel any shame in sharing that experience.

"So do you mind if I ask why you've been looking for me?" Mia asked.

Brian winced. "Oh, um, it's not—I don't mean to be creepy or anything."

"No, you're not. I mean, unless you've been following me for weeks now or something."

"No, no, of course not! I would never—"

Before he could ramble on about how not creepy he was in a way that would probably make him seem twice as creepy, Mia just giggled and said, "I was just kidding. Actually, I was really flattered that you came back for me. I didn't realize I'd left such an impression."

"Oh, you definitely left an impression."

They approached a dark staircase that might have raised red flags if not for the sound of music and chatter floating down toward them. Mia took hold of Brian's wrist, keeping him just a step behind them. Brian flashed his ID at the bouncer, but Mia just nodded to him. Then Mia dragged Brian through the crowded room full of writhing bodies and loud music. Bright lights danced across the dark walls, but he couldn't make out their destination through the never-ending sea of faces.

Then he felt a breeze as they burst through the edge of the crowd. This side of the bar sat open, the thinning crowd giving way to an outdoor patio lounge, where the vibe felt a little less flashy and overwhelming.

"You still haven't answered my question," Mia said, once they were somewhere he could actually make out their voice through all the noise.

"Question?"

"You know, why you were looking for me."

They stepped over to a quieter stretch of the bar where a TV hung playing some reality show, but the woman going on an angry tirade just didn't have the same ferocity with her shouts relegated to a black subtitle box. Mia took a seat on one of the chipped wooden barstools before turning back to him with a raised brow.

"Um, right," Brian said, taking the stool next to them. "It's not that I was looking for you, exactly, but I just kind of had you on my mind after the show. And then Kris mentioned you, and I couldn't help but ask."

Mia smiled. "You're an intern, right? You helped put on the show?"

Brian nodded.

"Sorry for putting you on the spot. I was just going to skirt right by you, but then I realized I could pull you in a little— well, it might have been overkill."

"No, it was fine," Brian said hurriedly. "I didn't mind."

"I can be a little fearless when I slip into costume, but I'm not usually like that," Mia said.

"Why the change?"

Mia paused, eyes flitting down to a small chip in the side of the bar counter. "Honestly, I'm not sure. I'm still figuring that out for myself." Then their eyes bounced back up, lighting up as they said, "But I'm really not that exciting. Tell me about you. You seemed like you were having a rough night. What happened?"

Brian winced. "Um, it wasn't anything important."

"No?"

The softness in their tone made Brian pause before he could insist it really wasn't worth the time. What was the worst that could really come from opening up to Mia? They weren't interning for the same company; they didn't run with any of the same social circles. And while there was always the risk that he might overshare and send them running, wasn't that exactly what Pearl had been lecturing him about before? That he needed to stop getting invested in people before he could honestly get to know them?

So he pushed any apprehension aside and said, "I broke up with my girlfriend. Or, well, I guess she broke up with me. I'm not entirely sure who did the breaking up, but it was a pretty shitty one either way."

"Oh, I'm sorry. How long were you together?"

"Almost a year."

A couple of different expressions warred across Mia's face for a moment, but when they finally spoke, they just opted for a sigh and, "That sounds rough. Sorry."

"It's okay," Brian said. "To be honest, your show was a nice distraction."

Then they smiled. "I'm glad."

The bartender slapped some napkins down in front of them, drawing Brian's eyes away from Mia despite the magnetic force trying to keep them there.

"You can just put it all on my tab," Mia told the bartender. "I'll have a Moscow mule."

And while Brian had no idea what that actually meant, he just nodded at the bartender and said, "Make it two, please."

Once the bartender stepped away, Brian turned to Mia and

said, "You don't have to pay for me. I mean, I can tell him to separate the checks."

Mia just waved him off. "Don't be ridiculous. You went through all this effort just to talk to me. I feel like I can at least buy you a drink. So, do you go to a lot of drag shows?"

"Um, no, not exactly. Yours was my first."

"Oh? Why does your voice sound like that?" they asked, a teasing lilt to the end of their question. "You don't like drag shows?"

"It's not that. I mean, yours was…nice." There were several other words he'd initially thought to put in that slot, but "nice" seemed the least likely to get him into trouble. "I guess I kind of feel like I don't belong there. Like I'm appropriating gay culture or something."

Mia threw their head back and laughed with the sort of reckless abandon that really made Brian wish he was in on the joke. Then they flashed him a grin. "Drag shows are for everybody. They're a celebration and a performance and a reclamation of self in the face of rigid gender rules. It's not appropriating queer culture to go to one."

"Well, that's good, at least," Brian said, a genuine weight lifting from his chest. "I hate overstepping."

"Oh, believe me, I get it. So what gave you the courage to go, if you don't mind me asking? I could use a little more courage."

Brian shrugged. "I have this brother who's always hounding me to get out and see the city, but I guess I don't know where to start. I really just came here to be with Anna, but all of her favorite places feel kind of weird now, and I don't know what I would even do now that she's gone—"

"Anna's the ex?"

Brian nodded.

"Well, there's your problem. You've got your feelings for the city all tied up in your feelings for the girl. You'll never be able to love New York as long as you can only see it through the lens of your ex," Mia said. "And you'll never be able to let her go so long as everything here reminds you of her. You have to sever the ties between them."

"Oh? And how do I do that?" Brian asked, but a smile tugged at his lips. Something about Mia's words sounded less like advice and more like an invitation, like she had something up her sleeve and was gently pulling him along for the ride.

The bartender returned, sliding their drinks to them, and Mia placed the glass in Brian's hand.

"You ever gotten a tattoo removed?" they asked.

Brian winced. "Thought about it, but no."

"Me neither," Mia said, "but I have this friend back home who used to have this huge Harry Potter tattoo on his bicep before that bitch came out as a TERF. He goes to ask about getting it removed, but the artist told him, if you just try to remove a tattoo, you're gonna leave scars. The best way to get rid of it is to cover it up with something new."

Brian raised an eyebrow. "Are you suggesting I get a rebound?"

Mia laughed. "Not exactly. But if you want to get over this girl who's ruining the city for you, you gotta replace her with something else. Make new memories. Rewrite what this place means for you. Then you won't have to see her face in every puddle or café window, you know?"

Mia picked up their drink, sipping it delicately for a moment before obviously thinking better of it and tossing the whole thing back. Once they cleared the glass, they set it back on the counter and turned to Brian with a soft smile.

"Anyway," they said, "that's just advice from a stranger who knows nothing about you and obviously talks too much. You don't have to take it."

"No, it's good advice," Brian said. "Now I just have to figure out how to start taking it."

"I can help."

Brian's eyes shot wide. "Wait, really? You want to help me get over my ex-girlfriend?"

As far as charity cases went, Brian doubted he was the most

promising, but Mia's face betrayed zero hesitation as they said, "Why not? It could be fun. And I've been looking for an excuse to explore the city some more, too. Although, I will say that soul searching is probably easier to do without any strings attached."

"I—what does that mean?"

Mia shrugged. "I just figure that if the whole point is to figure out what the city means to you on your own, it's probably better that you do that single, you know? No coupling."

"I—are you under the impression that we're coupling?"

"Not necessarily," Mia said. "But given the way Kris talked about you, it seemed like maybe you wanted to. Do you?"

Brian paused, letting the words soak in. When he first met up with them, something between the overwhelming city lights and the shock of realizing they were a real person had left him feeling airborne, but that was all it was. Sitting under the muted lights of the bar, he felt a little more grounded.

Was Mia objectively an attractive person with great energy, a good sense of humor, and an adorable smile? Sure, but anyone who spent a couple of minutes with them could figure out that much. That didn't mean that Brian was actually *attracted* to them in the sort of way Mia was referring to. After all, Brian was straight, and…

"Are you a woman?" Brian asked.

Mia spluttered. "Excuse me?"

"I—sorry, that was—I just meant—well, I'm straight, so like, I'm only into women, so if you're not a woman—"

And a part of him wished Mia would just throw a drink at him. At least that would stop whatever toxic sludge kept pouring out of his mouth.

But Mia just laughed. "Honestly, I'm still figuring everything out, but I would say I don't think I'm a woman. The rest is still to be determined."

"Oh, okay," Brian said awkwardly. "Um, well, good. Then no strings attached shouldn't be a problem?"

The words definitely weren't supposed to have come out like a question, but Mia didn't seem put off by his apparent uncertainty. They just smiled, holding out a hand to seal their agreement. "No strings attached it is."

10

"How did you manage to go through all of that and still come out of there without a date?" Kris asked after Thomas rejoined the group.

He'd walked in on some argument between Day and Kris over which Black musician had a bigger impact on country music—Darius Rucker or Lil Nas X. Really, the most interesting part had been how heated Day had been in their defense arguments given they typically had the sort of tranquil calm that was only rivaled by monks and stone statues, and thus far, the only adversaries capable of changing that were transphobes and Kris.

But the second Thomas sat down, Kris dropped the whole debate and whipped toward him so fast her lashes almost fell off.

Thomas grabbed the drink in front of Kris, taking a moment to sip it to avoid answering her question. Sharing drinks with Kris was always a bit of a gamble since she grew up in a family that brewed their own homemade moonshine in the backyard or something, but he felt a little uncomfortable sharing with anyone else at the table, and there was no way Kris was gonna let him go grab his own now that she'd put him in the hot seat.

Finally, Thomas lowered the drink and settled on, "We're friends now."

"Bitch, you don't give lap dances to make *friends*."

But Thomas just rolled his eyes. "It wasn't a lap dance."

"You know what I mean!"

If he were being totally honest with Kris, he'd have said he felt kind of relieved when Brian had agreed to a no-strings-attached friendship. Now that he'd nipped any romantic potential in the bud, he could actually let himself have a good time with Brian instead of stressing that he'd just be another Michelle.

"He's straight."

Kris spluttered. "Oh, please, that bitch is *not* straight. I saw the way he looked at you."

"He thought I was a trans woman," Thomas explained, "but now that he knows better, the attraction is gone."

"Now that he knows better? Bitch, *you* don't even knows better!" Kris waved him off with a dismissive eye roll. "This is the most convoluted type of denial I've ever seen."

Kris could call it denial, but Thomas called it self-preservation. What could he possibly gain by trying to sanitize his gender fuckery enough to convince Brian to be attracted to him?

And hanging out with someone he already knew could never love him was so much safer than trying to open himself up to someone new.

"Anyway, my point is, Brian *thinks* he's straight. He said so himself," Thomas said. "He's not interested, and I'm fine with that, *but* this could be my chance to help someone. I mean, Brian thinks he's so straight that it would be appropriating queer culture to go to drag shows. I can help him open up to exploring himself and dropping the toxic masculinity."

"Honey, if you want to help someone, go volunteer at a food bank. Adopting a baby queer and sending them the gay agenda is *not* gonna heal you."

Thomas pursed his lips. "Aren't you the one who said being

queer without the community is like mountain climbing without the rope?"

Kris rolled her eyes. "Bitch, *when* did I say that?"

"Literally when I tried to quit drag, and you told me you wouldn't let me."

Kris stared at him blankly for a moment before a slow smirk spread across her face. "You've got a great memory, you know that? Remind me to never have a bad hair day in front of you." Then she heaved a sigh, taking the drink out of Thomas's hand and setting it down on the table. "You wanna waste your time trying to break through the skull of a self-proclaimed straight guy? I'm not gonna stop you. But you should know, you're the most naive bitch I've ever known, and I'm from Nashville. My childhood babysitter thought she was gonna be the next Taylor Swift."

"I appreciate the vote of confidence," Thomas said, sarcasm oozing out of his tone, "but I've got this."

"Good. And you've got the next round, too, because you owe me a drink."

By the time Thomas threw himself out of bed Monday morning, he'd somehow already fallen fifteen minutes behind schedule and managed to go the whole night without actually charging his phone. Waking up at five a.m. to get to work on time probably could've qualified as a criminal offense back in Vermont, but in New York, the only unworkable hours were the ones after you were six feet under. And given that Thomas still had to prove that he even deserved to hold onto this job, he did his best to keep his complaining to his internal monologue.

Sometimes, living in New York felt like barreling down the freeway at seventy-five, but this highway lacked guardrails, and the lanes kept getting narrower and narrower.

Digging his backup battery out of the pockets of last week's unwashed pants, he rushed to gather the rest of his things before racing out the door. The café on the corner that carried the melon bread that kind of reminded him of the one his parents made had just opened for business when he rushed in to grab a quick breakfast. In Vermont, the shop owner would know his name and whole family line by now, but the cashier he'd spoken to almost every morning since starting this job gave him the same robotic send off before passing him his order.

Once he'd boarded his train and found a seat, Thomas pulled out his phone to check the battery. Just over thirty percent. He doubted his backup battery even had the necessary juice to get it to full, but hopefully it'd be enough to stay afloat until he could charge it at the office.

Back home, his phone battery never really caused him a lot of concern, but living out here, he could go sunrise to sunset and then a few hours into the night without ever stepping foot back in his apartment. Between work and socializing, it wasn't just his phone's battery that was perpetually chugging along in the red zone, yet the thought of returning to Vermont to go back to work at his parents' shop always managed to dig up some reserve energy.

But he doubted there was any amount of "upbeat and eager" that could make up for the fact that he didn't contribute a whole lot at the office. He'd downloaded the Agenda app as instructed, made his account, and tried to meet some people as a means of offering feedback, but he'd never been a social butterfly, and his messages were pretty quiet. And while he had a good deal of coding experience, he wasn't ever really allowed to use it. He was just another throwaway temp hire who'd be tossed aside at the end of the summer, and any hopes he'd had of avoiding that had dwindled faster than his backup battery.

And while the office culture was pretty friendly—and he actually kind of enjoyed working with people he also did drag with—bouncing ideas for the real programmers to flesh out wasn't exactly valuable work experience, so it wasn't like he could easily line up another job after this one, either.

Before his hopelessness could drown him completely, his phone vibrated in his lap, drawing him back to the train car.

"Hello?"

He'd answered before he could consider if he'd be better off letting it go to voicemail, but the sound of Theo's upbeat tone as he said, "Mooorning," assuaged any budding regret.

"Um, what are you doing up this early?"

"What? I can't be awake at seven?"

"Not unless someone's in the hospital." Which might be the only reason Thomas could think of for Theo to call him out of the blue like this, too. "Is Mom okay?"

"Yeah, she's fine. Everything's fine. I was just checking in."

"Um, okay?"

"I guess I just wanted to make sure we were cool. You know, after the other day."

A slight hiccup cut through Theo's voice, like maybe a kernel of doubt had seeded itself inside him just as it had with Thomas. And, as shameful as it felt to admit it, that nervousness did help to calm some of Thomas's own. At least he wasn't the only one feeling a little unsure of where they stood, which meant he also wasn't totally pathetic for letting it get to him.

"We're cool," Thomas said, words a little too rushed to convey the nonchalance he'd been aiming for. "I mean, if anything, I figured you'd be mad at me."

"No, I'm not mad," Theo said, also a little too quickly to be natural. "I mean, not anymore, anyway. Sorry for snapping at you. You know how I can be."

"Don't worry about it. And I'm sorry, too. How's Gabi?"

"Good. Fine. I mean, everything's good," Theo said. "Um, I'll let you go. Call me if anything interesting happens."

"Will do."

Thomas ended the call, looking down at his battery again. He'd drained it down to just under twenty percent even with the backup still plugged in, but all things considered, he wasn't too mad about it.

Working in an office lined with bright windows, pride flags, and a very carefully curated shrine dedicated to Marsha P. Johnson helped to counteract some of the bad vibes Thomas had to swim through in order to reach said office. The entire building was owned by Day's stepfather, but the man wasn't nearly as creative as he was wealthy, so most of the other offices held other startups he'd funded in the hopes a few would take off well enough to make up for all the others that would ultimately fold. If not for the familial connection, Thomas was pretty confident their little startup wouldn't exist at all, since most of the other projects had aims like "helping people triple their stock portfolios" or "reporting encampments of unhoused people to keep the streets clean" rather than "fostering queer community to build support for the city's most vulnerable."

Even if the work environment weren't so upbeat, Thomas would be grateful for the position. The fact that the project he was working on would do some good for the world really made the free coffee and welcome tablet carry a lot more weight.

Clearing the elevator and stepping into the office, he found Day and Felix standing at the coffee bar, tension already resting in the air. Their team was small enough that, day to day, they only carried about as much friction as the average book club. Well, maybe not a Young Adult one, but a normal one. Day, Kris, and Felix were the only full-time members of the team, with Thomas and five other temps only on for the summer, unless things went well, and Day could rally enough funding from their stepfather to keep the project going. And while Kris could be a bit of a drama queen, she also tended to keep to herself during work hours, so things ran pretty smoothly.

Apparently, until today.

"Um, morning," Thomas said.

Day and Felix turned to Thomas with mirrored looks that could only really be described as "tired." "Morning," they said in unison.

Thomas could only assume the two had known each other for a while since they ran the startup together, but he'd never seen them so in sync on anything. Even on a surface level, Felix was tall and lanky compared to Day's shorter, stockier build, with a light brown complexion compared to Day's rich, earthy skin tone, and a voice much sharper and more intense than Day's low, calming tone. A pit of anxiety settled in Thomas's stomach.

"Um, everything okay?" he asked.

"Have you been using the Agenda app much this past week?" Day asked.

Thomas froze. "Um, sure, yeah. I check it every now and then."

"Have you gotten a lot of matches?"

"A...few?"

Agenda Social worked like your typical dating app, but they'd designed it to focus on platonic connections and matching compatible friends with different activities they could do around the city. Since it was still in beta, the userbase remained pretty unimpressive, but the usability had been spectacular. Of course, he'd only checked it a few times since he'd gone on a spree the first day, only to match with people who mostly wanted dick pics or to meet up for quickies. It was actually pretty disappointing, given the app had recommended him some pretty cool hangouts that he hadn't actually had the chance to try out.

But despite Day's calm demeanor, the look they gave Thomas read a bit...frustrated? And Thomas couldn't exactly blame them since he was literally hired on to make sure the app could earn its mileage, and he hadn't spent nearly as much time with it as he probably should have.

But Felix just said, "I told you, the matches are fine. There's nothing we can do if people just aren't clicking."

"Okay, but getting them to click is kind of our whole job," Day said, "and you know how this works. Growth is the name of the game."

"Well, this is what you get for letting Kris do outreach," Felix said.

Day winced, turning back to Thomas. "Okay, tell me. What's it missing? Why aren't people coming back or shouting about it elsewhere? It's gotta be better than OKCupid, at least."

"I...don't know," he said.

The idea of test running a queer community app sounded like a great opportunity that only lost some of its shine when he realized most people just wanted to sleep with him, but there was no way that was every queer in New York. He probably just gave off the type of energy that made him seem good for sex but not much else, but that wasn't exactly helpful feedback.

"Maybe people just need a little extra...push?" Thomas ventured. "I mean, the meetup ideas are really cool, but I guess actually committing to getting together might be a lot for people?"

He had no idea if what he said was actually a good answer or not, but his palms were already getting clammy at the thought of having to explain to his parents how he got fired out of the blue.

Day just sighed, leaning back against the coffee cart. "We tossed around the idea of doing some sort of community event, but the whole goal is to reach people who may not come out to something new. Agenda gives them the comfort of meeting people at home, and then, once they're invested—"

"What about some ice breakers?" Thomas said. "Or maybe some suggestions for how to build connections in the app before the meetup? Agreeing to meet in person can be a big step, but if it maybe gave advice on working up to calls or something?"

Thomas cut himself off before he could ramble anymore and convince his literal boss that he was too smooth-brained to be in the office at all.

But after a moment, Day nodded. "That could be a start. Hopefully, if we can get some meetups going, it'll be a lot easier to encourage signups and get a press feature."

"Don't get too ahead of yourself," Felix said. "You had plans running wild two weeks ago, too, and what actually got done?"

Day sighed again, a little more frustrated this time. "Don't remind me."

Thomas awkwardly looked down at his shoes. He couldn't even recall what he'd been assigned to do two weeks ago, but if Felix was dragging him to his face, his fuck-up must have been pretty bad.

"Whatever," Felix said. "Thomas, can you just work with Kris on getting more signups? Hopefully, if it's a team effort, we won't have any more problems."

"Um, yup, I can do that," he said. "Um, I will go talk to Kris now."

And then he dismissed himself before he could face any more of the team's ire. The summer wasn't over yet, and neither was his position, so all he needed to do was help Kris get some more signups before they all realized how useless he really was.

11

"Wait, you *found* her? *How*?"

Pearl stared at Brian from her perch on the kitchen counter.

Dustin had some kind of art show on Sunday, so he and Pearl had barely been home at all, and Monday, Brian had thrown himself into work, conveniently providing him enough of an excuse to put off recounting all the details of his not-date.

But now that it'd been a few days since Mia had agreed to help Brian reclaim his love for the city, he felt a lot better about the arrangement. Not just because he and Mia had been texting off and on for the past few days, but also because he felt entirely confident that he wasn't rushing into anything. He and Mia were two platonic friends with no romantic feelings whatsoever getting to know each other in a totally normal platonic friend way.

Nothing else.

"Yeah, Kris connected us," Brian said as he pulled some leftovers out of the fridge for dinner. "You remember her, right? Princess Belle?"

"Yeah, I recall," Pearl said, "but I'm still not sure how you ended up in a social circle full of drag queens. I mean, I'm not complaining, because they're probably way cooler than you—"

Brian rolled his eyes. "Gee, thanks."

"—but I'm just saying…"

"It was just a fluke," Brian said. "I guess Kris just remembered me, so, yeah. Mia and I are gonna go discover the city a bit."

Brian shrugged, letting Pearl's imagination fill in the rest. As long as she didn't hurl that imagination at him, he figured that was the safest bet.

"God, that is wild," Pearl said, leaning back until her head rested against the cabinet door. "Like, I knew this story was bound to go somewhere weird, but you running through town trying to reclaim your youth with a drag queen was *not* it."

Brian rolled his eyes. "She just said she could help me get over Anna, and I couldn't really resist the temptation."

"Because you're falling in love with a drag queen?"

Brian spluttered. While he'd definitely had some…thoughts about Mia, it'd been easy enough to push those away before they got carried away by reminding himself that she wasn't a woman. Maybe not a guy either, but certainly not the type of person Brian was into that way.

"I'm not! She's not a woman, and I'm—"

"Yeah, yeah, you're straight. We got it. So, what happened to talking to Anna?"

"I mean, I was going to, but then I kept thinking about what you said."

Pearl's eyes shot wide. "What did I say?"

"About me only being in love with the idea of her?" Brian said, staring at the Tupperware of some sorry-looking pasta still in his hand. "I guess I realized you might be right."

Every girl Brian could trace back through his long line of failed relationships had been the same, all the way back to his first college girlfriend. It was like college had woven this idea into his mind that he needed a relationship to be whole—like seeing all his frat brothers and work friends always wrapped around some girl made him think he needed one, too—until he'd started seeing things in people that were never there.

But Maggie had been the worst, not just because she'd

broken his trust, but because she'd been horrible to his brother. Brian still resented her for that.

"Oh, sorry," Pearl said. "I didn't mean to break the illusion."

But Brian just shook his head, pushing his thoughts aside as he stepped over to the microwave to reheat his dinner. "It's fine. I mean, it's better this way. Now I can work on finding someone I can build an actual future with."

Pearl fake coughed. "Like Mia."

"Or, you know, an actual girl."

"Brian—"

"Besides," Brian said before Pearl could give him the impending *why are you so naive lecture*, "Mia's the one who suggested we keep things platonic, so I'm pretty sure she's not into me that way. And it wouldn't really be fair to put that kind of pressure on her."

"On her, or on you?" Pearl said. "Because it sounds to me like you're just running from accepting some hard truths about yourself and looking for an excuse to get away with it."

"You know, for someone who 'prefers not to use labels,' you sure seem awfully invested in mine," Brian said. "Is it really so hard to just let people live their lives without all the judgment?"

"When they constantly insist on making bad decisions? Yes, absolutely!"

But nothing about this situation constituted a bad decision as far as Brian could tell. He'd made a new friend, found a new means to explore the city, and matured enough to acknowledge any fluttering he felt around Mia was just his imagination getting carried away again. If anything, that was growth.

Needing a break from Pearl's scrutiny, Brian decided to take a walk. Since he'd arrived in New York, he'd come to associate long walks as just a means of transportation, but as he exited the old apartment building, he tried to really take in the block—the brownstones that'd probably been built long before his hometown had even been established, the rich green of the trees that looked like mere saplings compared to the ones back in Denver, and the uneven, partially uprooted sidewalks that Noah would probably call an ADA violation. The distinct urge to picture himself walking down the same sidewalk with another hand in his was almost overwhelming, but instead of Anna this time, it was Mia.

Well, Mia still in drag, the same way all of his fantasies tended to go.

He shook the thought away, trying to focus on the scenery, trying to keep his mind fixated on redefining New York. He desperately wanted to see it as it was, not connected to the people he explored it with, just…its own thing.

But the more he urged himself not to think about people, the more their faces bounced around in his head—first Mia, then Anna, then Pearl and Dustin, and Ella. He'd never attempted to unknot his experiences from other people before, and trying to do that now felt nearly impossible.

In a weird way, going from a huge group of casual friends to a tiny trio with Pearl and Dustin hadn't been that big of a change, thanks to Pearl chattering enough to compensate for ten people. And the way they'd both welcomed him in to hang out with their friends was enough that he could pretend he was being far more social than he really was.

But there was also something suffocating about it. Maybe it was the fact that his friendships had always been mostly casual, or maybe it was just the way his friendship with Pearl flipped his usual relationship dynamic on its head. Overseeing Noah's first relationship to make sure he didn't get into any serious trouble? Easy. Keeping watch over his frat brothers so they didn't end up with a DUI? An average Friday. Running whatever errands Ella asked for to keep her from getting too overwhelmed and forgetting something vital before a huge event? Exactly what he'd signed up for. But having an overprotective friend always on his back to make sure he wasn't making any major mistakes? He wasn't really sure how to handle that.

Not because he couldn't see the value in having a friend who reminded him to grab his wallet before he left and made sure he never ran out of his favorite breakfast cereal, but just because he was always the one holding the reigns. So, if that wasn't his job anymore, where was he even needed?

He drew out his phone, pulling up Mia's contact info. Despite texting off and on since they'd exchanged numbers at the bar, he still felt a little shy about being forward with her. Ordinarily, he could talk to a girl no problem, but this almost felt harder because things with Mia were just…different. Maybe because he wanted to be friends instead of a couple.

Why were friendships so hard?

Finally, he typed out, *Any chance you'd want to get ice cream or something with me?* and hit send before he could think better of it.

A squirrel skittered by his foot before racing into the bushes, and he typed, *Or I can just hang out with the squirrels. You know, whatever.*

After he hit send again, he paused, regret washing over him like cold water. Did he really need to add that follow up? He probably just sounded like a fuckboy at this point.

Then a reply came in, stopping his spiraling thoughts mid-whirl.

Aw, I wish I could, but I'm free Saturday? Say hi to the squirrels for me! Maybe you'll make a friend.

Maybe he should've expected that sort of cartoony response from someone he'd met in a Totoro costume, but more than anything, he was just glad they'd actually responded and actually sounded interested in seeing him.

I can do Saturday :) See you then!

Once he'd sent his reply and tucked his phone away, a seed of calm settled in him. Maybe it was okay if he didn't have a sense of direction. Maybe it wouldn't be so bad to spend an evening just hanging out on his own and communing with some squirrels.

Saturday, just after one o'clock, Brian caught a train to Brooklyn to meet Mia outside of an art museum.

Museums had always had the sort of academic energy that put Brian out of his comfort zone, so he couldn't say he frequented them, but this place was nothing of the sort. The street stretched out rough and unpaved and a little torn up around the edges, and almost every building on the block was covered in vibrant graffiti art.

"Interesting choice of venue," he said as he found Mia out front, bouncing idly on their heels.

They were dressed in plain jeans and an anime t-shirt, looking like just about any guy Brian might see wandering around on campus. But their energy was totally different—more feminine, definitely, but also just livelier and more infectious.

Mia smiled. "There's an exhibit in town this week that I really wanted to see. Come walk with me?"

When Mia first texted him the location, he'd felt pretty lukewarm about it, but the radiant excitement sparkling off of Mia's face spiked his own eagerness to match theirs.

Mia paid for both of their admission, even though Brian insisted he could do it. "I'm the one who dragged you all the way out here, after all. And I know you probably aren't making a whole lot from your internship."

Brian rolled his eyes. "Ah, as opposed to the competitive rates of drag tips."

Mia smiled. "You don't think I can make a lot in tips?"

Their playful, almost flirty tone felt like an invitation for Brian to guess how much people actually paid to get a closer look at her fishnets, but just the thought sent heat shooting through Brian's face. "I can still pay my own admission," he said. "Otherwise, it seems like we're on a date, doesn't it?"

Mia smirked. "Oh, so you're *ashamed* to be seen with me, hm?"

Brian spluttered. "I-I didn't—"

But Mia just laughed, waving him off. "I work in tech. It's not a very immersive position, but the pay's better than I deserve."

"Tech?"

"Well, officially I'm billed as a software designer, but I don't do a whole lot of actual designing. I mostly give feedback on what the company's developing." Mia snatched a pamphlet from the plastic holder at the edge of the front desk, flipping through the pages. "Oh, here it is."

"What is it?"

Mia just flashed him a wink. "It's a surprise, but I think you'll like it."

They turned, motioning for Brian to follow them as they headed down a dark, narrow hallway. The building as a whole hadn't looked that large from the outside, but whoever set the layout had really leveraged the space. The short hallway opened into a larger room, nondescript makeshift walls funneling foot traffic toward an opening bathed in red, like a beacon peeking out of the sea of gray. Mia headed toward the doorway, their footsteps practically silent against the gray carpet.

Brian fell into step beside them, saying, "So how'd you go from drag to software design?"

"Drag is a hobby. I went to school for comp sci."

"Oh, so you're like *smart* smart."

Mia laughed. "I'm literally the nerdy Asian stereotype. Overbearing parents and all."

But Brian was pretty sure the stereotype had no mention of eyes as deep as obsidian or thighs that were made to be draped in fishnets.

"Um, so if you're into all that stuff, wouldn't you be better off on the West Coast then out here?" Brian asked.

Mia reached the red door and paused, turning back to Brian with a pensive look. "You know, I've actually thought about it, and probably, but I don't think I could ever be that far from my family. Even now, I only left a couple months ago, and they still guilt me every time I see them."

"Where does your family live?"

"Vermont. It's super boring, very white, and the only thing's it's got going for it are a slightly left-leaning agenda and an astonishing lack of corporate chains."

Brian smiled. "I mean, it's not like you'd never see your family again. My parents live in L.A., and I go to school in Denver."

"Okay, but Denver isn't as far as Vermont. And it's got a major airport," Mia said. "Flying from Burlington to Seattle would be—" They winced "—let's just go with, not fun. Besides, my parents have a lot of expectations for me, and they can be kind of needy, so if I just up and run, they'll probably disown me."

They tossed the words out flippantly enough that Brian could have taken them as a joke, but their lips pressed together just a little too tightly when they finished speaking, like maybe they actually believed it.

"You really think they'd disown you?" Brian asked.

They shrugged. "Maybe not, but I think most Asian parents can only handle so much disappointment before they lose it."

"What makes you think you disappointed them?"

Before Mia could respond, a groan cut through the air. Brian turned to find a couple of teenage girls standing behind them, hand in hand and looking frustrated.

"Please hurry up," the one closest to them said.

Mia just winced, grabbing Brian's wrist and awkwardly stepping aside so the teens could pass them. "Sorry, just go ahead of us."

Once they were gone, Mia turned to Brian and laughed. "That was so embarrassing. We should probably check out the gallery now."

"Oh, right," Brian said, though he had to admit that he doubted anything in this museum could be as beautiful as the sound of Mia's voice.

They stepped through the red doorway, but all Brian's brain could process was *bright*. The walls were splattered with red paint that transitioned into orange further down like a gradient. The new hall they were in wasn't exceptionally wide, but pieces lined the wall, each one in a red hue. The only real reprieve from the richness of the shade were the small white placards put up with more information about each work.

But as he looked toward the end of the pathway, he could just make out how the color shifted a little more as it rounded the corner, starting to form a rich shade of yellow. Were the hallways forming a rainbow?

"It's cool, isn't it?" Mia asked, smiling. "The artist is queer and all about expressing queerness in ways that showcase depth and nuance. This exhibition is supposed to be all about the corporatization of pride and how absorbing queerness into the mainstream also leads to the erasure of queer history."

Brian looked toward the walls again, looking at the first piece that he'd largely mistaken as some sort of sculpture only to realize it was actually a stack of bricks. A little loose on the "art" as far as Brian was concerned, but "cool" definitely felt applicable.

"It's too bad it's a temporary exhibition," Brian said. "My brother would love this."

"Do you ever look at anything queer without thinking of your brother?"

Brian paused, the slight rise in Mia's tone difficult to discern. "What do you mean?"

"I mean, it seems like everything with you ties back to him," they said. "You can't even check out an art exhibit without mentioning him."

"He's just into queer community stuff," Brian said. "I mean, he blogs about it and everything."

"Yeah, sure, but," Mia said, stepping over to Brian and poking a finger into his chest, "he's also not here. It's okay to just...like queer stuff without consulting your queer brother."

Brian spluttered. "I'm not *consulting* him. Queerness is a big part of his identity, and it's really important to him, so I guess I just think about him when I see queer stuff. Is that so bad?"

"No, it's not bad," Mia said, but a wide smile had already overtaken their face. "And as far as being a brother goes, I think it's sweet that you think about him so much. It just seems…limiting to associate an entire community, culture, and history with one person, don't you think?"

"If this is about Anna—"

"It's not," Mia said. "Though you do have that problem, don't you? Associating things with one person."

"Okay, enough," Brian said, grabbing Mia's wrist and tugging them further into the exhibit.

He'd probably have to reckon with what they were saying, but at the very least, he could do it somewhere that didn't leave him feeling so exposed.

Most art left Brian with the same sort of impression—Confusion? Uncertainty? Like he was looking at something infinite enough to provide all the answers, but they were in some language he couldn't understand and was better off ignoring. But exploring the exhibit with Mia—listening to them rattle off their theories of how certain lines of history inspired certain brush strokes and figure placement—really breathed new life into the experience and actually made him think he might enjoy doing something like this again.

As they neared the end of the exhibit, Mia turned to him with an embarrassed expression. "Sorry, I'm probably boring the hell out of you, huh?" they said. "I tend to draw weird lines between things sometimes, but I probably just sound high."

"No, you're fine." The words rushed out on one quick breath, like he desperately needed to voice them before something precious slipped through his fingers. "I like listening to you talk."

Mia smiled. "Um, are you hungry? We can go grab dinner."

"Sure, yeah."

And while Brian wouldn't have been opposed to spending another half hour just listening to Mia wax poetic about the implications of lilac in contrast to the more popular indigo, he had to admit that food probably needed to be made a priority.

So they left the museum, Mia leading the way back toward the station.

"Do you like Korean food?" Mia asked.

"Yeah, why?"

"There's actually this really great place out where I'm staying," they said, "but, you know, that's in Queens."

"That's cool. I don't mind."

"Oh?" They raised an eyebrow. "Clearly, you're not from around here."

Brian laughed, though he couldn't refute it. Pearl would've gone on a twenty-minute-long rant if Brian had even suggested going out to Brooklyn for an art exhibition, but to then suggest a restaurant in *Queens*? Boroughs might as well be countries as far as the locals were concerned, but Brian grew up in a city where he had to drive ten miles just to go to his orthodontist, so a simple train ride out to Queens couldn't possibly be more convenient.

And taking the trip out there with Mia only made him wish the ride could be a little longer.

12

Donning the Mia persona was supposed to be as simple as stepping into a new pair of shoes. Sure, there might be a bit of a "breaking in" period, a couple blisters, even a missed step or two, but one didn't just *forget* how to ride a new pair of pumps. Muscle memory and all that.

But being Mia meant being everything Thomas wasn't— audacious, poised, *confident*—and without all the makeup and falsies and an extra twenty pounds of hair, he couldn't really trick himself into believing he could be those things. When he'd caught himself mid-info dump back at the exhibition, he'd nearly died of mortification. The final nail in his coffin was served in the form of the vacant-eyed confusion plastered across Brian's face.

And he wasn't sure at what point he'd slipped out of costume, but somehow, he'd ended up letting his guard down completely, the elegance and allure of Mia evaporating away to an awkward silence in the air. Thomas fiddled with his hands as the train barreled toward Queens, too nervous to even look at Brian, knowing he must be even more uncomfortable than Thomas felt.

The car finally squealed to a stop, and Thomas stood quietly, waiting for Brian to tell him he'd changed his mind and wanted to go back to Manhattan, but Brian followed him onto the platform and over to the stairs like normal.

It was only as they reached the crosswalk that Brian grabbed Thomas by the wrist and said, "Hey, you okay?"

Struggling to muster up enough "Mia" to not scare him away, Thomas turned to tell him that everything was fine. But the second their eyes met, Thomas's stomach twisted, like Brian could see through his carefully crafted image to the mess of a person beneath it. And before Thomas could tell himself to keep his cool, he was rambling again.

"I'm so sorry about earlier. I got caught up in everything, and I didn't even really think about what I was saying, and I didn't even ask if you *liked* art, and—"

Brian stared back at him in horror, and Thomas fought down the urge to run as far and as fast as possible.

Then Brian said, "I—wait, what are you apologizing for?"

"I—well, everything, I guess. Being annoying. And a nerd."

Brian laughed. "You shouldn't apologize for liking things. Or for being annoying." He paused. "I-I mean, not that you're annoying, because you're not! Or, at least, I don't think you are. I don't know if other people do, but I definitely don't, so—"

"Really? You don't?"

"No, not at all!"

They fell into silence for a moment, but the ice was gone. Finally, Thomas smiled and said, "Um, well, I'm glad to hear it. Sorry if I made things weird."

"No, you're fine, really. I… Well, I really like hanging out with you, so…"

Brian trailed off, but Thomas could feel a dorky grin spreading across his face.

Brian liked hanging out with him even though he was a rambling mess, and that meant the only person keeping Thomas from being happy in this moment was Thomas.

So it was time he stopped doing that.

"Um, so, dinner?" Brian said.

And Thomas laughed. "Yes, right! Sorry!"

Thomas punched the crosswalk button so they could clear the line of traffic. The small shop sat nestled between a convenience store and some shop that had since closed down, but even the tinted windows welcomed him warmly, given how often he'd been there. His apartment lay two blocks over, and because the food was excellent and the owners were friendly, he'd quickly carved a safe haven out of the place, his one familiar beacon in a city that moved too fast.

As soon as they entered, the old woman who owned the shop with her husband motioned them over to an empty table. In a lot of ways, she reminded him of his own mom—even though his mom would probably slap him if he said that, since this woman was about twenty years older and quite a bit heavier—but he still took comfort in her presence. He slipped into the open table, Brian hesitantly following behind him.

Thomas grabbed two of the paper menus sitting in the holder and passed one to Brian. One thing he appreciated about this place was that they hadn't transitioned over to digital-only menus, so he didn't have to worry about his shitty Wi-Fi connection.

"Pretty much everything's good here," Thomas said as his eyes scanned the menu, even though he had most of it committed to memory. "I've tried almost everything."

He looked up to find a deeply concentrated look on Brian's face before he slapped the menu back down onto the table with a look of triumph. "Okay, I think I know what I want."

Thomas whistled. "Ain't that the dream."

Brian raised an eyebrow, and Thomas just winced.

"Sorry, I don't know why I said that."

Brian laughed, and the cheerful melody quickly chased any insecurity away. "You apologize too much, you know that? You're super cool, multiply talented—"

Thomas blushed. "Really? You think so?"

"I mean, software design, drag. And you obviously have a penchant for art."

"Oh, I don't make it, but I do appreciate it," Thomas said,

awkwardly looking down at the menu. "Well, except the costumes. Those I do make."

"You think making costumes and doing makeup don't count as art?" Brian asked, but his tone was teasing.

Thomas looked up, an eyebrow raised. "Yeah, well, you think hitting on a guy is straight if he's wearing a leotard."

Brian's jaw dropped, and Thomas clapped his hands over his own mouth.

"I'm so sorry. I don't know why I just said—"

"It's not—" Brian started before heaving a sigh. "Okay, it's—it's not like I have a problem with being queer or anything. It just feels kind of—I just don't want to overstep or—"

Thomas shook his head. "I'm sorry. I shouldn't have said that. You can explore your identity in your own time, and you don't have to answer to me. That was so uncalled for."

Brian stared back at him for a moment before a small smile tugged as his lips. "So, is that what you're doing? Exploring your identity in your own time?"

"What do you mean?"

"Well, I asked if you were a woman before, but you never really told me what you were so—"

Thomas bit his lip. "Oh, yeah, that. I guess so. I've read a lot about gender expression throughout history, especially outside of Western colonial standards. And even in modern times..."

He froze, catching himself before he could launch too far into territory that would only bore Brian out of his mind. But then, Brian had said that he didn't find Thomas annoying, and even now, as he was about to ramble them both to death, Brian's face seemed intrigued, like he was still waiting for Thomas to continue, so maybe...

"Um, I don't want to bore you—"

"I—but you can't just end on a cliffhanger," Brian said. "I wanted to know what you were gonna say."

And a small smile tugged at Thomas's lips as he continued, "Well, there's just a lot to consider. Like, did you know that some people see gay and lesbian as distinct genders, too? Because of the unique experiences queer people have in relation to their gender as opposed to the way allocishet people experience it? Sometimes I think it'd be easier to just think of my gender through my sexuality. I've basically always known I was gay. It feels a lot easier to figure out. Either you're attracted to someone or you aren't."

Brian winced. "I...guess."

Thomas grinned. "Okay, well, maybe that's not that easy, either. I guess it doesn't really matter, you know? We don't even have to use labels if we don't want to. I think I just feel bad because..."

Brian raised an eyebrow. "Because everyone else has everything figured out, and now you feel like you're too late to the party, and you're just taking up space from people who need it more than you do?"

Thomas stared back at Brian for a moment before bursting into a fit of laughter. It was enough to make his sides ache and his throat sore, but wow. He hadn't even realized what he wanted to say until the words had flown flawlessly out of Brian's mouth like Thomas had scripted all of it.

As Thomas sobered up, he said, "Yeah, I guess it's something like that."

And Brian just smiled back at him.

The old woman who owned the shop walked up to them with a paper pad in hand and a scrunch to her brows. Thomas resisted the urge to offer up an apology for how loud he'd been a moment before and, instead, rushed to give her an order.

Once she left the table, Brian turned back to Thomas and said, "So you made the sexy Totoro costume?"

Thomas grinned. "Oh, Brian, don't ask me about costuming if you aren't prepared to be saddled with tons of information you don't need and probably won't understand."

"I'm fine with that. Are you working on anything new?"

Thomas jerked forward, balling his hands into fists in his lap to keep himself from shooting out of his seat in excitement.

"Well, I stalled for a really long time, so to keep myself focused, I wanted to keep all my new costumes on theme. So my next project is a gender-bent Howl Pendragon. It's like eighty percent done, and the bodice looks great. Also, the fabric for the cape was all but impossible to find, so I actually ended up recycling some of my old costumes to—" Cutting himself off, Thomas smiled and said, "Anyway, the point is it's coming along. But enough about me. I know I've been dominating the conversation all day. What do you do for fun?"

"Um, does partying count?"

"It counts, but it's not exactly original."

"Fair. Actually, now that you mention it, I guess I don't really know."

Thomas paused, going back over the question to figure out if maybe he'd worded it weirdly. "How do you not know what you like?"

Brian laughed awkwardly. "Well, for the past eight months or so, I've just been doing whatever Anna liked. So, going to the movies, drinking with her friends. She was really into plants, so sometimes we went to nurseries and stuff."

"But you don't like any of those things?"

"It's not that I don't like them, exactly," Brian said. "I enjoyed doing all of them with her. I guess I just kind of like everything, so I didn't really care what we did."

Oh, no. This guy needed more help than Thomas had originally thought. "Nobody likes everything."

"Well, I'll let you know if I ever find something that I hate."

"It's not just about hating things. When you find something you really like, everything else will look dull in comparison."

Brian paused, staring back at Thomas, who awkwardly shifted under his gaze.

"Did I say something weird?"

"I—no," Brian said hurriedly. "Um, I guess I'll let you know if something stands out."

Thomas smiled. "I'm sure we can find something you'll love. The city's got everything. So, why'd you and your girlfriend break up? I mean, if you don't mind me asking? I find it hard to believe you just didn't see eye to eye given how agreeable you are."

Brian sighed, picking at the edge of his menu. "Yeah, about that. She, um, wanted me to meet her parents, but they didn't like me very much."

"How come?"

Brian looked up then, lips pressed together. "Guess they were kind of racist."

"Oh, gross."

Brian smiled. "Gross?"

"I mean, is there really another response to that?" Thomas asked. "No offense. I imagine you still care about her."

"None taken," Brian said. "Honestly, when it happened, all I could think about is how badly Noah would judge me for it. He's...well, he's very decisive."

"There's that brother talk again."

"Oh, sorry."

Thomas laughed. "You're fine. I just think it's funny how you frame everything in your life around other people."

"I guess I'm just...trying to figure out what I want, you know?" Brian said. "Like, as pathetic as it is to be jealous of your younger brother, I think about how Noah has this perfect relationship, and I wonder what I'm doing wrong."

Thomas smirked. "You date a lot of white girls?"

Brian laughed. "To be fair, Denver has a lot of white girls."

"Long-distance exists for a reason."

"Yeah, that's what Noah's doing, but I don't think I could pull it off. Physical intimacy's huge for me."

Thomas's eyes shot down to the table, warmth flooding his cheeks before he could remind himself that Brian's sexual preferences really had nothing to do with him. Really.

But the thought of physical intimacy was also one of those things that left him feeling a little ungrounded, like he was floating awkwardly inside of his own body instead of steering it. From a hypothetical perspective, sex was great. Sex in books, sex in movies, sex dreams—he could get swept up in a finely tuned sexual fantasy as well as just about anyone else he knew.

The catch was that, in his fantasies, he never really had to exist. He could observe without ever having to think about the mechanics and the finer details and the way his details often felt like some typos and smeared ink that'd accidentally gone to print.

Thomas looked up at Brian, struggling to shake off some of his awkwardness as he said, "Um, so does that mean you don't want to find anyone in New York?"

Brian sighed. "I don't know. Part of me wants to find someone just because I don't have Anna anymore, but what's the point if we're just gonna go our separate ways in a couple of months, you know?"

Thomas could definitely say that he did not, in fact, "know," but his stomach still sunk a little as Brian said it. Not because anything was going to come out of their strictly platonic friendship, but just because…well, maybe there was a part of him that wouldn't hate it if something did.

"It's okay to have a relationship just for fun," Thomas said. "It doesn't have to last forever."

"I know."

But for five letters, those words carried way too much weight.

Thomas reached for his silverware, even though what he really wanted was to reach for Brian's hand and ask him to open up about whatever he'd buried away in those two words. But Brian had made it abundantly clear that he wasn't looking for anything serious, and Thomas was confused enough about his own life without making things more complicated for the both of them.

13

While Brian had been keeping track of the number of drinks he'd had, the tally was something like one and half bottles of soju in his mouth and another half bottle down his shirt. But by the time Mia offered to take him back to her place to lend him a shirt and introduce him to her sexy Howl costume, the tally had long been lost.

"That's the problem with soju," Mia said as she shuffled around in her pocket for her keys. "It doesn't have as much bite, so you almost don't notice how much damage it's doing."

"Noted," Brian said, a laugh bubbling up in his chest. "Remind me of that next time."

Mia flashed him a grin before finally getting the door unlocked and pushing it open.

Brian stepped forward to follow her into the apartment, but before he could, she jerked the door closed again, quickly turning to him with a neutral expression.

"What happened?" Brian asked.

"No, nothing. Um, do you mind if I go in, and you just wait out here for a second?"

"Um, sure?"

"Thanks!"

Mia slipped inside the apartment, quickly closing the door behind her. Even from a few feet away, Brian could hear some shuffling furniture and slamming doors before, finally, some footsteps, and Mia pulled the door open again. "Sorry about that! Come in!"

The apartment lacked square footage, which Brian had come to accept as a basic New York requirement. A small living room sat to his left and a smaller bathroom to his right. Just past the kitchen counter, the full-sized bed lay hastily made, and just a few feet from that sat a long wooden table that was probably supposed to be a dining table but was now buried under messy sketches and pin cushions with a sewing machine at its center.

Mia's quick cleanup job still left the apartment in a state of disarray—the coffee table lined with empty glasses, a couple books open and face down on just about every surface, and an overflowing laundry basket spilling onto the floor at the foot of the bed. It wasn't uninhabitable, though, and as Brian kicked off his shoes and left them on the shoe rack by the front door, he couldn't help but appreciate the entertaining space she'd carved out between all the costuming materials and craft books.

"Um, sorry for the mess," Mia said with a quick laugh. "I just kind of got used to it."

"It's okay," Brian said, following them to the couch and getting comfortable against the plush throw pillows.

As chaotic and disorganized as the space was, the colorful decor and artistic clutter felt very Mia, and that made the whole room feel warm.

"Just one more thing to disappoint my Asian parents, I guess," Mia said.

Brian couldn't help but laugh. "It's okay. My mom's the exact same way, but she raised some pretty messy kids."

"Is your mom Japanese?" Mia asked.

Brian paused. "I—yeah, how could you tell?"

Mia blushed, sitting down on the couch next to Brian and pulling one of the throw pillows into her lap as she pulled at the frills. "I—you have Japanese cheekbones. Sorry if it's weird to, like, say that."

As far as racial comments went, Brian couldn't say it was much of a gut punch, though it was a bit unexpected. It was more common for people to ask what he was or pose completely inaccurate guesses than it was for someone to actually clock him, but the flustered look on Mia's face made the comment even sweeter, like she hadn't really *meant* to see him for exactly who he was, it just sort of happened, and here they were locked in this bubble that felt weirdly intimate.

No, it wasn't weird. Because they were friends. It was just a friendship level of intimacy, nothing that Brian needed to pry too deeply into.

Brian forced his eyes away, instead saying, "Um, so about that costume," before he could let himself get too wrapped up in the moment.

"Oh! Right! I totally forgot!" Mia stumbled off the couch, half-tripping over the pink, frilled rug before quickly righting herself. "Um, just a second. Oh! Do you want something to drink or something while I'm gone?"

Brian just smiled. "No, you're fine."

Mia smiled back before turning and heading into the bathroom.

Brian's mind was already racing with too many ideas of what Mia might look like when she finally emerged, so he pulled out his phone, seeking a distraction from his daydreams. The last thing he wanted to do was make her uncomfortable, so getting a hard-on on her couch before she even showed him the costume was completely out of the question.

He scrolled through his missed messages—a few texts from Pearl, each more harried than the last.

You coming home for dinner?

Yo, Ramirez, where the hell did you go?

What do I have to do, call the cops???

The last message had only been sent a few minutes ago, but Brian quickly fumbled over the phone, calling her before she could send any police to come kicking down Mia's door and probably shooting him in the face.

"What the hell?" Pearl snapped by way of greeting. "Where are you?"

"Sorry, I've been hanging out with Mia all day. You didn't call the cops, did you?"

"No, I just knew it would get your attention."

Brian rolled his eyes, kind of wishing she were in the room just long enough to see it. "Okay, well, you got my attention."

"Where are you now?"

"At Mia's place," he said with an exasperated sigh. He wasn't sure why he felt self-conscious talking about it, but he dropped his voice lower so Mia wouldn't overhear him, anyway.

"Seriously? You went home with a stranger? What is *with* you men?"

"She's not a stranger! Besides, I moved in with you, and you were just as much of a stranger as she was."

"We met through work," Pearl countered.

"I met her through work, too."

"As a *contractor!*"

Brian wasn't really sure that the technical distinction mattered, but fighting with Pearl over this felt like a waste of a good night. "Whatever," he said. "Unless you have something important to tell me, I'm just gonna go now, okay?"

"Drop me a pin, so I know where to find your body."

"Don't call the cops unless you want me to haunt you for eternity."

"Yeah, yeah."

Brian hung up the phone, quickly sending his location to Pearl. He doubted someone who'd sewn their own sexy Totoro costume was particularly likely to try to butcher him, but if it gave Pearl some peace of mind—and kept her from calling back—he figured it was worth the trade-off.

A few minutes later, Mia stepped out of the bathroom dressed in the signature white and pink Howl outfit, but instead of the usual shirt and pants, a skintight body suit traced her silhouette down along her hipbone before cutting off mid-thigh. Replacing the pink jacket typically worn over the shoulders, an identically patterned pink cape curtained her upper half until she swung her arm out, the fabric billowing around her in waves as she struck a pose.

Without the makeup and glitter and heels, she looked less like a drag queen and more like a regular cosplayer, but the word "regular" felt painfully out of place. Mia didn't need glitter to glow. Even in the cramped, cluttered living room, her smile was enough to bathe her in light.

"What do you think?" she asked, slinking over to the wall and draping herself against it like a swimsuit model posing for a shoot.

Not that she, in any way, needed to do that. Brian had been holding his breath since she left the bathroom, and it was only as he said, "Beautiful," that he was able to let it out again. Then, he sucked in a gulp of air before saying, "I mean, it looks good. Great, even! Do you have a show in mind for it?"

Mia smiled, stepping over and sitting down next to him on the couch. "Nah. To be honest, I don't do nearly as many shows as I'd like."

Brian was almost painfully aware of how close she sat, the smooth, exposed skin of her bare thigh only a few inches from his own leg. He struggled to pull his eyes back up to her face as he said, "Oh, um, why not?"

But Mia didn't seem to notice. She'd moved on to playing with one of the throw pillows again, saying, "I just run out of venues. Plus, I have a bunch of other things that take priority, so I don't really get as much time to look into events as I'd like."

"Right, yeah, that makes sense," Brian said. "I'm glad it has nothing to do with your family."

Mia's eyes shot to him, and Brian froze. He'd been so concentrated on avoiding staring that he'd forgotten to avoid any awkward conversation.

"My family?" Mia said, an eyebrow raised.

Brian laughed uncomfortably, waving her off. "Earlier, you mentioned not wanting to disappoint them, so I'm glad that isn't it. It'd be sad if you were neglecting your passions over—"

Mia sighed, looking down at her hands for a second. "Right. I mean, I'm not gonna stop doing shows because of them or anything, but I guess I can't say they have nothing to do with it. My parents can't know about drag. I think their heads would explode."

"Are they homophobic?"

"No," she said, but the word dragged out a little too long to be natural. Finally, she sighed, running a hand through her hair. "They're not homophobic, but they don't have a wide imagination, you know? My brother's gay, and they accept him and have basically welcomed his boyfriend into the family, but…"

"But?"

Mia shrugged. "I'm not your token TV gay, you know? I'm not your *Will & Grace* or *Queer Eye*. I'm a flaming, faggoty queer. And couple that with the fact that I'm supposed to be the good, wholesome son who's gonna give them grandchildren—"

Brian took Mia's hand in his. The move probably reeked of audacity, but he hadn't been able to resist springing to action after seeing the sadness nestled in her eyes. "Being queer doesn't mean you can't be a good son."

"I know. It's the 'wholesome' part I worry about it." Mia laughed humorlessly, throwing herself back among the couch cushions. "I'm not family friendly. I don't think I ever could be, you know, assuming I even wanted to. And my parents already lost a lot when my brother came out, so looking at me? Well, I can't even tell them *what* I am. I mean, I think 'mom, dad, I'm actually a woman' would be easier than 'mom, dad, I'm literally just a freak,' you know?"

"I don't think you're a freak at all," Brian said, hoping he'd infused enough earnestness into his voice to convince her. "But you could always…try out being a woman. See if it suits you."

Mia raised an eyebrow. "I'm literally a drag queen."

"No, I know. I just meant… Well, drag is a performance, right? So it's not like it would feel like you should feel every day.

But you could try just, like…living as a woman. Or anything else, for that matter"

Mia laughed. "I wouldn't even know where to begin. I don't really feel safe going out in public like that, and they probably wouldn't mind at work, but I don't want to tell them to address me differently when I'm not even sure——"

"Okay, well, maybe you can just experiment a bit with someone you trust not to judge you, until you find something that makes you more comfortable."

Mia stared back at him for a moment before a small smile spread across her face. "You mean, like you?"

Brian winced, his face warm. "I-I didn't mean *specifically*——"

But before Brian could finish his sentence, Mia closed the space separating them, her lips finding his.

Any logical thought Brian had been trying to form evaporated at her touch. His body flipped into autopilot as he kissed her back, one arm sliding around her waist to steady her. And while she was only a few inches shorter than him without the heels, the way his arm fit around her slim waist made her feel smaller, like he might accidentally overwhelm her if he wasn't careful.

Mia slid forward, her hip brushing against his as she maneuvered herself almost into his lap. Her lips felt soft under his, her hands warm and gentle as they reached along the sides of his face, but her fingers were callused—probably from all the sewing.

Then she froze, jerking back a moment later with wide eyes and heavy breaths. "Sorry," she said through a breathy laugh. "That was kind of sudden."

But Brian's head was already shaking before she could finish. "I don't mind," he said, reaching to pull her back to him.

So, she fell into his touch, their lips crashing together again.

The weight of her body against his felt so real compared to the retreating apartment around them. The smooth, softness of her skin as he ran a hand up her thigh, the warmth of her as she straddled his hips and slid her tongue into his mouth. Her kisses stole the breath from his lungs, like clawing his soul from his very body and transporting him into a world that was just Mia.

But he didn't mind in the slightest. Hell, he was grateful. Air had nothing on the girl in his arms. Oxygen had never ignited his blood or made him feel as whole as cradling Mia's body did.

As she slid against him, his hand slipped just beneath the fabric of her body suit, gently teasing the stretchy spandex away from her skin. His fingers caressed her hip before sliding back against the side of her ass.

A small gasp escaped her lips as her hand fell to meet his. She held it in place for a moment before gently prying it away, twining their fingers together before shoving him back against the couch arm.

From this angle, there was no denying how slim her physique really was—narrow hips, tiny shoulders, a completely flat chest. Brian's eyes hovered there for a moment as his brain recalled the fact that Mia had only ever had breasts as part of a costume, but this wasn't his sexy Totoro wet dream. This was the real Mia.

He pushed any intruding thoughts away. Now wasn't the time to overthink things. It was like all of his dreams were slowly slipping into reality, and the reality was even better.

She lowered herself onto him, lips trailing along his jawline. This wasn't anything like it'd been with Anna or Maggie or any of the other girls he'd made out with over the past few years. Mia was a force of nature, crashing into him like a tornado, intimate and precise with its destruction, picking each point of weakness with acute accuracy.

Her fingers slid along the hem of his shirt, toying with the fabric. Then they carefully crept up his chest, her nails tickling fine lines along his skin before digging in deeper.

He gripped her arms tight, holding her in place as she leaned into him, her mouth gliding along the base of his throat.

Releasing her, he let his hands fall to her waist, his fingers slipping down to where the fabric began to crinkle along her thigh. As he slipped his fingers underneath, he could feel every curve of her body, the gentle ridge of her hipbone beneath her skin, sliding down to the crest along her thighs. His fingers slid lower, feeling for the swell of her body, which mirrored the swell he felt in his own pants.

But then she jerked back, half tumbling out of his lap as she stumbled to her feet, breath rushing out of her and cheeks flushed. He could still see where his left hand had been twined in her hair just a minute before as she rushed to brush the untidy locks back into place.

"I'm sorry," Brian said, words tumbling out of him. "I'm sorry. I shouldn't have—"

"No, no, it's fine," she said, letting out a breathless laugh. "You're good. *Very* good, I might add."

Brian smiled. "I didn't mean to make you uncomfortable."

"No, no, you didn't," Mia said, still running a hand through her hair. "I mean, I'm not uncomfortable. I'm very comfortable. Maybe too comfortable."

"I don't—"

"It's just been a long time since I've really…done anything like this," she said, eyes awkwardly falling to the floor. "I know that's not exactly the impression I give off, but—"

Brian quickly shook his head before she could downplay her own boundaries. "No, it's fine. I get it. Don't worry."

Mia took a deep breath before sitting down next to him again, though it was virtually impossible not to notice the foot of space she left between them this time. "I just think this was really fast. Especially for two strictly platonic friends—"

"Right, yes, say no more. I totally get it. I think I just got a little carried away because—"

But he couldn't imagine anything more inappropriate in that moment than waxing poetic about how amazing Mia's body had felt against his. That was the last thing he needed to throw at someone trying to hit the brakes.

Hell, maybe he needed to be hitting the brakes, too. Because whatever had just happened between them wasn't like anything he'd experienced before, and now didn't feel like the right time to be interrogating all of that.

But Mia smiled back at him like she'd filled in her own satisfactory answer. "You're sweet," she said. "And I know you've probably been a little lonely since the breakup, right?"

Brian nodded. "Um, yeah, that's probably it." It made more sense that he was just spiraling into a desperate rebound than that he really was spiraling into someone he wasn't even supposed to be attracted to.

"I'd actually like to keep, you know, doing *this* general thing," Mia said, gesturing vaguely. "I mean, you know, a little on the tame side, but—"

"No, yeah, I mean, absolutely. I'm totally cool with that."

Mia laughed. "Okay, but actually, let me change first. No need to tempt the Fates."

Which Brian couldn't really refute, given how he'd almost torn the bodysuit off just a few moments prior. But as Mia got up and headed to the bathroom, he also couldn't shake the eagerness in his body telling him that whatever it was about Mia that had him so deeply enraptured, the clothes had very little to do with it.

14

"You did *what* with him?"

Kris's words all but echoed off the walls of his small office, and Thomas waved a hand in his face, motioning for him to drop the volume. The last thing he needed was for everyone else to start peeking their noses into his love life. Or, his not love life, but whatever exactly it was that he had going on with Brian.

"I said it wasn't that serious!" Thomas said, fiddling with a pencil on Kris's desk, though he knew the qualifier didn't help his cause much.

He and Brian had been texting for a little over a week, and the past few days especially had been pretty committed. After Brian left Saturday night, he'd texted Thomas a "goodnight" followed by a "good morning" the next day, which had then barreled into a full day of talking about absolutely nothing. Common Sense and Self-Preservation had settled in on Thomas's shoulders, belting a duet about him being in denial, which only compounded now that Kris was singing the same song.

Thomas had been officially assigned to help Kris get more signups, which really meant being Kris's bitch around the office. All things considered, it wasn't the worst assignment, since being friends with Kris basically meant being his bitch anyway, but since his tasks thus far were "grab me another coffee" and "can you seal all of these envelopes real quick," he figured catching Kris up on the Brian situation might as well be on his work to-do list.

"Bitch, you move fast," Kris said, not looking up from whatever he was deeply scrutinizing on his computer screen. "That's all I'm gonna say."

"I don't," Thomas said. "Mia does. I'm actually discovering an awful lot about her."

Kris rolled his eyes. "Well, I hope she has great health insurance, so you can both get that therapy you need."

Thomas raised an eyebrow. "What's that supposed to mean?"

Kris looked up slowly, his piercing blue eyes cutting straight through Thomas with a single, slow blink. "You just almost jumped in the sack with this guy on the first date."

"You're one to judge," Thomas scoffed, "considering you're practically the queen of one-night stands."

"Oh, no, that's not what I'm judging," Kris said, a glittering purple nail cutting the air in front of Thomas's face. "In fact, if you wanna go to town, I'll be the first to congratulate you. But what happened to no strings? What happened to being careful? What happened to *Michelle*?"

Thomas's head jerked back, but Kris's tiny office was far too small to escape the sound of that name. "That's so unnecessary."

"Okay, whatever," Kris said, though his tone almost sounded apologetic. "I just don't want to see you jump without any landing plans. I worry about you, baby."

Kris turned back to his computer, and Thomas just stared at him for a moment before getting up and stepping over to him.

"What's wrong with you?" Thomas asked. "Niceness? On the nose? What are you, terminal?"

Kris rolled his eyes. "Obviously, I'm stressed. And horny."

Which, often enough, went hand in hand for Kris, but if he was stressed enough to go spiraling into a full-blown manic episode, things with the app must be going worse than Thomas realized.

"Are the signups really that bad?" Thomas asked.

"Please, capitalism gonna capital."

Which was exactly the sort of non-answer Thomas could typically expect if Kris was avoiding something, but he doubted it was something he could actually pry out of him.

"So what do you need me to do?" Thomas asked.

"Face reality and stop signing up to ride a mechanical bull with buttered asscheeks."

Thomas groaned, trying to shove the gruesome visual out of his mind. "I meant about work."

"Oh." Kris looked up just long enough to slide his travel mug in Thomas's direction. "Get me another coffee, will you?"

Thomas grabbed the mug with an annoyed huff, but the mindless task just gave him more time to stew on his thoughts of Brian, which he figured was a more worthwhile use of his time.

"So, if you could live anywhere, where would it be?"

Thomas paused to think over Brian's question, watching a woman walk by with a golden retriever eagerly trotting along at the other end of the leash. Meeting up during the week had been harder than anticipated, thanks to both of their work schedules. Even without any real assignments in the office, Kris had insisted that Thomas make sure to check the Agenda app every evening and spend some time talking to anyone who matched with him to give them a little more confidence in the kinds of connections they could make. But that also meant Thomas's social life was basically just his work life now on top of already spending forty hours on the job.

So, it wasn't until Friday afternoon that he'd been able to meet up with Brian again, and with nothing interesting planned, they'd ended up in Central Park over lunch, since it was the first place Brian had gone with Anna. At the very least, Thomas hoped that helping Brian pick up some good memories of the place might help balance out any Anna remnants.

"Mmm, assuming my family would still be nearby? Maybe San Francisco?"

Brian smiled. "You're into California?"

"I mean, good Asian food, a big queer population, and a lot of dogs? Sounds pretty great. What about you?"

"I don't know," Brian said pensively. He leaned one elbow against his knee, resting his face against his hand. The gesture seemed to be Brian's go to when he had something that needed heavy thought. "I guess I'm just indecisive."

"You can't think of any place you'd want to live?"

"No, it's not that. It's just that anywhere sounds fine. I mean, not like Utah or something, but Miami was cool. Denver's cool. California sounds—"

"Cool?" Thomas supplied.

"Call me cliché, but I feel like anywhere could be home if you make it that way, right?"

"Let me guess," Thomas said, "you're an extrovert."

Brian laughed. "Okay, fine, that's fair. But you're the one with, like, a trillion hobbies. It can't be that hard to meet people, right?"

"Definitely an extrovert."

Brian laughed again.

And the sound of it was becoming comfortingly familiar. Learning someone's sense of humor was the gateway to really knowing them, but Brian had been pretty easy to crack. Puns, sarcasm, dark humor—he pretty much ate it all up the same. Actually, he had the sort of easygoing mirth that made Thomas wonder if maybe he should give standup a try, even if he knew Theo would never let him live that kind of humiliation down.

It was just so nice making Brian laugh. And no matter how silly the joke, Brian couldn't be bothered with the sort of office laughter you tossed around to keep people in your good graces. Every chuckle felt so genuine and natural and warm, and Thomas could easily get lost in it if he let himself.

Finally, Thomas said, "I've always liked the idea of that

whole 'found family' thing, but I'm not so great at it. Maybe that's why I'm so reluctant to leave my parents. I just…don't really do friends besides a couple of stragglers here and there."

"Really?" Brian said, his tone already giving away just how ready he was to challenge that whole notion. "I mean, I don't know your whole life or anything, but Kris seems to care about you a lot."

"You got that from one conversation?"

Brian laughed, that warm, honeysuckle laugh. "I guess I speak from experience, but she butted into your life in the way only a real friend would."

Thomas couldn't help but smile at that. "We met through a mutual friend at school, but neither of us really talk to him anymore."

He didn't want to get into the whole smear campaign that nuked that friendship, how Kris had been the only person to take his side when everything went down, or how he'd been the only person who'd stuck around to help stitch Thomas back up. It was all a bit too heavy for this otherwise light-hearted conversation.

But Thomas also always felt a little weird trying to figure out exactly where Kris fit into his life. Once upon a time, he and Kris hadn't even been close. They'd just been two guys who occasionally talked because of their mutual friend and shared drag scene.

But, now, Thomas wasn't sure what his life would be without him.

"Kris is kind of…a unique situation. We only got close because of this whole fall-out with our old friend group. I don't think I could ever replicate something like that again."

"That may be true, but she's still your friend," Brian said. "I mean, she obviously cares about you, and even if the situation might be kind of weird, that doesn't mean she wouldn't care about you if you'd met some other way. You're really great to be around, so I'm sure plenty of people would gravitate toward you."

A smile tugged at Thomas's lips. "Oh? You think so?"

Brian winced. "Oh, sorry, was that weird?"

"Extremely flattering, actually."

Brian smiled.

"I guess, I just worry that I care about other people more than they care about me," Thomas said. "Especially with Kris. She's so good at making friends and cutting people off like they never meant a thing to her. I have to wonder if I'm just here to fill in the space until she moves on to someone else."

Thomas glanced over at Brian to find him staring back at him blankly, and Thomas winced.

"I—sorry to be so morbid."

Brian shook his head. "No, you're fine. I-I guess that was just shocking to hear because you're—"

"Because I'm...?"

Brian just shook his head again. "Anyway, about Kris—I don't know her super well or anything, but if she makes you feel replaceable, maybe you should just talk to her about it."

But Thomas wasn't sure what he'd say to her. It wasn't even really Kris's fault, per se. It was just hard for Thomas to believe someone that confident, ballsy, and generally exciting could feel any deep investment in Thomas beyond whatever utility he brought to the relationship. And more and more, Thomas had to wonder what that even was.

But he also didn't want to ruin his afternoon out with Brian by saying all of that. If there was one thing he was grateful for, it was the warmth and sunlight Brian could so naturally infuse into Thomas's life, and he wasn't about to waste it.

Visiting Central Park with Brian may have been the perfect way to spend an afternoon, but Thomas probably should've prepared himself for just how perfect it might be. By the time he realized he was enjoying himself a bit too much, he was knee deep in feelings he was never supposed to catch and twenty minutes late getting back to work.

The second didn't concern him too much, but as he rushed

back to the office, the warm feeling in his chest refusing to ebb even with Brian out of sight, Thomas had to wonder if he'd made a colossal mistake. Not just meeting up for lunch, but all of it.

Was he really about to let himself fall for a straight guy?

He pushed the thought out of his head as he cleared the elevator and headed toward Kris's office. He could still hear the tone Kris had used when he'd mentioned Michelle, and the sound of it made Thomas's stomach lurch.

Michelle was an entirely different situation. Thomas hadn't meant to hurt her. Hell, when she'd confessed her feelings to him, he thought he was doing her a favor by trying to make it work, even if he knew he couldn't really love her. At least he was giving her a chance. Maybe things would be different if he just gave it time.

But maybe that was what Kris meant. Brian was pretty sure he was straight, so maybe the other night at Thomas's apartment had been nothing more than *experimenting*, trying out every flavor just to decide which ones were too bitter.

Maybe the warmth Thomas was feeling was entirely one-sided, and all he was doing was delaying the inevitable by pretending there was actually something between them.

"Do *not* stand there making that face at me when you're the one who's late."

Kris's voice startled Thomas back to the real world, standing in the doorway to Kris's office as Kris and Day stared at him.

"Oh, um, sorry," Thomas muttered.

"Jesus, you don't know the first thing about workplace etiquette, do you?" Day said, leveling a look at Kris that Thomas couldn't make out from his current angle, but their tone seemed to have ramped up all the way to mildly annoyed, so he imagined the look was equally harsh.

"With *Thomas*," Kris said, lip curled back. "I don't gotta respect that bitch."

"*Kris.*"

"It's fine," Thomas said, stepping over to Kris's desk. If Kris's bitchiness was a battle he needed fought, he would've stopped being friends with him years ago. "Sorry for being late. I got…caught up in something."

Kris turned to him with a piercing glare that said he saw right through everything Thomas wasn't saying, but Day just gave him a look of mild disappointment and said, "If you need a longer lunch break, just let someone know, okay? We can work something out."

It was probably the single calmest scolding Thomas had ever received in his life, but he still felt the need to say, "I—right. Sorry. It won't happen again."

Day nodded before leaving the office, and Thomas turned back to Kris to find him making obscene gestures at Day's back.

"What is your problem?" Thomas asked.

"*Moi?*" Kris shot back. "*They're* the one going full-blown autocrat, and you're the one too full of shit to do your damn job!"

Thomas raised his hands in surrender. "Okay, *first* of all, you're the one who hasn't really given me anything to do. And *second* of all, what's your problem with Day? They're probably the single chillest boss on the planet."

"Oh my God, do you even *hear* yourself?" Kris snapped.

But not only could Thomas hear himself perfectly, he had no idea what Kris was even mad at. Being twenty minutes late might be a nuisance if he actually had work to do, but this felt more like Kris was throwing a fit because Thomas was ignoring his advice.

So Thomas just said, "If you have work for me to do, tell me what you need, and I'll do it."

Kris stared back at him tensely for a moment before rolling his eyes. "We have to send an update to the boss end of next week. If we don't get our signups out of the goddamn gutter, Day's gonna get chewed out, which means they're gonna chew me out."

"What's the worst they can do? Say they're mildly disappointed in you?"

"You'd be surprised," Kris said. "I know you don't have a lot of friends, but go tell everyone you know to make an account, or, I don't know, put your ass up online and lure people in that way."

"Yeah, I'm not doing that, but I'll ask around," Thomas said, though he already knew he didn't actually have anyone he could pitch the app to. Anyone he knew, Kris already knew and had probably done a far better job selling to.

Well, except Brian, but asking a straight guy to join a queer community app probably wasn't the answer to his problems.

But it did kind of give him the excuse to talk to Brian again, even during company hours.

Kris groaned. "Okay, you are *pissing* me off. Get out of my office."

Thomas balked. "I—what did I do?"

"I don't have time for whatever Hallmark bullshit you're trying to live out right now. I have actual things to do. So get out!"

Thomas just rolled his eyes, turning and leaving the office. Whatever Kris was pissed about probably had little to do with him, and all things considered, his temper was probably just short, which meant practically non-existent since "short-tempered" was pretty much his default.

But whatever warmth had remained in Thomas's chest after his chat with Brian had been cut out by the sharpness in Kris's tone. Thomas's biggest concern had been getting dropped from this job at the end of the summer, but he probably should've realized that would mean getting dropped by Kris, too.

It was practically a law of physics—what goes up, must come down, and every bitch gets dropped eventually.

As far as supervisors went, Ella kind of had it all—nice, fun, reliable but understanding—and Brian felt indebted to her for getting him this internship, which just made it harder to have to break the news to her that her latest event idea just wasn't it.

"What's wrong with it?" she asked, looking up at him from her cluttered desk like a groundhog peeking out of its burrow. Her eyes were a little baggy from lack of sleep, and there was something almost feral in her pupils as she desperately sought to crack this ever-important code.

Brian paused, crossing his arms before uncrossing them again. "Well…"

"People do fundraising auctions all the time," she said, quickly shuffling through the papers on her desk like she could produce the magic proof that would guarantee this event's success. "And it's all going to a good cause. I think people would have a lot of fun with it."

"That may be true, but when the thing you're auctioning off is people—"

"It's just a date," she said.

"Okay, but the second you put a Black person up there, it just sounds like the slave trade."

Ella stared at him blankly for a moment before the light

slowly drained from her eyes. "Maybe we can auction off art instead."

Brian nodded. "Good thinking."

A bubble of guilt welled up in Brian's chest at quashing Ella's dream, but while people argued that even bad press could be good press, he doubted getting canceled over a racism scandal was the kind of press Ella was looking for. Especially since all the chaos around the office lately went back to the donors and needing to impress them with another big event to ensure there weren't any disruptions to their funding.

The drag show had gone over so well that, at least for a moment, things had seemed pretty safe, but when Ella had pitched a bigger drag show as their big event to reign in the Fall, the Board had deemed it "uninspired," so now the pressure was on again.

"Why is brainstorming the perfect event so hard?" Ella asked, as she slumped back in her rolling chair.

Brian didn't bother mentioning that if it were easier, neither of them would've gotten hired. But as difficult as it was to organize an event that brought the community together while also honoring everything the organization stood for *and* bringing in enough people to appease their corporate overlords, the biggest hiccup to Brian's creative process was still Mia.

Well, his inability to stop thinking about her.

They'd yet to repeat that evening in her apartment, but ever since, Brian couldn't get the taste of her off his lips, the feeling of her body off his skin. He'd thought spending some time apart might ease the ache he felt whenever he thought about her, but not seeing each other during the week had only caused her grip on him to grow to the point that even lunch in Central Park on Friday and drinks on Saturday had done little to quench his thirst.

And the more insatiable his appetite grew, the more Pearl's words echoed in his mind. After all, Mia was aloof, occasionally distant, and as much as he hated to admit it, he didn't really know anything about her. Hell, their whole not-relationship was built on his desire for her drag persona, and what spark there was beyond that—well, he'd avoided thinking too hard on that for a multitude of reasons.

Then there was what Mia had said about wanting to keep things platonic. He wasn't sure at what point they'd smeared all the lines like running their hands through pools of wet ink, but he had no idea how to keep their boxes neat and tidy when his hands were already this stained.

"Brian, *focus*," Ella snapped.

"I—what? Yes, totally here for it."

"I didn't pitch anything."

"Oh, right. Sorry."

Ella rolled her eyes. "Okay, look, you're obviously distracted, and I can accept that, but I just need you to hold on for a little bit longer. Once we have a couple of good ideas, we can pitch them all and just pray on the rest."

"Got it."

Which meant he just needed to focus for a couple of hours, and then he was meeting up with Mia for dinner, so maybe he could finally satisfy the gnawing in his gut, once and for all.

Pearl's nagging circled through Brian's mind as he waited for Mia to arrive. He already knew Pearl would launch into a whole tirade if she found out he'd invited "a random stranger" to their apartment while she and Dustin were out, but since she wouldn't actually have to know that, he figured it was mostly harmless.

Since he'd already been to Mia's place, it only seemed fair he invite her to his. But there was also a part of him that was hoping some alone time would mean a little more intimacy than they'd been able to have since going to her place. She may not want anything serious with him, but maybe if he could have just one more real taste of her, he'd finally be satisfied enough to move on.

Mia arrived carrying a tray that she quickly held out to him. "Sorry if this is weird, but I had some free time on Sunday, so I made some Japanese croquettes, and I thought you might want some?"

Brian took the tray, a dorky smile already spreading across his face. "Really? That's so sweet."

Mia shrugged, nonchalantly stepping over to the couch and sitting down even as a small blush spread across her face. "I was feeling kind of homesick, so I thought I'd cook something up."

Brian was maybe just a little bit smitten by how adorable Mia was, smiling and blushing and bringing him snacks. She was basically someone's grandmother, except with perfectly unlined skin and wearing white and purple color block jeans.

"You cook when you're feeling homesick?" Brian asked, setting the tray down on the coffee table before taking a seat next to her.

"Not always, but food always reminds me of my family," she said. "Guess that's what growing up in a café does to you."

"Well, it's nice of you to bring something. I was just gonna order delivery, but this is probably better," Brian said. "Sorry. I didn't think to make anything."

"Do you cook?"

Brian winced. "I...used to? Kind of? It was just a hobby."

"Why'd you stop, if that's not super rude to ask?"

Brian laughed. "Don't judge me, okay? I mostly cooked for my girlfriend, but I guess after we broke up, it was hard to find the motivation anymore. I just didn't have anyone to share it with."

"Anna?" Mia asked.

"No, before her."

"Ah," Mia said, but there was a sort of finality in her tone that would've felt painfully damning if not for the way her face always showed everything she was thinking. "So did you actually enjoy doing it, or was it just for her?"

Brian shrugged. "I think I liked it, but I guess I'd have to try again to figure that out."

Mia smiled. "Well, let me know if you ever need any pointers. I'm happy to share."

Brian went into the kitchen to grab plates, napkins, and drinks before bringing them back over to Mia, who'd already pulled the aluminum foil off the tray. The big, golden brown balls of fried potato and meat wafted a savory smell through the air, and Brian's stomach rumbled in response. He quickly bit into one, the salty crunch hitting him in a rush of sheer euphoria.

"I'm so happy I know you," Brian said, his unfiltered thoughts rolling right off his tongue.

Mia laughed. "Happy to be of service. Honestly, it's nice feeling useful."

Brian raised an eyebrow. "Did something happen?"

Mia frowned. "Just...work stuff. You know."

"Boy, do I know," Brian said with a laugh. "My supervisor's ridiculously stressed trying to plan our next event, and the chaos is really dragging the whole office down."

Mia nodded. "It's the same for me. I mean, not the events thing, but apparently, we're getting some pressure from upper management to get more people to..." She trailed off, her entire expression shifting from frustration to shock to deep contemplation.

"Everything okay?" Brian asked.

She turned to him then with wide eyes. "You work for a queer organization."

"I—yeah, I do."

A smile spread across her face. "Okay, so here's the thing. The app that we're working on is all about bringing queer community together, but we've really been struggling with signups. I think the biggest thing is just getting the word out, you know? But it's hard to find people who are interested, and the app is still kind of slow right now, so—"

"So, you want my help spreading the word?" Brian asked.

Mia crawled closer to him, taking his hand in hers. "It would mean so much to me if you could tell people around work to check it out? It's okay if you can't, but we really need to increase our signups if we want to keep the project going, and I really believe it could be a great thing down the road if just—"

"Of course," Brian said, already folding under the weight of her smile. "I'd be happy to. Can you just send me a link?"

Mia squealed, throwing her arms around him. "Thank you so much!"

"I—"

Then she jerked back, eyes wide and face flushed. "I-I'm so sorry! I don't know what came over me."

"No, you're fine. It's fine. I mean, I don't mind."

She spared him a small smile before leaning back against the couch, and he longed to pull her closer again but settled on just watching her from the few feet that separated them.

"Um, and of course, if there's anything I can do to help you out, I will," Mia said. "Can't say I'm great at event planning, though."

"Don't worry about it," Brian said. "I'm sure Ella will think of something."

They fell into a sudden quiet, and as the seconds ticked by, the weight of it became overwhelming. It wasn't the silence itself that closed in around him so suffocatingly, but the desperate urge welling up inside of him to pull Mia closer. He didn't want to sit around making small talk or discussing work or sitting in silence. He wanted to meld their bodies together, let their breaths mingle, surround himself in every inch of her skin until she left a mark on him that never faded, no matter how much time he was forced to spend away from her.

But, instead, what broke the silence was the soft sound of his phone vibrating on the coffee table.

He stared at it blankly for a moment before realization struck him. "Um, sorry, just a second."

Mia didn't speak as he checked the name on the screen. Pearl.

"Yeah?" he said, but Pearl was already cutting him off.

"Did you eat? We're picking up dinner and coming home."

Brian's eyes widened. "I—wait, now? I thought you were meeting up with some high school friends?"

"We were, but now we're not." Pearl heaved a deep sigh. "It's a long story. Anyway, do you want anything?"

"I—no, I'm fine. How long till you get back?"

"Eh, fifteen minutes maybe? Why?"

"I gotta go."

"Brian—"

He hung up the call before she could say anything else.

Mia watched him apprehensively for a moment. "I'm getting kicked out, aren't I?" she said.

Brian winced. "I-I mean, it's not—"

"It's okay," she said, flashing him a smile. "I don't really want to have to do a super awkward brush in with your roommates. Maybe I can meet them another time."

Brian nodded, but what he really wanted to do was wrap her up in his arms and beg her not to go. God, when had he gotten so hooked on her? They'd only known each other a few weeks, and he was already doing everything Pearl had chastised him for.

Mia stood up, and Brian rushed to stand with her. He at least wanted to kiss her goodbye, at least feel the pressure of her lips on his, even if only for a moment, before she'd have to slip out of his arms again.

But he'd promised her friendship.

A nice, safe, platonic friendship with no strings attached.

So he just told her to get home safe and watched her leave without another word.

When Pearl and Dustin returned, Brian asked what brought them home so soon, but Pearl just stormed off to eat her sub in their bedroom, and Dustin shrugged and said, "Pearl started picking fights with people, so we left."

All-in-all, it sounded pretty par for the course, but Brian couldn't deny his annoyance that Pearl's short temper had also cut his date short.

Well, not a date, but...whatever it was.

He reminded himself that it was better this way. He was

supposed to be working on untangling his life from Mia, and spending an evening nuzzling her neck like he wanted to probably wasn't the way to go about it.

But he also hated trying to stay away from her. Maybe Pearl thought they were rushing into things too fast, but did he really need to let Pearl dictate his life, especially when she was the type of person who couldn't even visit high school friends without getting into a scuffle? Maybe he was better off just being upfront with Mia—telling her that she was all he could think about day and night—and, for the sake of his own sanity, he'd really like if she'd consider leaving their platonic promise in the dust.

Well, maybe not exactly that, but something with the same sentiment.

Tuesday morning, he texted Mia to ask if she'd want to meet up sometime that week, but the next day she had open was Friday evening, so he decided to work on his spiel until then. Maybe if he could word his argument *just* persuasively enough, she'd realize she didn't really want to be platonic at all, and he could finally know peace.

Keeping his mind focused on work was even harder with the knowledge that he might destroy everything between them come Friday evening. As much as he longed to fill the space dividing them, the thought of burning it all down was almost enough to paralyze him.

But if all they were doing was forming a foundation that could never stand, was it fair for either of them to keep dragging this out?

By the time Friday rolled around, Brian's restlessness seeped into all of his muscles, his entire body vibrating with excess energy with no safe target.

Just after three, Ella pulled him aside and said, "You can go home, if you want."

"I—what? Sorry."

She just shook her head. "Whatever's bothering you—just work it out this weekend, okay? I'd like to get some work done next week."

He didn't know what to do other than apologize before gathering his things and leaving.

But that also left him too much time to kill before meeting up with Mia, and without anything to distract him—no matter how weak of a distraction work ultimately was—he found himself even antsier than before. He ended up just walking around the block, using the consistent motion to burn off some of the restless energy.

As he stopped at a crosswalk, he pulled out his phone, sending off a quick text to Mia to let her know that he was off work early, and they could meet up whenever she was free. Then he resumed his walk, this time letting the words he'd rehearsed into his phone camera flow through his mind again.

I appreciate everything you've done, helping me see the city…

I know you said you wanted to keep things platonic…

It's just that when I think about you…

Suddenly, his phone vibrated in his pocket, and he quickly fished it out, answering it before he could lose the nerve.

"Um, hey," he said, "so I was thinking—"

"Brian?"

He froze in the middle of the sidewalk, an older white man with a briefcase clipping him in the side with a disgruntled snort as he walked past.

"Um, hi, Anna."

His words squealed out like rusted gears grinding to a halt, but he couldn't course-correct. Not right now. Not when he was so caught off-guard.

Hell, it'd been weeks since he'd heard from Anna, and in all the time he'd spent with Mia, she'd barely come to mind at all. Even if their main goal had been helping Brian forget about her, he hadn't really needed much help once Mia walked in the door.

"Oh, thank God," Anna said breathlessly. "I've been trying to reach you forever. I thought you blocked my number."

"Um, no, of course I didn't," he said, slowly regaining

enough of his self-control to take a few steps forward. Regaining his stride was a lot harder, though, and passersby kept jostling him as they shot past with far more speed and confidence than Brian could muster.

"Well, good." The relief in her voice struck Brian like a punch to the gut. "Listen, I'm sorry. I talked to my parents, and they said they're sorry, too. They want to try again."

"I—your parents said that? Really?"

"Yeah. I know the situation was really awkward, but my dad explained it to me. He said it wasn't about you at all. They're just really protective of me, you know, because I'm their only daughter. They're really sorry they took that out on you, though."

A pit formed in his chest, the kind that only really reared its ugly head when you finally got everything you'd asked for, only to find it was never what you really wanted.

Obviously, his brain was still struggling to catch up. Anna calling him back in wasn't just everything he wanted, but everything he *needed*. This was his invitation to stop floundering around aimlessly, chasing someone who'd made it clear they could never be anything concrete or permanent. He hadn't been wrong about Anna; Pearl had. And now he could go back to building the perfect life he wanted with the girl who fit into it seamlessly.

If only that damn pit would just disappear.

"Um, Anna, I gotta go," he said, hoping that some time to collect himself would get his brain working the way that it should. "Can we talk about this later?"

The other end of the line fell quiet for a moment before Anna sucked in a deep breath. "You're still mad."

"I-I didn't say that."

"You didn't have to. If you weren't still mad, you'd be saying how excited you are to see me, but now you don't even want to talk."

"It's not that I don't want to talk, it's just—"

But what could he even say? *I'm not sure what my feelings for you really are, now that I met someone else* probably wasn't what your girlfriend wanted to hear at a time like this. Well, *ex*-girlfriend.

But then, did it even matter when Mia was supposed to be a friend?

"It's just what?" Anna repeated, her tone tense.

Brian sighed. "No, you're right. I'm sorry. I do want to see you."

"Good," she said. "Can we do dinner? I'm free right now."

"I kind of have plans—"

"Oh, right. I guess another time, then."

But the disappointment in her voice cut through him harder than anything she'd said thus far.

A small voice in the back of Brian's mind told him that it didn't really matter if she wanted him to drop everything to get dinner with her.

But didn't it? Didn't he at least owe her a chance to fix things? Didn't he owe it to the both of them and the future they could have together?

"You know what? Now's fine. I'll just reschedule with my friend."

And he could practically hear the smile in her voice as she said, "Perfect!"

16

While Thomas was used to getting canceled on, Mia certainly wasn't, and Thomas was starting to lose track of the line between the two.

The cancellation text sat open on Thomas's phone screen as he sat on his couch, contemplating what to do next. The growing pit of disappointment in his chest had gnawed at his insides since he'd first read the *Hey, do you think we can reschedule?* as he'd left the office, but now that the commute home couldn't pull his attention away, the dull ache only grew in force.

And it didn't help that, as much as he'd picked on Brian for letting his sense of self get so wrapped up in other people, there was a part of Thomas that only existed when Brian was around. Mia. Not Mia Sake, the performance, but something in between the version of him he stepped into once he donned the wig and the version of him that always hid somewhere beneath the surface, too afraid to peek out.

The best version.

It was just one night. Just one dinner. None of it should've had the chokehold on him that it did, and he was ashamed to even acknowledge the sort of twisting that nestled in his gut at the thought that maybe Brian had canceled because he didn't *want* to see him. Maybe Thomas had completely soured whatever was between them when he'd backed out as things had started to heat up the other night. Maybe Brian had realized then that Thomas couldn't ever give him what he really wanted, and that was it.

Thomas splayed out on the couch, staring up at the popcorn ceiling as thousands of pounds of guilt and shame buried him.

He pulled out his phone, scrolling from one page of apps to another. A small seed of hope had started to bloom in his chest that Brian would text to say he'd finished whatever he needed to do and wanted to meet up now, or that canceling had been the biggest mistake of his life. But the tiny sapling wilted the longer Thomas stared at his phone, not a single notification in sight.

Then an incoming call filled the screen.

And along with it, a bubble of disappointment seeing that it wasn't Brian's name attached to it, but Theo's.

Thomas sighed, reminding himself to stop being so pathetically hopeless before taking the call. "Hey."

"God, you sound miserable. Who died?"

Thomas groaned. "You got all that from 'hey'?"

"Eh, you've gotten more dramatic since you moved to New York. Did something happen?"

Thomas stared at his ceiling, weighing his options. Theo might be his only relative who could actually understand what he was feeling, but that made the vulnerability even harder.

"Nothing worth mentioning. What's up with you?"

The other end of the line was quiet for a moment before Theo said, "Planning a trip to New York. You wanna hang out?"

"Wait, what? Why? When?"

"Well, Gabi was saying we didn't really get a chance to do a whole lot when we were there last, so I figured we might as well make a trip out of it. Go see a musical or something."

Thomas sighed. Of course Gabi would have that brilliant idea. Very like him.

"Thomas?"

"Um, yeah, sure. Just let me know when you're coming, and I can work something out. And I take it Gabi will be there."

The resounding silence slammed into him with so much force that he barely managed to stay on the couch. He replayed the last few lines in his head, trying to hunt down the conversation killer.

Then Theo said, "Seriously? You're seriously still gonna act like that?"

"Act like what?"

Theo groaned. The sound of a scraping chair and a slamming door cut through the other end before Theo spoke again. "So what's your problem with Gabi now?"

"I-I don't have a problem," Thomas said. "I just—I mean, is it really so bad to just want to hang out with my brother without someone else in the way?"

"In the way?"

Thomas winced. "I didn't mean it like that."

"Gabi and I are a package now, so you're gonna have to learn to deal with that," Theo snapped. "Jeez, you're worse than ā mā."

Thomas spluttered. "Look, I don't have a problem with you being with Gabi, okay? I'm just saying he's not my brother."

"No, please, Thomas, say what you really mean. Gabi's not part of the family, right?" Theo shouted. "*That's* what you really want to say? You don't think he belongs here. Well, guess what? He is part of the family now, whether you like it or not."

"Oh, please, Theo, you two are dating, not married."

The line fell quiet for a second, and Thomas felt a pit settle in his stomach. "You're *not* married, are you?"

"Oh my God, shut up! Obviously not. But we will be one day. We've already talked about it."

Thomas wasn't sure what to say to that, but he could already feel bile rising up in the back of his throat. "Right."

Theo groaned. "You know what? Forget it. Gabi and I just want to have a nice trip without all the drama, so I'll just see you whenever."

"Theo—"

But the call ended.

Thomas stared down at the phone for a moment, chest tight. Part of him longed to hurl the device across the room and scream at the top of his lungs, but he'd never been capable of big outbursts or temper tantrums. He was "the good son." Always. The pathological people-pleaser.

Which was why pissing Theo off felt so viscerally painful, like someone had pumped shards of glass into his bloodstream. Every awkward word, every misplaced sigh—they all tore through him, carving up his insides.

But it wasn't just Theo. It was Kris. And Brian.

And Michelle.

Thomas shook his head, trying to shove any remnants of Michelle's face from his mind. Not now. He couldn't do this right now.

He bee-lined for his apartment's tiny kitchen, pulling a bottle of sake out of the cabinet. If he couldn't distract himself with Kris or Theo or Brian, he could at least let the sake wash away the guilt and regret that pooled in the pit of his stomach every time he thought about Michelle. Even if he couldn't get over the pain of the lies she spread about him and the community she cost him, he could at least let the burning liquid wipe away some of the stains she'd left long enough for him to get lost in someone new.

Thomas pulled up the Agenda Social app, taking a drink to drown out the sound of Kris's voice in the back of his head, lecturing him for not using it more. As uncomfortable as he'd already been using the app to try to make friends, there was a part of him that had started feeling guilty once he and Brian had begun hanging out regularly, almost like Thomas was cheating on him by talking to other people. But all of that was nonsense. This wasn't even a dating app, and whatever Thomas and Brian had was never meant to be anything other than friendship, and he could have as many friends as he wanted.

Even if that number always seemed to fall back to zero.

He took another drink.

His inbox was full of missed messages from people he'd never actually spoken to before. A couple were downright sexual harassment, so he just blocked and reported them so Felix could take care of it later. Then he scrolled through the rest, finally settling on one that looked pretty friendly.

Hi, Thomas! I'm Jeff, a recent transplant from Colorado. You mentioned liking comics and anime in your bio. Do you have any recommendations?

Thomas eyed the message for a minute, looking at the newly added little suggestion box that popped up on the side, showing their mutual interests as prompts to discuss. The whole thing felt a little tedious, but he wrote up a couple of recommendations before hitting send.

The reply came back almost immediately.

Those sound great! :)

Thomas stared at the message for a while, waiting for Jeff to supply something else, but that was it. As far as conversations went, it wasn't exactly riveting. Throwing himself back against the couch, Thomas dug around for something else to add, but his mind kept drawing a blank.

Maybe the problem with Agenda Social had nothing to do with the app at all. Maybe certain people just naturally clicked, like two stones somehow weathered down into just the right shape so that when the currents brought them together, they clung perfectly to each other's grooves and ridges.

And maybe, at least for a moment, Brian had fit perfectly against all of Thomas's grooves and ridges, too.

So maybe all of this was his own fault for pushing him away.

17

Red light spilled over him like wine as Brian stepped into the restaurant Anna had chosen.

The place was more elaborate than any he'd been to in the city—the type of large, ritzy spot that he'd normally have been repelled from with magnetic force. The guilt he'd felt at canceling on Mia gave way to nervousness as he stepped toward the host, who was collecting hats and suit jackets like something out of a movie.

The host eyed him with a look of thinly veiled disgust, which he supposed was par for the course when a single appetizer probably cost more than his wardrobe.

"Brian!"

His head whipped to his right, taking in the dining room full of carefully set, tableclothed tables.

Then he caught sight of Anna as she stood, the kitchen behind her outlining her silhouette in a light glow. And she looked even prettier than he'd remembered—her dark hair tied up in a bun with loose rivulets around her face, a long red dress hugging her hips before flowing loosely down her legs, and her bright smile rimmed by red lipstick.

Brian turned back to the host, saying, "Um, that's my girlfriend, so—"

The host just eyed him in annoyance as Brian quickly turned, skittering off toward Anna's table.

He offered her a smile, careful not to leap into anything too physical. If they were going to make things work this time around, he needed to make sure he didn't accidentally sabotage things from the jump.

And a part of him felt almost guilty for wanting to kiss her at all, even though it didn't make any sense.

But Anna seemed completely unreserved as she leaped over to him, arms encircling his neck and her lips falling onto his before he could sit down. The kiss didn't last long, but he could still feel the tingle of her lips on his as she pulled back with a wide grin.

"God, I really missed you," she said.

"I missed you, too."

Anna sat down, motioning for Brian to join her.

The table was set for two—a white tablecloth set with two wine glasses, small plates, and silverware wrapped in red cloth napkins. Brian took his seat, quickly pulling out his phone camera to check his face. A bit of Anna's lipstick had smeared onto his mouth, so he quickly tried to wipe it away, but the rouge stained his skin, leaving his lips looking puffy and swollen.

Brian grimaced, lowering his phone and biting back the last of his guilt. It didn't matter if his lips looked like Anna had done far more than offer him a quick peck. She was his girlfriend, and he wasn't doing anything wrong by being with her.

"You look beautiful," he said.

"Thank you," Anna said with a radiant smile. "I knew I had to do something to win you back."

"Win me back?"

She raised an eyebrow, one hand resting on top of the other against the white linen of the table. "Am I really supposed to believe you've just been sitting around here waiting for me to come back? That's not really your style."

His eyes widened as her comment sunk in. "My style?"

"*Please*, you think I don't remember that I was your rebound girl? What was her name? Jenny or something?"

"I—it was Julie, but you weren't a rebound," Brian said with as much conviction as he could force into his voice.

His relationship with Julie had been about as empty as a relationship could be. It'd only lasted three weeks, and on top of being awkward and clingy, the only thing that had really drawn Brian to her at all was the fact that they had a mutual friend. Well, and that she made really good pancakes. But all in all, it hadn't been a relationship he particularly needed help getting over, nor one he'd really thought about much at all until Anna brought it back up.

"Right, sure, I believe that," Anna said, her tone teasing. "Let's face it. You're hot, you're sweet, and you dress like you actually own more than two shirts. The last five guys I've met like you were gay, and the one before that was married. You're a rare find."

Brian's eyes locked onto his silverware. "Um, about that—"

Anna raised an eyebrow. "Please don't tell me you're married."

He looked up. "What? No! I—never mind."

Anna stared back at him for a moment before leaning back in her seat. "Okay, so, if I wasn't a rebound, what was I?"

A laugh bubbled up in Brian's throat. "Not subtle, for one."

"Oh, come on, a girl can't be curious? I remember when we first met, I thought you were just gonna be another dumb jock with a good tongue."

"And then?"

"You ended up being a smart jock with a good tongue."

Brian smiled. "Gee, thanks. I don't know if you want to know what I was thinking about you when we first met."

"That bad?"

"Bad? No. But it's certainly not rated G."

A waiter stepped up to their table, and Anna quickly flashed him a smile. "Can we get the chef's special? Tell them Pete's daughter is in."

Looking a bit flustered, the waiter stuttered out a quick, "R-right away, miss," before rushing back toward the kitchen.

Brian just stared back at Anna a moment before saying, "Oh, so you're like rich rich."

Anna blushed, her eyes darting down toward the table. "My dad called in a favor before we came. He said he wanted to make it up to you after the other day."

"With a fancy dinner handmade by one of his servants? I'm impressed."

Anna slowly raised her gaze to meet his, but surprisingly, her eyes lacked any defensiveness. "Brian, I'm really sorry. About everything. And my parents—they're sorry, too. And I told my dad that this was overkill and you'd appreciate it more if my mom cooked for you or something, but they were insistent. I don't think they realize our generation just isn't that into capitalism."

Brian laughed, shaking his head. "It's fine. Don't worry about it."

"I want to start over," Anna said. "Well, maybe not *over* over because…what we had back in Denver? That really meant a lot to me, and I—well, I was hoping we could just restart our time in New York, you know? Pretend none of it ever happened."

The offer was almost too tempting to refuse, to pretend that they'd just landed in New York this afternoon and wash away any of the remaining residue from that evening with Anna's parents.

But then, New York hadn't been all bad. As nice as a clean slate would be, he couldn't deny that he'd laid down marks on this city that he wasn't ready to wash away just yet, especially the ones he'd drawn these past few weeks.

Taking in a deep breath, he said, "Anna, I care about you a lot, and I want to make this work."

"Really?" she asked, an uninhibited smile stretching across her face.

And for a moment, looking at that smile, all he could think of was Mia—the way every thought and feeling showed on her face. But this wasn't about Mia or how she'd helped him reshape the city. This was about Anna, with her bright—albeit, a bit lipstick-stained—smile. She wasn't some aloof, unreachable beauty who'd only ever really existed in his dreams. She was someone here, present, someone he could really build a life with instead of constantly setting himself up for disappointment.

"Really. So let's just start over."

By the time Brian stumbled back home, it was just after three a.m.

They hadn't even been drinking, but between making out in the back of a movie like a couple of high school kids before getting a private karaoke room to sing and talk and fuck, Brian had to admit he was a little love drunk.

He hadn't even realized how much he missed being in a relationship until they'd fallen back into place, like having her around had somehow filled a hole in his chest he'd only just realized was there.

As he stepped into the apartment—hoping it was late enough that everyone would be deep asleep—the disappointment slapped him across the face as he caught sight of Pearl standing in the kitchen doorway, a mug in hand.

"You're home late."

He shrugged. "It's early."

She rolled her eyes as she sipped from her mug. "Seems like you had fun."

Brian locked the door behind him before kicking off his shoes and heading into the kitchen. If Pearl was still awake, he might as well give her what she wanted before heading to bed.

"Yeah, it was great."

"You were with Mia?"

Brian paused halfway to the cabinet. "Um, no. I was with Anna."

In all the kissing and cuddling and talking about their future, Brian had mostly forgotten about Mia. At least, he'd definitely forgotten about canceling on her and the inherent guilt that followed. Not that he really had anything to feel guilty about.

Pearl spun toward him, her eyebrows furrowed. "Anna? I thought you two were ancient history?"

"That might be a bit exaggerated."

Brian walked over to the cabinet and grabbed a glass to pour himself some water from the tap. Pearl padded over, her footsteps too heavy and loud in the silence of the early morning, and the eagerness in every step felt like a jab in Brian's side.

"So are you two back together, then?" she asked, angling herself to get a better look at his face.

He took his time drinking water to avoid answering.

Anna had been so happy to see him again that she'd lobbed herself at him without bringing up any major details, and Brian had enjoyed the ride enough that he didn't bother interrupting her. The new lines of their relationship were still waiting to be drawn, but Brian figured that wasn't a cause for concern. After all, they'd agreed to start over, so if they were going back to their first days in New York, that meant they were basically back on with full force.

Which meant that things were back to Brian's most comfortable state. That was, except for the way his mind kept awkwardly bringing up Mia at inopportune times.

Pearl eyed him expectantly as he finished the water and stuck the cup in the sink, officially ending his attempts at stalling.

"We haven't really set any ground rules," Brian said, "but Anna asked to start over, and I told her I was fine with that."

Pearl slowly placed her mug down on the counter. "So what about Mia?"

"What about her?"

"You seemed really into her. Are you not into her anymore?"

Brian rolled his eyes. "You know, you really shouldn't be drinking coffee this late. The caffeine'll fuck up your sleep cycle."

"It's chamomile tea, and my sleep's already fucked, so answer the damn question."

Brian laughed, but he turned back toward the fridge, if only to keep Pearl from reading too much into his face. "I don't know if I was ever really into her."

"Oh, boy, shut up, you were so into her."

"I mean, don't get me wrong, she's cool," Brian said. "I really like her as a person, and I'll admit that I was definitely attracted to her at the drag show, and even maybe a little after that. But it's kind of what you said before."

"Meaning?"

"Meaning," he paused, trying to choose his words carefully,

"Anna's real. I know her. And yeah, things were kind of awkward with her parents, but they did this whole apology dinner, and she seems really sorry. We really reconnected tonight, and I could maybe even see myself spending the rest of my life with her. But I can't see any way that my feelings for Mia were really concrete I've only known her a few weeks, and I don't even know her real name. It's just what you said. Letting go of Anna to chase the idea of this person just seems like a terrible idea, you know?"

"Agreed," Pearl said, "but it also seems like a terrible idea to hold onto Anna if you don't really have feelings for her."

Brian shook his head. "It's not like that. I really do like Anna. I think I'm just getting over this awkward hump because of how things ended before."

"Like?"

"Like what?"

Pearl rolled her eyes. "You said you *like* Anna? Because you were just saying you could see yourself spending the rest of your life with her."

Brian waved her off. "Love her. Whatever. You know what I mean."

Pearl took a step up to him, placing a hand on his shoulder. "Well, look, if you really do love Anna, then I say go for it. I know I got into your head the other day, but the good thing about advice is that you don't have to take it."

"Ah, but you're usually right, so ignoring your advice sounds like self-sabotage."

Pearl smirked. "Flattery will get you nowhere, Ramirez. Well, maybe somewhere, but probably not where you want to go. Anyway, I'm sorry if I made things weird for you. I didn't mean to, like, try to throw you off of Mia or anything. I can hold in my unsolicited advice until it becomes solicited."

Brian paused because Pearl's tone sounded both sadder and humbler than he was used to ever hearing it. "Everything okay? That's very… humble of you."

Pearl just rolled her eyes. "The point is, I'm not trying to be a bitch, so if I crossed the line, you can just tell me."

Brian smiled. "No, you're fine. Honestly, I think it helped a lot. For a minute there, I got really wrapped up in Mia, you know? And she seems cool, don't get me wrong, but I know there can't really be anything permanent between us, so I'd rather focus on building up a relationship with substance."

"So are you done talking to Mia, then?"

The words sent a sinking feeling into Brian's stomach. "I mean, I wouldn't say that."

Pearl raised an eyebrow.

"She said she wanted to be friends, right? I don't see why we can't still be friends."

Pearl eyed him suspiciously for a moment before shrugging. "Okay, just be careful."

"Mia's not dangerous."

"That's not what I was referring to."

18

As the days rolled by, Brian reaching out to reschedule only to not have any real free time, Thomas came to the conclusion that this was one of those weak excuses people used as a means of cutting you off. Part of him wished Brian would just give up the whole hoax of trying to plan something so he could rip off the Band-Aid and move on, but the other part of him was quickly realizing just how badly he'd failed at "no strings," because each "sorry, maybe a different time?" text left a gaping wound in his chest.

So when Brian finally agreed to a midday tea break on Friday, Thomas wasn't sure if he should be elated or embarrassed. All he knew for sure was that he'd been stringing Brian along for far too long. He needed to be honest with him, no matter how painful that might be.

They agreed to meet at a food court, the place already packed with people grabbing lunch before getting back to their workday. Thomas had scouted it because it also held one of his favorite boba shops, but standing amidst the haphazardly placed tables and bustling crowd, he felt over-exposed and under-prepared.

Well, he mostly felt exposed because he'd opted to dress up a little.

Since Kris was too busy at the office to really pay him much attention, and Brian's absence had left him feeling a little lackluster, Thomas had spent the week trying out some new looks. Subtle stuff only, because he didn't want to have to explain any of it, but Monday, he'd let himself wear some blush and a little mascara. Tuesday, he'd worn a women's shirt that he'd buried under his jacket despite the encroaching summer heat. And that led him to today, standing in public in a nice blouse and a pair of heeled boots that he hoped didn't draw too much attention. The only makeup he'd bothered with was a soft lip gloss, but he was pretty sure his face had managed a rosy flush all on its own.

He idly shifted his weight from one foot to the other, contemplating whether he should just hide in the bathroom until Brian texted him that he'd made it.

But then he looked up, eyes locking on Brian's as he made his way over. And Brian paused, his eyes darting all over Thomas's body with a look of awe. Thomas's face warmed, but instead of the humiliation he'd been bathed in a moment before, this warmth left him feeling almost cozy, like Brian had pulled him into a tight embrace.

"Um, hey," Brian said, flashing him a smile.

"Hey," Thomas said, not even realizing how tense his shoulders had been until they'd started to relax at the sound of Brian's voice. "I was worried you weren't coming."

"I'm not that late, am I?" Brian asked, pulling out his phone and checking the screen.

"No, no, you're good," Thomas said with a rushed laugh. "I guess I was just a little worried after you canceled the other day."

The words crash landed between them, and Thomas silently berated himself for saying something so uncomfortable. So *insecure*.

Brian laughed awkwardly. "Right, sorry. It was, um, just something I had to deal with."

"I understand," Thomas said, rushing to sweep some of the

discomfort away. "It's okay. Really."

"I like your outfit," Brian said, something in his voice hitching as he said it.

Was he…nervous?

"Thank you," Thomas said. "Unless you're making fun of me."

Brian quickly shook his head. "No, I'm not! I mean it. You look…" But he just trailed off like his mind had gone blank.

Ordinarily, Thomas would take rendering a man utterly speechless as a compliment, but this time, it just added to the nerves already twisting his gut.

"I thought I'd follow your advice and try branching out a little."

"And?"

"Well, so far I don't totally hate it," Thomas said. "I do feel kind of awkward, though. Like everyone's staring at me."

Brian took a quick glance around the food court, but Thomas already knew he wouldn't find any prying eyes. This was still New York. But it wasn't the actual eyes that mattered. It was the way the fear of their eyes made the room press in around him, even if nothing was actually moving.

"Um, so, do you want to grab a drink and sit?" Thomas asked.

"Sure."

Thomas led him to the boba shop, keeping his eyes trained on the menu even if he got the same thing every time. It wasn't his order that had him antsy, but if he let himself think too much about what he was about to say to Brian, he knew he'd chicken out before he could even get his mouth open.

"So, what are you thinking?" Thomas asked, hoping to distract himself with a little bit of boba chat.

"Me?" Brian stammered out. "I-I'm not thinking about anything."

"I meant what are you ordering?"

"Oh, right," Brian said. Thomas turned to him to catch him ducking his head as his cheeks darkened. "Um, I always get the same thing. Original milk tea."

Thomas wasn't sure what was so shameful about his drink order, but Brian's face was buried in guilt. "Well, nothing wrong with being certain about what you like," Thomas said, hoping to reassure him.

Brian heaved a sigh. "I'm not certain about anything anymore."

Thomas raised an eyebrow. "Honey, it's just tea. You'll be okay."

"Uh, yeah."

They placed their orders and stepped out of line, Thomas keeping his hands in his pockets until he finally had a tea and straw to hold in them. He kept opening his mouth to speak before closing it again, dancing from one foot to the other like they were in a ballroom instead of a food court. Sometimes, he felt like a classical musician with how bad he was with words, but the tinny air struggling to whistle its way out of his windpipe in that exact moment made for the sorriest sonata his ears had ever heard.

He led Brian over to a table, sitting down across from him and quickly tearing through the straw wrapper before punching it through the plastic film lid.

Speaking up was just like using his straw. Just punch a hole through the silence and keep going.

"I—"

"Mia, there's something I've been meaning to tell you," Brian said, eyes glued down to the table even as his hands clasped and unclasped his cup.

"Okay?"

Not only was Thomas distinctly of the "you go first!" variety, but as he looked up and caught sight of his own nausea mirrored perfectly on Brian's face, a small bubble of hope welled up in his chest. Was Brian thinking the same thing he was? Were they about to realize that all of their nerves were pointless because they both wanted the same thing all along?

Brian sighed, staring down at his plastic cup again. "So, you know how when we first met, I told you about my ex, and you offered to help me get over her?"

Thomas pushed down the butterflies in his stomach. "Yeah?"

Keeping his eyes glued downward, Brian said, "Well, I've just been trying to really reevaluate what I want, you know? Because for a long time… Well, the point is, I'm really grateful for everything you did to help put things into perspective for me."

Thomas smiled.

"If not for you, I don't think Anna and I would've ever gotten back together."

Thomas frowned. "I'm sorry, what?"

Brian laughed. "Sorry, I meant, Anna reached out to me the other day. That was why I had to cancel."

Thomas's heart crash landed into the pit of his stomach, exploding on impact and going up in flames.

"She told me she regretted everything that happened between us, so we made up, and now we're back together. I mean, things are still a little gray, but we're gonna try to make it work."

Thomas grimaced. "How cute! I'm so happy for you."

Brian stared back at him blankly. "Are you okay?"

Thomas coughed, reaching up and clapping a hand over his mouth. "Sorry, I choked on boba."

He'd hoped that if he said it with enough conviction, he might convince himself that that's all the burning in the back of his throat was. Not the disappointment or heartache that he really had no right feeling when he was the one who told Brian they should keep things platonic.

No, worse than that, it was exactly what Kris had said. It was his own fault for being dumb enough to pursue a straight guy in the first place.

"Let me know if you need me to do the Heimlich," Brian said. "I learned that at my old job."

Thomas smiled, or at least the closest approximation of a

smile he could muster, but he clearly did a piss poor job because Brian said, "Are you sure you're okay? You seem kind of upset."

Thomas just shook his head and said, "Sorry. I'm happy for you! I just…have a lot going on."

"Do you want to talk about it?"

But the last thing Thomas wanted to talk about was how close he'd been to confessing his feelings before Brian had told him he was in love with someone else, so he decided to pivot completely. "I guess it's just my brother."

"Your brother?"

Thomas fiddled with his straw for a moment. "He called the other day. Said he was coming to New York and wanted to meet up, but then we had a little spat, and he doesn't want to see me anymore. And I tried calling back, but he won't answer. I'm wondering if he blocked my number."

"Oh, wow," Brian said, his voice low, and the amazement in his voice only made the weight of Thomas's distress sink in deeper. "Are you two close?"

Thomas laughed. "Yeah. Or…we kind of are? It's a recent development, though. We used to be at each other's throats."

He didn't add the part about how much that contributed to his fear that they'd end up there again. It'd been three years since Theo had broken down in front of him while their parents' shop was struggling, and Thomas was still haunted by the brokenness in his voice sometimes.

"That's all that I'm good for! Theo, the son who ruins everything and makes everyone's lives harder. Do you think it's easy to follow in your footsteps?"

Thomas hadn't even realized how much resentment had built up between them until Theo had lost it on him that day, and he still felt guilty. About not supporting his family like he should've. About letting Theo come out first and take all the attacks alone. About failing to be the perfect son his family needed him to be.

Brian could say whatever he wanted about how Thomas could be queer and still be a good son, but his queerness wasn't the problem. Or, at least, it wasn't the *biggest* problem. Because Thomas was the oldest son, and that meant he had to keep the family together, protect Theo, inherit the shop, and yet, he'd failed. Theo was the one who healed the family and saved the shop, and all Thomas had done was be too much of a coward to accept the blows he should've taken on Theo's behalf.

"Sometimes I think he hates me," Thomas said. "And sometimes I think he's right to."

Brian raised an eyebrow. "All this because you used to fight sometimes? I feel like that's pretty normal."

"Is it?"

"Sure. I mean, when you're kids locked in the same house, siblings are infuriating, but then you leave, and suddenly you start to miss them, and you realize what an important part of your life they are."

"Yeah, I guess so," Thomas said, though he wished he could borrow some of Brian's confidence.

He struggled to believe Theo missed him a whole lot. Not just because they barely talked—definitely less than siblings were supposed to—but simply because he knew what he looked like in Theo's eyes, and he wasn't sure how anyone could *not* hate someone like that.

"What was your spat about?" Brian asked.

Thomas whistled, eyes downcast. "His boyfriend."

"Oh." A pause. "You hate the guy?"

And even though Brian's tone made it sound like a question, the whole thing felt like an accusation.

"No! I don't!"

"You sound like you do."

Thomas wanted to immediately shoot back that he didn't have any hard feelings against Gabi, but Brian calling him out on his tone gave him pause. It was exactly the kind of thing Theo would've said, so maybe his voice was betraying him in ways he hadn't expected.

"I mean, he's nice," Thomas said tentatively. "A little awkward, but nothing fatal."

"So, what's the problem?"

But that was the thing, wasn't it? If he knew how to give a reasonable answer to that question, he probably wouldn't be in such dire straits with Theo right now.

"I guess I just don't feel comfortable with him," Thomas said honestly, hoping Brian would get over it even if he accidentally said something unforgiving in a way Theo never would. "The thing is, I want to be happy for Theo, and I'm glad he found someone who makes him happy, but it's just so annoying to not even be able to see him without you-know-who popping up out of the woodwork. Am I the asshole?"

"I don't think so," Brian said. "You sound kind of jealous, though."

Thomas laughed. "That's ridiculous. Why would I be jealous?"

"It just kind of reminds me of what happened with my brother, I guess," Brian said. "A couple years ago. I was dating this girl, Maggie, and he felt kind of weird because of the way things had changed, so he lashed out a bit. Ultimately, she was terrible, so he wasn't exactly wrong, but the point remains the same."

Thomas looked down at the boba cup in front of him, his fingers tugging at the edge of the plastic lid. "It's not like I don't want them to be together, you know? I think Gabi's probably good for him. They balance each other out."

"But?"

Even at one word long, it was the hardest question Thomas had fielded in a long time.

"I guess I just…don't know why he needs me anymore."

The words sounded so miserably pathetic, even to him, but he hated how much everything clicked into place the second he said them.

Because if he was being completely honest with himself, he knew the only reason Theo really had for keeping him around was to solve his problems for him. To be the one to make sure he did his homework and remind him to put things in his calendar and keep him from saying something that would make the family lose their damn minds.

But Theo wasn't a kid anymore, and now he had Gabi to help manage his life, and he was happy.

And Thomas desperately wanted to be happy for him, but all he could manage was fear. Fear at being replaced, fear at never seeing his brother again, fear at the painful finality he always returned to—the knowledge that, in the end, nobody really needed him.

Thomas sniffled, quickly reaching up to wipe his eyes.

He glanced up to find Brian staring back at him with so much pity in his eyes, it made Thomas feel like he was drowning in it. He didn't want Brian to look at him like something pathetic and weak and miserable. He wanted to go back to crawling in his lap and kissing his lips and digging his hands through his hair.

But Brian didn't need him, either.

Finally, Brian said, "I don't think that's how it works."

"Isn't it? Theo said it himself. My role in the family has always been 'the good son.' The one who makes sure things get done. But they have Gabi now. Boy wonder. And that doesn't even touch the fact he's not some gender-confused freak like me."

"Okay, one, you've got to stop talking about yourself like that, okay? That can't be healthy."

Thomas rolled his eyes. "Who cares if it's healthy when it's true?"

"It's *not* true, Mia," Brian said with a sharpness that stopped Thomas mid-thought. "You're amazing. Brilliant and funny and talented and caring. Who cares if you don't know what your gender is? Or if you aren't keeping your family's schedules for them? You really think the only reason you matter to them is because they can use you? I'm sure they don't feel that way. Or, at least, I really hope they don't, or they wouldn't deserve you."

Thomas fought to blink the tears out of his eyes before they could spill over. "Thank you."

"Of course."

"I'm sorry for dumping all of that on you," Thomas said, quickly wiping his eyes. "That was so messy of me."

But as embarrassing as it was, a massive weight had lifted from his chest. He couldn't exactly argue that Brian had magically patched things up between him and Theo, but at least things between them felt a little less hopeless.

Brian smiled. "I'm glad I could help." Then he pulled his phone out of his pocket and groaned. "Um, but I should probably go now. Lunch break is long over."

Thomas laughed. "Yeah, of course. I'm sorry for keeping you."

He'd probably get chewed out by Kris when he got back to the office, but considering how little attention Kris had paid him over the past week, that might even be refreshing.

Brian smiled at him and said, "It's fine. There are much worse ways to waste an afternoon."

Heat rose in Thomas's cheeks as he quickly looked down, pretending to make himself busy cleaning off their table. Then he paused, looking up and calling out to Brian again, just before he could head for the door. "Um, I almost forgot, but some friends and I were gonna go out for drinks later. Interested?"

Something small fluttered in Thomas's chest as Brian said, "I'd love to."

19

Brian wasn't sure if people got "fired" from internships, but he suspected he'd find out soon if he didn't stop playing with fire.

When he got back to work, he told Ella he'd be happy to stay an extra hour to help her organize some files as an apology for strolling back almost an hour late. She flashed him that usual look of annoyance, but the whole thing was short lived, since her phone pinged a minute later with an incoming email.

"We're approved," she said, her face frozen in such dumbfounded shock, Brian wasn't sure if she'd ever be able to screw it back into shape.

"Approved for what?"

"The *fall event*, Brian."

"Oh!"

Part of the reason Brian hadn't been able to meet up with Mia for so long had been because Ella had shoved him into a work Discord for which he wasn't allowed to turn off notifications while the team tried to get their next event cleared by the board. Considering they had no event planning experience, they sure had a lot of feedback that basically amounted to "no" and "this sucks, but we don't know why."

"So what did they settle on?" Brian asked.

"A masquerade ball," Ella said.

Brian almost choked. "I—isn't that overkill? Who came up with that?"

Ella shrugged. "Don't know. Probably Trisha, but whatever. They turned down everything else, and we were pretty much out of options. Not that you really contributed anything."

Brian spluttered. "I'm part of the chat!"

"Okay, but are you really?" Ella said. "Because all you really offered were emojis, and my grandmother could do that much. She's ninety-four."

Brian just frowned. "Dragging me like that feels kind of unnecessary, don't you think?"

"No, Brian, I don't think," Ella said. "Look, you were a great help until the drag show. What happened to *that* Brian?"

He just winced, because he didn't really have an answer. Even if he said that the breakup had had a huge impact on him, it wouldn't explain why he was still feeling a little unfocused at work now that he and Anna were back together. Actually, the only consistent thing was Mia, but that felt like ill-placed blame.

"Do you know why, out of everyone who applied for your position, I picked you?" she asked.

"Because you needed a token straight?"

"No," Ella deadpanned. "It's because you have this natural charisma that really moves people. You're agreeable, sure, but you really help people open up and feel comfortable, and that's everything in this line of work. Communities aren't built on identity labels, Brian. They're built on trust and care. I need you to act like you actually care about the people we're working with, even if you don't actually feel that anymore."

"It's not—" But Brian didn't have the words to refute that when his performance said otherwise.

It wasn't like he didn't care about queer youth anymore. Hell, if anything, being around Mia so much made him care more now. But maybe it was just too hard to be at work without thinking about Mia, which was exactly what Mia wanted him to stop doing, which only meant thinking about her more.

He sighed. "Sorry. I guess I just got a little distracted."

"And I get that. I really do. I happen to have a girlfriend that I really love, and I would love to get lost in her tits for a while instead of working all the time."

"I—"

"But you accepted the job, Brian, so I need you to do it, okay? You're just an intern! You even get to clock out! So the hours that you're here, I need you to actually be here, at least until we get this masquerade set, okay?"

Brian nodded. "Yeah. You got it."

So he stayed the extra hour—spending most of it reaching out to his coworkers about Mia's app since it'd only taken fifteen minutes to organize Ella's files—before heading back to his place to change and get ready for his night out. Mia had texted over the details after they'd parted ways, but he didn't look them over until after he'd taken a shower and thrown on a fresh shirt.

They were meeting at seven at the same bar he'd met Mia at after the drag show. Mia had included a list of names, but Brian wasn't sure he really knew any of them besides Kris.

He wasn't about to try to compete with a bunch of drag queens in terms of attire, but after what Anna had said about him dressing well, he wanted to put his best into it. Not that seeing Mia had anything to do with that, as they were strictly platonic, but he still didn't want to embarrass her by looking like a slob.

Once he was convinced that his leather jacket and dark jeans were nice enough that he wouldn't be instantly clocked as the token straight, he shouted a quick, "I'm going out!" to Pearl before leaving the apartment.

It hadn't been that long since meeting Mia at the bar that first time, but the familiarity he felt as he reached it gave the whole place a different vibe now. The side stairs felt exciting instead of sketchy, the bright lights and pumping bass almost familiar and cozy. He headed back out to the patio they'd hung out on before to find Mia at a table with seven other people. Fortunately, only two drew attention decked out in full drag attire, so he didn't feel too horribly underdressed as he joined her.

"Glad you could make it," she said with a smile.

And Brian couldn't be sure if it was the neon purple glow that haloed her face or if it was just the way she'd done her makeup—pink lips and a rosy blush lending a feminine cuteness to her otherwise masculine getup—but his heart instantly skipped a beat.

"Um, thanks for inviting me."

Brian's phone vibrated in his pocket, and he quickly slipped it out to find a new message from Anna.

Busy tonight? I have something you might like to see.

Warmth bloomed in Brian's cheeks as he typed out a quick, *Sorry, can't, maybe tomorrow?* And hit send.

Shame and nerves started an eager tango through Brian's stomach, but he did his best to ignore them. He was just hanging out with a friend. He didn't need to lend any more scrutiny to it than that.

"Oh, honey, you look like you need a drink," Mia said. "Everything okay?"

Brian gave her a smile that felt a little more like a grimace. "Fine."

Mia patted him on the shoulder as she stood. "I'll go grab you something. Kris, let's go."

Brian hadn't recognized her at first without all the makeup, but once Mia said it, it was pretty clear that the guy next to her was Kris—same bone structure, same too-curious eyes, same perfectly manicured nails.

She raised her lip at Mia and said, "You're so needy," but obediently got up and followed her toward the bar anyway.

With Mia gone, Brian awkwardly crossed his arms as he leaned back and tried not to look too long at anyone. Social situations served as Brian's natural habitat, but something about this group left him feeling out of place.

Of the six of them, the two in full drag looked somewhat familiar, so he imagined they may have been at the show with

Mia. They both looked southeast Asian, though that was as far as the resemblance between them went, and they were both dressed extremely professionally—one in a pink pantsuit and the other in a black pencil skirt and blazer—like their drag personas were actually lawyers or something, but their massive wigs and stage makeup made it pretty clear they hadn't just clocked eight hours at a local law firm.

The person sitting closest to Brian had a gender expression that was entirely ambiguous, though they weren't exactly dressed androgynously. Their hair was shaved, and their shirt lay buttoned up only as far as their rib cage, revealing a sliver of their flat chest beneath, but from the haphazard way they sat half leaning against the light-skinned Black guy next to them, Brian could make out the heeled boots on their feet and the wicked glitter eyeliner on their face.

And as Brian's eyes bounced from person to person, taking in how different they presented compared to the average subway patron while still laughing as casually as kids on a playground, it suddenly struck him why he felt so out of place. This whole group seemed so natural and comfortable with each other that their energy formed its own little bubble no outsider could breech. It was like catching a glimpse of a single island, floating alone in a vast ocean, and wondering what sort of life the people on it were living. He was a foreign invader, accidentally washing up on shore where he wasn't wanted and imposing on the locals.

So much for that "natural charisma" Ella was talking about.

He was just about to slip away to ease his own discomfort when one of the queens turned to him, grinning at him. "So, what's your name, hun?" she asked.

He blinked for a second, making sure she was actually addressing him before saying, "Brian."

The light-skinned guy got as far as, "Oh, you're friends with Th—" before the gender-ambiguous one said, "He's the one *Mia* was talking about, right?"

"Oh, *right*, Mia. My bad."

The gender-ambiguous person—who introduced themselves as Day—went around introducing everyone else, though Brian struggled to latch on to all the names.

"Poor thing," the queen in the pantsuit—Lola—said. "Your girl just up and left you, huh?"

"Oh my God, don't say that," the light-skinned guy—Felix?—said, each word dragged out with oozing sarcasm. "Mia says they're not together."

"I—we're not together," Brian clarified.

Felix flashed him a vaguely passive aggressive smile. "Right. I just said that, didn't I?"

Brian wasn't sure how to respond to that, but he figured the safest bet was to steer the conversation as far away from himself as possible, so he said, "Um, Lola, that's a nice outfit. Is that...part of something?"

Lola glanced down at her pantsuit for a second before laughing. "You mean, like, a costume? No, I bought it at Macy's."

The other queen—whose name Brian couldn't remember—jumped in with, "We were meeting with city officials before this to talk about the importance of letting queer people exist in 'family friendly' spaces."

Brian's eyes widened. "Oh, wow. I'd be way too intimidated to do something like that."

Lola laughed. "Do it scared, babe."

The white person on Lola's other side raised their glass to her saying, "Oof, mood." Brian couldn't remember their name either, but from their shaved brown hair to patchwork tattoo sleeve, he was kind of surprised by how timid they looked saying it.

A shot glass appeared in front of Brian's face, and he looked up to find Mia standing over him, passing him the drink. "That'll help."

Brian smiled. "Thanks."

The drink in his hand made him a little more comfortable, until one of the guy's whose names Brian couldn't remember said, "Mia, dear, never leave your *drink* unattended, or a thirsty bitch might snatch him up."

Brian wasn't sure how warm his face could physically get, but he was pretty sure he was about to find out.

Lola slapped the guy's arm and said, "If you're offering favors, at least be direct about it."

"I'm just saying, it seems impolite to bring a hottie around and then just leave him all alo—"

"I'm straight," Brian said, the table falling quiet despite the pumping bass in the background. "I-I mean, I have a girlfriend. So, I'm not interested."

Brian turned to find Mia's face completely flushed, like maybe his outburst had completely humiliated her.

Then Day broke the silence by saying, "Well, alright then, ladies. Claws back in, please."

"You bitches gotta stop being so messy before I get a chance to get wasted," Kris said, downing a shot for good measure.

"You're one to talk," Felix snapped. "I've yet to meet a guy in the Tri-State area who couldn't recognize you by your dick."

Kris smirked, but Brian couldn't help but notice that compared to the flirty grin she'd offered while teasing him about his "crush" on Mia, this held a lot more…bite. "Is that supposed to hurt my feelings, Felix? I can't help that I'm memorable."

"Of course you are. Who could forget the slut that got dragged out of their apartment in a strait jacket?"

Brian wasn't entirely sure what the comment actually meant, but it sounded a bit too pointed to still be within the realm of friendly banter. He glanced over at Kris, confirming his suspicions with the look of pure venom in Kris's eyes. Mia went rigid next to Brian, but she didn't say anything, just toyed with her drink instead.

Day grabbed Felix's arm like they were trying to reel him in. "We all get a little rowdy sometimes. Better to leave it in the past."

"Sure thing," Felix said before turning back to Kris. "After all, you'll always have the restraining order as a souvenir, right?"

Kris stood up, lip curled back slightly. Then she just smiled and said, "Must suck being so boring that all you can talk about is someone else's life. I'm getting another drink."

Then she stormed off.

Mia winced, quickly standing up, but before she could chase after Kris, Day grabbed her wrist and said, "It's fine. Stay with your friend. I'll handle it."

Mia frowned. "Are you sure?"

Day just winked at her before getting up and rushing off after Kris. Once Day was out of earshot, Felix burst out laughing, and a moment later, the rest of the table, excluding Mia and Brian, joined him.

Mia turned to Felix, shoulders tense. "I don't get it. What's so funny?"

Felix waved them off. "Oh, come on, you know how Kris can be."

Mia just raised an eyebrow.

"She's such a *diva*," Felix said. "Just makes everything about her and throws a fit when it doesn't go her way." Then he dropped his voice low enough that only Mia and Brian could hear him as he said, "It's just the way the white gays are."

Mia still looked a little uncomfortable, but after a moment, she just said, "You didn't have to make it about her mental health, though."

"Oh, come on, Mia," Lola said, "Felix was just messing around. It's not his fault Kris loves to dish it but can't take it."

Mia fell quiet, and Brian felt...well, he only really followed half of the conversation, but he had to admit he kind of hated the way the energy of the group changed once Kris and Day were gone. Like things had suddenly become more hostile, with Mia slipping into the line of fire.

So, Brian just said, "Um, Mia, come with me to get another drink? I don't really know this place that well, so—"

She looked up at him and immediately nodded, the look in

her eyes telling him she was grateful to have an out.

"So, what was that all about?" Brian asked once they'd moved to the other side of the bar and ordered another round of shots.

Mia grimaced. "Kris is really sensitive about mental health stuff, so I guess that's why she freaked out, and as for the rest of the group...I don't think they really like me that much, so taking Kris's side was probably a bad idea."

Brian paused. "I—why don't they like you? You're amazing."

Mia smiled weakly, but her voice was sad when she said, "I'm kind of new, and I stick out like a sore thumb. They only let me in because I'm friends with Kris, but I don't think they really wanted to do that."

"Well, if they don't care to have you around, maybe you should go find better friends," Brian said.

Mia just winced. "I'm not great at making friends, but I'm pretty great at losing them, so sometimes you just have to cut your losses."

Before Brian could comment on just how ridiculous that notion sounded, Mia said, "Sorry for dragging you into all this drama. Let's just drink and pretend none of this happened, okay?"

Brian nodded. He wasn't sure if drinking to forget your problems was a healthy way to approach it, but spending the rest of the night with Mia, away from the drama, sounded like a brilliant idea.

They grabbed two more shots before returning to the table with everyone else, and by the time the third one hit Brian's throat, he realized the jokes were getting a whole lot funnier and everyone's faces a whole lot prettier and the feeling of Mia's hand on his shoulder a whole lot warmer.

Whatever tension had settled over the table before dissipated once Day returned, saying Kris wasn't feeling well and headed home for the night. They easily steered the conversation back to safer waters, and suddenly the night blurred by in a haze of laughter and camaraderie. Before he knew it, Brian felt like part of the gang, like they'd all been friends for years instead of him being the awkward interloper who'd tried to infiltrate their clique.

By the time he and Mia headed out to the street, he was glad he'd come. Next to him, Mia wobbled slightly down the sidewalk, drawing Brian's attention to the heels on her feet.

"I thought you wanted to play it safe in public," he said.

She followed his eyes down to her feet and shrugged. "Yeah, but I've been looking for the perfect excuse to wear these."

She said it so nonchalantly, but Brian couldn't help but feel a little warm at the fact that Mia had grown a little less self-conscious in their time together. He couldn't take all the credit, but even knowing he may have had a small hand in it filled him with joy.

They weren't far from Brian's apartment, but Mia still had to get to the train station, so they headed in that direction.

"I can ride the train back with you, if you want," Brian offered.

Mia shook her head. "And then you'd have to come all the way back here? It's fine. I can get back on my own."

"You're a little tipsy."

"Yeah, so are you."

But Brian didn't feel too foggy. He couldn't be sure whether the night air had helped clear his head once they'd exited the bar or if the way his heart had sped up when Mia had suggested they walk together forced the alcohol out of his system, but he felt pretty alert. And then there was the feeling of belonging that had settled over him. That feeling of being welcome, even in a space he wouldn't have ordinarily considered his, had left him feeling remarkably grounded.

The word "community" surfaced in his mind, but he pushed it aside. It wasn't his community, no matter how welcome they'd made him feel. But he got what Ella had been talking about, now, about why she was so invested in keeping the nonprofit thriving, why Noah was so committed to helping the queer community. If he could spend every night feeling like he had tonight, he wouldn't ever give that up.

Mia bumped into him, giggling as she leaned against his arm to steady herself. "I think the ground's a little uneven."

He laughed, draping an arm around her to keep her upright. "I'm pretty sure you're just drunk."

"A convincing argument, but I refuse to give the concrete the benefit of the doubt."

"Are you sure you don't want me to take the train back with you?" he asked.

She pulled away from him, flashing him a quick smile. "You're sweet, but really, I'm fine."

It wasn't that he didn't believe her, because he had little doubt she could ride a train on her own, but the thought of something possibly happening to her felt like a knife to the gut.

Mia leaned against him, staring into his eyes for a moment before saying, "I'm glad you came tonight. I had fun."

He nodded. "Yeah, me, too."

And then she kissed him, her body melding perfectly into his own as her lips traced his. The same electric fire he'd felt between them before shot back into him, urging him to pull her closer, to trace every inch of her skin with his tongue.

But a moment later, she jerked back, eyes wide. "Oh, oh God," she said, hands shooting up to cover her mouth. "I am so sorry. I don't know what came over me."

"It's okay—"

"No, no it's not," she insisted, her words pouring out of her before he could try to pull her back in. "I mean, you have a girlfriend, and I—"

Right.

A girlfriend.

But for a second, with Mia pressed against him, Anna hadn't existed at all. He probably wouldn't have even recognized her name if someone had shouted it at him.

And even now, watching Mia's flustered face in the flickering streetlight, Anna felt like the furthest thing in the world—the smallest, most irrelevant blip in the back of his mind.

Because all he could think about was how perfectly Mia had fit against him.

She laughed awkwardly, taking a step backwards and nearly tripping over the drain hatch in the sidewalk. He reached to steady her, pulling his hand back at the last moment to keep from making things worse.

"I'm so sorry," Mia said. "The alcohol got the better of me, but at least I think that sobered me up a bit."

Brian shook his head. "Let me walk you home."

She stared back at him for a moment, a small smile tugging at her lips. But then she shook her head, stumbling toward the subway. "No, it's okay. Um…I'll see you later, okay? And sorry again."

And while every part of his body longed to chase after her, the last functional part of his brain kept him planted in place.

So, he stood there, frozen on the street, feeling like a complete fool.

20

"I told you this was gonna happen," Kris snapped.

And while Thomas couldn't technically argue that he was wrong, she really wasn't in the mood for an "I told you so." She'd chugged about a gallon of water since waking up, but it hadn't done much to get rid of this morning's hangover. Combined with the twisting in her stomach, she hadn't had the energy to get out of bed, so she'd texted Kris to pick up something she could eat other than stale pocky and graham crackers, and Kris had shown up an hour later with a reasonable meal and some Tylenol.

All things considered, Thomas figured she was lucky Kris showed up at all. Between their tension at work and whatever had happened between Kris and Felix the night before, a soberer Thomas wouldn't have called in the favor. But she was so out of her element that she hadn't even considered that it might be kind of shitty to do it until Kris showed up and immediately started ranting.

However, any guilt Thomas had felt about dragging Kris to her apartment quickly shriveled up, both because the lecture felt like payback enough, and because she figured Kris was getting a kick out of beating Thomas up over her problems instead of having to think about his own.

"You're such a dumb bitch, you know that?" Kris said. "You really thought you could do no strings despite all the evidence to the contrary?"

"Okay, so what was I supposed to do?" Thomas asked.

"Well, not go and fall in love with a straight guy, for starters."

Thomas leaned back against the couch, closing her eyes to quell some of the roiling in her stomach. Nausea had been swelling and crashing over her like the tides all morning, but only a small pool of it could really be blamed on the hangover.

She could still taste Brian's kiss on her lips. Well, the kiss she'd forced on him during a complete lapse of judgment. The guilt of being the type of slut who kissed straights guys with girlfriends was weighing on her heavier than the alcohol-induced stupor.

Well, guys with girlfriends, straight or not.

Any respect Brian had for her had probably shriveled up as the space between them shrunk. Thomas's own self-loathing was surging to an all-time high.

She popped some Tylenol into her mouth, desperately looking for any way to turn some of Kris's scrutiny away from her fuck up with Brian, so she just said, "What was all that with Felix last night?"

Kris froze, his falcon-sharp gaze turning to Thomas like a challenge. "My dear, I have no idea what you mean."

Thomas rolled her eyes, but as it sent the room spinning even more than before, she reminded herself not to do that again. Kris could pick a fight with just about anyone, but last night's scuffle had seemed a bit less "in jest" than Thomas was used to. Especially since Felix went so far as to bring up Kris's mental health, which anyone who'd known him for more than a few hours knew was a near-fatal mistake.

But Thomas just said, "Okay, fine, if you don't want to talk about Felix, what about Day? They seemed worried about you."

Kris radiated a sort of tension that warned Thomas to stop prodding, but she couldn't help it. In the time she'd been friends with Kris, it was always Kris lecturing her about what he thought she should be doing, but it never went the other way. Hell, whole chunks of Kris's life were a complete enigma to Thomas, so it was impossible not to be curious after the whole subtextual fight that had clearly transpired last night.

And there was a part of Thomas that had to wonder if he'd made a mistake in backing Kris up. The last thing he wanted was to estrange another drag group by taking the wrong side, and everyone had made it pretty clear that they thought Thomas was out of line for calling out Felix.

Kris physically moved himself away from Thomas, stepping into the kitchen and leaning against the counter. "Why do you even care?"

Thomas raised an eyebrow. "I'm not allowed to care about what's going on with you?"

"I mean, if it's you asking, then maybe, but I'm not interested in giving you more dirt to pass off to Felix."

Thomas's head jerked back at the accusation. "What the fuck are you talking about? I don't even talk to Felix outside of work."

"Oh no?" Kris said, disbelief oozing from his tone. "Because you sure didn't give a shit about my life at all until what? Last night? And now you're asking about Day like that isn't suspicious as hell?"

"I tried to ask you about shit before, but you pushed me away like you always do!"

"Please, spare me your pathetic, desperate damsel act," Kris snapped, his tone getting more and more unstable as his volume ramped up. "Everything's always about you. Poor, innocent Thomas, so persecuted! The whole world is falling apart at your feet."

Thomas spluttered. "*Me?* There hasn't been a day since I met you that the whole world didn't revolve around Kris! And as for Felix, I don't even know what you're accusing me of, but it sounds to me like you need to up your meds because you're downright delusional."

The room plunged into a heavy silence, and Thomas did her best not to back down. She'd definitely gone too far with that line, but what else was she supposed to say? Kris had been getting bitchier and bitchier as his mania progressed, and now this? Thomas had pretty much sacrificed her place in their group just to take Kris's side, and here he was accusing her of what? Colluding with Felix to take him down? It was the most paranoid accusation Thomas had heard in a long time.

And it reminded her a bit too much of Michelle, of the way she'd twisted everything, taking a simple case of unrequited feelings and turning it into Thomas being some sort of aggressor, turning everyone against her when she hadn't done anything wrong. She didn't want to believe that Kris would ever do something like that to her, not after he'd seen everything Thomas had been put through and helped her pick up the pieces. But then, she hadn't wanted to believe it about Michelle either.

Then there was the fact that Kris had always held the power in their friendship. Kris was the one with all the connections, the privilege, the confidence. If he was about to cut Thomas off over some paranoid delusion, she couldn't afford to cede any power. She couldn't do anything except ride the wave and try to keep from sinking.

Kris stared back at Thomas like she was something he should crush beneath his heel.

But after another moment of silence, Kris just said, "You're a cunt, you know that? You think you're the victim in everything, so you go around screwing other people over and acting like you're just too innocent to do damage. But you're not a fucking victim. Seems like you're the one who needs a dose of reality. Not me."

And Thomas was absolutely livid. Everything Kris had thrown at her—this was exactly why she hadn't wanted to trust him in the first place. She should've known that Kris would take everything he'd learned about her and use it to stab her through the chest at the worst possible moment.

But the part that hurt most was the voice in the back of her head telling her that he was right, that Kris knew her better than anyone, so if he thought she was just a manipulative bitch, he must be right.

Thomas turned away, doing his best to push down the tears already building in his eyes. "Whatever. We were never really friends anyway, so you might as well go."

Thomas waited for Kris to curse her out or say some shit about how all of this was her fault and she had it coming, but he just turned and stormed out of the apartment without another word. And the pain in Thomas hung so heavily in her chest that it was only as she reflexively reached up to wipe her eyes that she realized she'd started crying—or that Kris had been teary eyed, too.

Thomas technically had plans with the group for later that evening, but they texted Day saying they weren't feeling well. Not only were they not overly eager to meet up with a friend group they were pretty sure didn't want them around, but they didn't want to run into Kris. Plus, Kris's words were still circling through their head like water refusing to go down the drain. The last thing they wanted was to come face to face with how shitty of a friend they really were.

So, Thomas spent the next few hours lying on the couch while they waited for their sickness to subside, and going back and forth on whether or not they should call Brian to apologize. They'd both been pretty wasted, so maybe they'd gotten lucky, and Brian had completely forgotten about the whole thing.

But Thomas knew that had to be wishful thinking. They'd been far more drunk than Brian, so if *they* remembered everything, the odds of it having slipped Brian's mind were probably zero. And he doubted Brian would forget something so awful.

The more he dwelled on that guilt, the more it sunk in that maybe Kris was right. It was clear that Brian had only entertained Thomas's crush because he felt bad for them, but he was back with his girlfriend now. Thomas had crossed the line, so if Brian hated them and wanted nothing to do with them, they really had no one to blame but themself.

They did the back and forth dance for a while before finally deciding to pick up their phone and at least pretend they'd come to a decision. Then they found the screen marked by two missed calls, but both were from their mom.

"Thomas? I assumed you were working," she said when they called her back.

"You assumed I was working, but you called me twice anyway?"

"I assumed you were working after you didn't answer. If you're not working, why didn't you answer?"

They sighed, quickly running through their mental stock of mom-approved excuses. "I wasn't feeling well today, so I was resting."

"Are you okay?"

The concern in her voice broke their heart. More than anything, they wanted to say no, to break down crying and tell her that they messed up and that they just wanted to come home.

You think you're the victim in everything.

Thomas just rolled their eyes. They may not be confident about a lot of things in their life, but the one thing they could be sure about was that they were far removed from the version of themself that could go crawling home to their mom, bawling their eyes out. It'd been years since they could even be honest about the pronouns they used or the friends they hung out with or what they really wanted in life.

So, they just said, "Yeah, I'm fine. How's everything at home? And with the shop?"

"The shop is good," she said. "Have you spoken to Theo?"

Thomas froze, the last conversation they'd had resurfacing in their mind. They couldn't be sure how much Theo had mentioned to their mom or if he'd even brought it up, but they definitely didn't want to be the one to introduce that conflict if she was mercifully in the dark about it.

"Um, not super recently," they said. "Why? Is he okay?"

"He booked a hotel for New York, but I told him to just stay with you. Did you tell him he couldn't stay with you?"

"Uh, no, I didn't. He didn't ask. By my apartment is really small, so I'm sure he and Gabi just want some privacy."

"He's just stubborn-headed is what it is," their mom grumbled. "Never wants to ask anyone for help."

Thomas chuckled humorlessly. "That is how you raised us."

The line fell quiet for a moment, and that sinking feeling in the base of their stomach started to form again.

The old Thomas—the one his parents loved—would never have talked back like that. The old Thomas always did what his family needed. He always buried his own needs, never took up too much space, never got into fights with people.

They weren't sure where the old Thomas had run off to, but they desperately wished they could switch places with him. Let the chronic people-pleaser fix their relationship with Theo and with Kris and with all of their friends. Let him remind them that staying in line wasn't so bad. That pleasing others at their own expense was worth it if it meant they never had to go through the heartache of losing everyone they loved.

Because the new Thomas wasn't so sure they believed that anymore, but the alternative was also too much to bear. No matter what they did, they always ended up alone.

"Thomas? Did you hang up?" their mom said.

"Uh, no, sorry," Thomas said.

But they weren't really sure what else they could say, like any word that came out would out them as the exact opposite of the son she thought they were. Like even making small talk would betray that the kid she'd raised and loved was gone, and Thomas was just the changeling who'd taken his place.

Finally, they said, "Mom, I'm sorry. I have to go."

"What happened? Are you okay?"

"I'm fine. I just think I'm gonna lie down for awhile."

The line fell quiet again. Then their mom said, "Okay. I love you. Call me soon, okay?"

They still weren't used to her expressing verbal affection, and the words forced tears to their eyes. They knew that odds were, she wouldn't be saying any of those things if she really knew the truth, but they still held the words close to their chest, hoping they could wrap themself up in enough of their mother's love to forget they weren't the kid who deserved it anymore.

"I love you, too."

21

The smell in the air should've been sweet and refreshing, but the tickle to Brian's nose left him desperately fighting down a sneeze.

Anna had asked to meet up, and even though he hadn't been entirely in the mood, Brian couldn't turn her down—especially after what happened with Mia. Not that he was eager to tell Anna about it.

The drunken kiss felt pretty irrelevant. Just two friends making dumb choices when their heads were too heavy to think clearly. But he also knew Anna wouldn't see it that way, which made him all the more hesitant to open that can of worms. He told himself that he'd tell her, just when the time was right, and when he wasn't worried about her taking it all wrong.

So, when Anna said she wanted to visit a nursery, Brian had agreed, even as his conversation with Mia replayed in his head. It didn't matter that plants weren't all that exciting to him. He didn't mind the walking or the fresh air, and he liked the giddy look on Anna's face as she raced from one little pot to another, looking at each plant like some diamond she'd personally excavated.

But more than that, he took comfort in spending time with her, in knowing that he could do this forever, the two of them *179* falling easily into each other's lives and finding simple pleasures in the mundane. She was exactly the type of girl he could build a life with, and he had no problem doing whatever activities she needed to make that happen.

Which was exactly why he forced Mia's face out of his mind every time the memory of her smile interrupted his view. He couldn't pretend he didn't enjoy flirting with her, the playful kissing, the banter, but he couldn't imagine anything more pathetic than throwing away his perfect future with Anna over someone who'd made it very clear she saw him as nothing more than a summer fling.

"How about this one?" Anna asked, raising a little clay pot with some sort of yellow flower in it.

"It's nice," he said.

She rolled her eyes. "You said that about the last three."

"Well, they're all nice. I'm not gonna pretend they aren't."

She laughed, placing the pot back down among the crowd. Then she shrieked, eyes shooting outlandishly wide. "Oh my God! Look!"

He followed her gaze down to her wrist where a ladybug had camped out on one of her freckles. Brian had never been particularly fond of bugs, but Anna shouted, "Look how cute!"

"Yeah, sure, cute."

Anna grinned. "Did you know that ladybugs can lead you in the direction of your true love."

"Well, lucky for you, you don't really need an insect for that."

Anna laughed. Slowly lifting her arm closer to her face, she blew lightly on the bug until its little red wings fluttered and it took off into the air in the opposite direction. Anna huffed, her eyebrows scrunching. "Well, that didn't work. It was supposed to fly to you."

The frustration on her face seemed like overkill, but her commitment to the bit was cute anyway.

Brian laughed, slinging an arm around her waist. "It's just a silly superstition."

"Yeah, I know," she said with a disappointed sigh. "But to be honest, I was kind of hoping to get some magic on our side. Or at least a little bit of luck."

He raised an eyebrow. "What do you mean?"

Instead of answering, she eyed him warily for a moment, slowly stepping in front of him and taking his hands in hers. "Well, our relationship has had some hiccups."

"It doesn't matter. All relationships have hiccups."

She looked up at him, her brown eyes big and round. "I know. It's just—I really want this to work out for us, you know? I love you, and—"

He closed the distance separating them, letting his mouth fall against hers, trying to infuse enough reassurance into his kiss to chase away the fear in her words. He soaked up the warmth radiating off her skin from standing in the direct sunlight, and her arms circled his waist, a gentle pressure holding him in place and fitting them together perfectly.

When he pulled away, she smiled. "I'll take that as a good sign?"

"Of course. I want things to work out for us, too. I mean, I wouldn't be here if I didn't."

She pursed her lips, pulling back slightly. "Your sentence is still missing something."

Which felt like a weird complaint, given he was already giving her everything he had. Then it clicked, and he forced down the guilt at not having realized it sooner.

"I love you, too."

She smiled wider than he probably deserved, pulling him to her again and kissing him.

"Don't forget about dinner next week," Anna said as Brian unlocked the door to his apartment.

"How could I forget?"

It really wasn't a lie. Ever since she'd pitched the idea to him as they'd left the nursery the day before, he hadn't stopped thinking about it, though probably not in the way she wanted.

If he was going to attempt dinner with her parents again, he needed to be alert. He couldn't claim to have a magical solution if they came out swinging again, but at least if he went in prepared, he could keep himself from saying anything to her that he might regret later.

At the end of the day, he was dating Anna, not her parents, even if ideally he'd want to marry a girl with a big family. Either way, their kids would still have one set of grandparents, so he could worry about the rest later.

"It'll be better this time," she assured him as he stepped aside, letting her enter the apartment ahead of him. But despite the certainty of her words, her tone sounded like she'd said them as much for her own benefit as his.

He didn't know how to admit it to her, but her uncertainty actually helped to quell some of his own. At the very least, it meant she was aware of how wrong things had gone the first time, so hopefully she had a plan for preventing a part two.

Pearl and Dustin had gone out for date night, so Brian was excited for him and Anna to have some alone time. Despite the largely foreign environment, Anna quickly crossed over to the couch, plopping down and making herself at home as she kicked her feet up on the arm.

"You wanna order pizza or something?"

"Actually," Brian said, "I was thinking about cooking something."

Anna's eyes widened. "You cook?"

"Eh, it's kind of an on again, off again hobby, but I've been thinking about picking it up again." He didn't bother mentioning that Mia had inspired him to get back into it. Anna didn't really need that kind of detail to get the point.

"Well, in that case, maybe we better play it safe and go with the pizza," Anna teased. "I'm not over-eager to start my week off with food poisoning."

He laughed, sitting down next to her. "That's fair," albeit a little disappointing. He didn't have to cook for Anna, exactly, but having her back in his life felt like a good excuse to cook for someone again. Of course, taking some time to practice and get back into the swing of things wasn't the worst idea, especially if he was about to stake his relationship on his ropa vieja. "Maybe I'll just bring something to dinner, then?"

Anna smiled. "Oh, my mom would love that. She's big on food. She's always saying you can't land a better guy than one who can cook."

Brian pushed his nerves down as he said, "Okay, well, I guess that means I better get practicing."

Anna offered him a sympathetic smile. "Don't worry about it too much, okay? I'm sure whatever you come up with will be great."

It struck him just how lucky anyone would be to have a girlfriend like her, someone perceptive and kind and reassuring. Not that Mia couldn't also be all of those things, but all-in-all, Anna was a real catch, and he should be glad to have someone like her in his corner.

He *was* glad to have someone like her in his corner. He wouldn't give up a relationship like that so easily.

"So, what's the best pizza place around here?" Anna asked as she pulled out her phone, scrolling across the screen.

Brian shrugged. "I haven't lived here that long."

She raised an eyebrow. "You're telling me you've been here over a month, and you still don't have a decent pizza place?"

"First of all, you said 'the best.' That's a really high standard to set! And second of all, I haven't ordered that much pizza."

Anna gasped, dramatically dropping her phone in her lap as her hands shot up to cover her face. "What kind of monster goes almost six weeks without pizza?"

Brian laughed, but a defensive bubble rose up in his chest. Was it really a bad thing to find something better than pizza while in New York City, of all places? But she was just joking, and it wasn't worth defending. She'd start to understand as he got her to branch out a little more, slow and steady.

The front door opened, and Brian whirled around to catch sight of Pearl and Dustin stepping inside.

"Oh, you're here," Pearl said, a smile creeping across her face as she caught sight of Anna. "Bad timing?"

Brian just groaned. "You two were supposed to be going out."

"We did, and now we're back."

With guests being few and far between, the living room hadn't been properly spaced to hold a crowd. There were only a deflated bean bag chair and two small couches, one of which was currently littered with some of Dustin's art supplies. Pearl threw herself down onto the other couch, half-draped over Brian, who just rolled his eyes before shoving her off onto the floor.

"Rude," Pearl snapped, crawling over to the bean bag chair.

"Like it isn't worse to throw yourself all over me with your boyfriend right there," Brian said.

Dustin just shrugged as he grabbed a chair from the kitchen island and spun it around to sit down. "I don't care."

Brian glanced at Anna to see if Pearl's maneuver had elicited any jealousy from her, but she looked unbothered as she tucked her phone away. Then she nudged Brian's shoulder, mild annoyance seeping into her tone as she said, "Aren't you gonna introduce us?"

"Oh, right," Brian said. "Uh, Anna, this is Pearl, and that's Dustin. They're my roommates. Roommates, my girlfriend, Anna."

"Ah, yes, the infamous Anna," Pearl said, pretending to fiddle with an invisible mustache. "We meet at last."

Anna smiled. "Pleasure. Now, where's a good place to order pizza around here?"

"Oh, Dustin!" Pearl said. "Get the drawer!"

Dustin dutifully stood up and headed into the kitchen without complaint.

"The drawer?" Brian asked.

Pearl grinned. "Duh. The all-important takeout drawer."

"The what?"

Dustin stepped back into the room and passed Anna a stack

of little paper pamphlets and fliers. "It's where we keep all the takeout menus."

"It was the first thing I set up when we moved in," Pearl said. "You know me, always thinking about the important stuff."

"That's a very mom thing to do," Brian said.

Anna smiled. "It's brilliant is what it is." She rifled through the menus before finally settling on one that looked promising.

Pearl beamed like it was the highest of compliments, and Brian opted to just let her have this one. Pearl and Anna getting along like they were old friends was better than the alternative, even if it meant he was outnumbered in terms of pizza lovers. Finding someone who actually got along with his friends only boded well for their future together.

"Oh, by the way, Anna," Pearl said, grinding any optimism coursing through Brian's brain to a halt, "you're invited to game night."

"Game night?" Anna asked, peeking up from the menus.

"Oh, right," Brian said, rushing to fill in the conversation before Pearl could shame him for forgetting. "Uh, Pearl and Dustin are hosting a game night this weekend, if you want to come. We're just gonna play Uno or something and get wasted."

"Ah, classy," Anna said. "Sure, I'll come."

Pearl clapped her hands together. "Great! Also, Brian, don't forget to invite Mia."

Anna paused, her head cocked to the side. "Who's Mia?"

For a moment, Brian's entire life flashed before his eyes, even as he insisted that this wasn't a big deal. No problem. Nothing to worry about.

Anna eyed him quizzically, as he said, "Um, no one. Just a friend from work. So, what pizza do you want?"

Anna's gaze remained on his face for a moment longer before she shrugged, turning back to the menus. Brian let out a breath, turning back to Pearl and sending her a pointedly annoyed glare, but she just pulled out her phone and proceeded to ignore him.

He hated how nonchalant she looked, as if she hadn't nearly started a new world war right in the middle of their living room. It was probably intentional, all part of her convoluted plan to get him to prioritize him bringing Anna up to speed about Mia. And of course he would, eventually. He had no intention of keeping her a secret forever. But he also knew Anna, and, well, girls in general, and he didn't want to start some sort of fighting by accidentally implying there was something there when there wasn't.

Because there *really* wasn't anything there.

Even if he'd finally forced himself to admit that there had been a time when he'd wanted there to be, there *definitely* wasn't anything there now.

22

After spending the weekend running from his past, his problems, and his own self-loathing, Thomas woke up Monday morning feeling far too winded to be enthusiastic about work, but he forced himself to go in anyway.

During the commute, he reminded himself that all of this would fade. Maybe not his problems or his self-loathing, but he'd certainly be let go by the end of the summer, and then he could just move back to Vermont with his tail between his legs and restart all over again. Maybe this time he could rebrand himself as the useless brother so he wouldn't have to disappoint anyone else. Hell, with Gabi working the shop now, his parents didn't even need his help, so they could just throw him out on the street, not that they ever would.

He reached the office in a miserable stupor before reporting promptly to Kris's office. The door lay closed, and when he tried the handle, it jimmied a bit but wouldn't budge.

Given their fight over the weekend, he wasn't surprised that Kris didn't want to see him. He wasn't even surprised that Kris would carry his petty grudge over to their work environment and turn everything upside down.

But Kris could've at least gotten him fired so he wouldn't have to come in at all.

"Is the door still locked?"

Thomas turned as Day walked up behind him, a tired but resigned expression on their face. "Afraid so," he said.

"Just ignore her," Day said. "She's been pissy all weekend, but she'll get over it eventually. Why don't you come lend me a hand?"

Day didn't wait for a response, just turned and walked down the hallway, so Thomas scrambled after them.

Day was a few inches shorter than Thomas and didn't have a particularly long stride, but they walked with a confident gait that left Thomas hustling to keep up. Their office was the largest, a wide rectangle with a wall full of windows. Where Kris's office felt more like a sort of storage closet with a desk shoved in, Day's was equipped with an L-shaped desk, a wide cork board littered with sticky notes and memos, and a potted cactus in the corner that may or may not be a real plant.

Day motioned for Thomas to take a seat in one of two gray armchairs, but he felt painfully out of place as he slid down into one. He'd always liked Day—always kind of admired them from afar—but it was only setting in now how much his acceptance by them felt contingent on Kris's acceptance of him. In fact, as much shit as he'd given Brian, it was easy to say that Thomas's entire life in New York hinged on his friendship with Kris, and now, navigating any of it felt like navigating the slew of New York sewer grates in a pair of needle-sharp heels.

"I was really impressed with what you and Kris managed to pull off," Day said as they sat down on the other side of their desk and clicked around with their mouse.

"I—what do you mean?"

"Well, I don't know what you all actually did, but we got a huge surge of app downloads recently," Day said. "It's the happiest I've seen my stepdad since this whole project started, and he is notoriously hard to impress."

The news was certainly good, though Thomas wasn't sure what he really had to do with any of it until he remembered asking Brian to circle word of Agenda Social around his internship. He must have come through.

"Anyway," Day continued, "it couldn't have come at a better time. I think my stepdad was kind of expecting this whole venture to crash and burn. You know, give me some start-up capital so he could turn to my mom and pretend he tried. But now that we're actually getting some traction, he's talking about putting real money into the whole thing."

"Like…the kind of money to hire us on long-term?"

Day laughed. "I mean, I'm still waiting to get the details finalized, so I won't make any promises, but I think so. You've all put so much time into helping this app land; it only seems fair that you get to see it grow. Plus, Kris has really hyped up your abilities. I'd love to see you write some new code."

"Wait, really? Kris did?"

But the whole train of thought sounded foolish even as he voiced it. Obviously, Kris must have said something good about him, or Day wouldn't have hired him in the first place. But Thomas hadn't really thought about it, especially since he hadn't been able to flex any real skills.

There hasn't been a day since I met you that the whole world didn't revolve around Kris!

Thomas knotted his hands together, digging the tips of his shoes into the tile of Day's office to brace himself as he shoved the memory deeper into his mind. Regret settled over him like chains, and not just for that line, but for all of them. Telling Kris they were never really friends, using his mental illness against him. At the time, Thomas hadn't even stopped to consider if maybe he was pulling those words out of a place of vindictiveness rather than accuracy, but with a couple of days' time between them, he realized it didn't matter. Even if everything he'd said had been right, he'd still feel like a piece of shit for having said it.

Flexing their mind reading skills, Day said, "You okay?"

Thomas ducked his face, hoping he hadn't accidentally given too much away. Kris may have been the one to lock the door, but Thomas didn't need to hang their dirty laundry from an office window, especially not an office window that Thomas could only reach because Kris had referred him for the job.

"Sorry. I guess I'm just a little…"

But he didn't know what he could say that wouldn't just make things more uncomfortable.

Finally, he looked up to find Day offering him a sympathetic smile. "It's okay," they said. "Whatever Kris is pissed about will be water under the bridge in a week."

Thomas winced. "Sorry. I didn't mean to bring this into work."

Day waved him off. "Really, it's fine. You and Kris are obviously close, and I know it can be hard to keep your head on straight when you're in a fight with a friend. Besides, Kris is notorious for causing a scene out of something she'll forget about by next week. You really don't need to stress about it."

But as reassuring as their tone was, Day's words made Thomas feel even guiltier. If even his boss could see that he and Kris were good friends, why was *he* the only one who'd apparently missed the memo?

We were never really friends anyway, so you might as well go.

He'd spent the whole summer waiting to get dropped again, but the more his words from the other day haunted him, the harder it was to pretend that Kris was the reason they weren't talking anymore.

"Do you want my advice?" Day asked, calmly twirling a pen around their fingers like a magical girl readying her staff for the final strike.

Figuring it couldn't possibly make things worse, he said, "Yes, please."

"Let's find something to take your mind off of it, and I'm sure Kris'll be back to apologize in a few days or something."

Thomas sighed. "I'm not sure he's the one who needs to apologize."

Day laughed, and as embarrassed as Thomas felt at the moment, at least the sound was kind of soothing.

"That's even better," Day said. "Kris sucks at holding a

grudge, and you obviously already know what you need to apologize for, so this'll blow over in the blink of an eye."

Thomas didn't feel nearly as confident as Day sounded, but maybe their optimism could sustain the both of them.

23

There was a chill in the air as Brian entered the office to find Ella furiously pounding away on her phone keyboard.

"Everything okay?" he asked, though a part of him instantly regretted drawing attention to himself.

Ella slowly looked up at him like his arrival had just singlehandedly thrown the entire world off its axis. The feverishness in her eyes forced him back a single, involuntary step, his hands already rising in front of him in a show of surrender.

Then Ella just rolled her eyes, motioning for him to take a seat. "We're in trouble."

"Trouble?" Brian echoed as he sat down across from her, grateful that the wooden desk served as a barrier against whatever she might throw at him.

"This masquerade ball? It's going up in flames, and we haven't even locked in the venue or purchased insurance yet."

Doom hung heavy in Ella's tone, but Brian actually felt pleasantly surprised. It sucked that their big event of the year was falling through, but Ella's terror had him expecting some sort of major injury or lawsuit, so comparably, this wasn't too bad.

"We managed to get the event approved," she continued,

"but they don't want to give us any real funding for it! How are we supposed to throw a masquerade ball without funding?"

"Why don't we just half-ass it?"

She stared at him with a look of abject horror. "You want to half-ass a masquerade ball for a bunch of gays? We'll never hear the end of it! We might as well call it quits and shut down the organization now."

Which sounded a bit dramatic from Brian's POV, but he valued his own safety enough not to mention that to Ella.

"Okay, well, what if we just do something cheaper?"

But she was already shaking her head. "Be serious, Brian. It took weeks to get this event approved! If we have to go through the process again, we'll never get things finalized before fall."

Right. Brian leaned back in his chair, trying to dig through his mind for some alternative solutions.

"If we just need more money for the event, what about a crowdfund?" Brian said. "Or getting some sort of event sponsor?"

Ella rolled her eyes. "This isn't like charging for tickets. We can't plan anything without money, and until we plan anything, how are we supposed to convince people to put their money behind us? It's just not really practical."

He picked his brain for more ideas, but considering he'd tried a couple different suggestions only for them to fall flat, he figured it might be better he just keep his mouth shut for a while.

Ella ended up calling more of the interns in, breaking them up into groups to workshop solutions, but all they really managed to do was make Brian feel better about his own suggestions. Once Chad suggested a "virtual ball," Ella told everyone to go home early, and Brian didn't need to be told twice.

He was already a bit stressed thinking about his upcoming dinner with Anna's parents, so more time to prep could only work in his favor. Of course, while the dinner itself had him too antsy to sit still, he was actually looking forward to flexing his cooking skills again.

When he was a kid, wandering into the kitchen to help his mom churn out some of the old recipes she'd inherited from the family had been a pretty common practice, but after going to college and turning his little family hobby into his big gesture to win over Maggie, something about the recipes had lost their shine. Or maybe it was just that the nostalgia of the flavors had bled out, leaving something far more bitter in their place.

Either way, pivoting to cooking for Anna and her parents both rekindled the spark and left him feeling a little anxious. As much as he loved Anna and longed to have someone he could share his cooking with, he couldn't help but feel like cooking for someone new only meant sullying the recipes even more.

He could always try experimenting, playing around with whatever Pearl had tucked away in the kitchen until that creative spark kindled something exciting. But he also didn't want to run the risk of giving Anna's parents food poisoning and walking back whatever progress they'd actually made. And even if he managed something edible, it didn't feel like enough to bring something over that they'd just leave to mold in the fridge. He wanted to do something that could really show how committed he was to Anna, really serve as a representation of the life they could build together.

But if he was going to manage something that good, he needed some honest feedback.

So, before he could think better of it, he texted Mia, *Busy?*

Always, but I'm easily swayed.

I'm trying to cook up a masterpiece but will probably end up with something lethal. Want to come taste test?

Be there in an hour!

Brian didn't even realize how giddily he was smiling until he set the phone down and caught sight of his own reflection on the oven. Suddenly, a rush of shame filled him, and he quickly turned his face away before he could watch his guilt chase away his own happiness.

He leaned over the counter, resting his head in his hands. There was a reason he hadn't invited Mia to game night despite Pearl's insistence, but he'd been able to avoid acknowledging it by drowning himself in work and makeout sessions.

Because the second Mia and Anna were in the same room, there was no way Brian wouldn't be stuck comparing the two.

And he knew, without question, how absolutely ridiculous it was, like refusing a perfectly nice apartment in Hell's Kitchen because he'd rather be on the Upper East Side. What could be more foolish than throwing away a perfectly happy life to chase something unattainable, incompatible, and that had blatantly told him it wanted nothing to do with him?

He hadn't lied to Anna the other day when he'd told her that he loved her. He'd been meaning to say it ever since he'd gotten to New York. Because he did. He was certain of that. She was the type of person who just made everything easier— getting out of bed, working through a day job, planning for the future. She'd taken smelly, exhausting, hectic New York and turned it into something comfortable, safe, and homey. In every daydream Brian had, he always saw himself settling down with a girl like Anna, someone he could bring home to his parents and start a family with. Someone who fit perfectly into the life he'd dreamed of having since elementary school.

So why did he have to keep thinking about Mia at the most inopportune times?

Shaking his head, he turned toward the pantry. He needed to stop wasting brainpower overthinking impossible scenarios and just let himself get lost in his craft.

Anna had said that her mom would be cooking them dinner, so he decided to focus on an appetizer or dessert. He didn't have a whole lot of dessert recipes memorized, but maybe this was a good chance to try something different. There were a couple he'd saved from his mom's recipe book that he hadn't had a chance to fool around with yet.

Was it too optimistic to hope Pearl had the ingredients lying around? Probably.

Brian threw open the cabinet door, pulling out some basics—sugar, vanilla, baking soda. Unsurprisingly, most of the ingredients his mother leaned on were nowhere to be found.

Brian turned back to his phone, quickly typing out a *Would you mind grabbing a few things for me?* and sending it to Mia.

He pulled up the recipe photos he had, comparing the ingredients with what he'd set out on the counter before running off a list of some of the absent parties—red beans, glutinous rice flour, corn starch.

Mia sent him an *I'll see what I can do!* and he forced down the fluttery feeling in his chest. A friend offering to do him a favor wasn't something that should have him feeling giddy, so he must just be excited to see what he could make.

Since he couldn't get started baking until he had the rest of the ingredients, he set out prepping the kitchen—digging out measuring cups, washing any dishes he needed, separating what he had into categories.

An hour later, Mia arrived, a reusable bag slung over their shoulder with the ingredients Brian had asked for.

"You're lucky I actually know what all of this shit is," they said, placing the bag down on the counter. "A white bitch could never."

Their tone pulled a laugh out of Brian's chest, but he also felt a little uneasy, like they were specifically dragging Anna. Brian pushed the thought away as he accepted the bag of ingredients. The last thing he wanted was to project some sort of bitterness onto Mia.

"Sorry. I'm still trying to figure out what to make, but Pearl doesn't have a lot of the basics."

"What are you cooking for?" Mia asked. "Like, for fun or…?"

"Um, dinner," Brian said, turning so he wouldn't have to see the look on Mia's face as he explained. "Well, not literally dinner, but I'm bringing it to *a* dinner. With Anna's family."

"Oh."

The kitchen fell quiet for a moment, and Brian turned back

to find Mia simply pulling out a chair and making herself comfortable at the kitchen island.

"Um, yeah," Brian said. "I hope that's okay?"

"Why wouldn't it be?"

Brian wasn't sure if there was a slight edge to Mia's voice, or if he was just hearing one because a part of him wanted it there.

No. No, he *didn't* want that.

It was a *good* thing that Mia was totally unbothered by him getting back together with Anna. Actually, it was great. He had a really cool friend who was supportive of his relationship. He couldn't have been happier.

"Um, no reason," Brian said. "I-I just realized it might be kind of rude to ask you to help me cook for someone else."

Mia shrugged. "I used to work at a café. That's literally all I did."

"I kind of forgot about that, but I guess this is perfect, then. You can keep me from accidentally poisoning anyone."

Mia smiled. "Yeah, I guess so."

Brian pulled out a large mixing bowl, drying it off with a towel by the sink before setting it down on the counter.

"Oh, by the way," Mia said, "I wanted to thank you for sharing the app around. You may have single-handedly saved my job."

Warmth rose in Brian's face. He *had* been a little aggressive in blasting emails out to everyone he worked with, but he hadn't thought much of it. Just a little favor for a friend. But the smile Mia was throwing in his direction now blotted out the kitchen lights, and he wasn't sure what to make of that.

"Um, no problem," he said, trying to fix his attention on his recipe. "I've been kind of useless at my job recently, so I'm at least glad I could lend you a hand with yours."

"Oh?" Mia asked. "What happened?"

Brian shrugged. "Nothing serious. We're just having trouble getting the funding we need for an event, so I suggested getting a sponsor, but I don't know. I'm only working this gig for the summer anyway, but I do feel kind of bad not being able to help since the org does so much for the community."

The *queer* community, he probably should've specified. Of which he had no part in.

But the words died on his lips. Somehow, it just didn't seem as relevant anymore.

Standing in the kitchen with Mia carried an unexpected sort of charge to it. It felt right being in what was now his home as he did something as domestically mundane as whipping up food with Mia casually sitting a few feet away like it was no big deal.

It sunk in then just how unfair he'd been in viewing Mia as almost otherworldly ever since the drag show. In his mind, he'd put them on this weird pedestal, separating them out from mere mortals like Pearl and Anna, and treating them like someone who couldn't belong in his daily life, like some untouchable goddess.

But watching as they flicked idly through their phone for a moment before setting it down, it was clear to him just how wrong he'd been. Not because Mia wasn't kind of ethereally magical, but because they were so clearly human, just as at home in the mundane parts of his life as they were on stage or at the bar or raking their fingers through his tousled hair.

They looked up at him, an eyebrow raised. "You okay?"

Brian winced, quickly nodding and turning back to the task at hand. What had he been working on?

Rising from their chair, they rounded the island as Brian turned toward the utensil drawer in search of a mixing spoon. He knew he was acting weird, and of course Mia would catch onto that, but he wasn't sure how to calm his nerves.

Finally, he pulled out a wooden spoon before turning around to face them. "Are you free on Saturday?"

"Free is a bit ambitious, but I might be able to make time if it's worth my while. What's up?"

"Uh, nothing big. My roommate, Pearl, is hosting a night of games and drinking, and she said you're welcome to come. Um, but you don't have to if you don't want to."

Mia eyed him suspiciously for a moment before saying, "I could probably make it."

"Okay, I'll tell—"

"But I guess the question is whether *Pearl* is inviting me, or if you are."

Brian paused, mouth gaped. "I—what's that supposed to mean?"

"You just made it all about Pearl, so I wasn't sure if maybe she told you that you had to invite me, or if you actually wanted me there," Mia said, voice dipping lower. "The last thing I really need right now is to show up at a party where no one wants me."

Brian's head was already shaking before they'd even finished talking. "No, it's not just Pearl. I mean, I *do* want you there. It wouldn't be nearly as fun without you."

Mia stared back at him for a moment more before a slow smile spread across their face. "Okay, if you say so."

They offered to lend Brian a hand, since Japanese desserts had so many steps and parts, it'd probably take him most of the evening to finish if he worked alone. The second pair of hands helped cut the task load, and Brian had to admit that having someone who knew their way around the kitchen to keep him on track proved extremely useful.

But Mia being so close made for its own distraction.

"Ow!" Brian yelped as he jerked back, the newly formed burn on his finger already blistering. It was in good company given how many times he'd accidentally brushed the griddle over the course of the past two and a half hours.

"Are you sure you're Japanese?" Mia said, a cheeky grin slipping across their face as they casually leaned against the side of the oven. "Your heat tolerance sucks."

Brian rolled his eyes. "Oh, yeah, I'm sure that's the problem here. Not the insistence on cooking everything on scalding."

Mia smiled. "Without the right amount of heat, everything'll be limp and lifeless."

Suddenly, Brian's cheeks decided to compete with the stove

top for highest temperature. "What is *that* supposed to mean?" he spluttered. "Just because—there's plenty of heat, okay?"

Mia blinked back at him. "Okay. I just don't think you should take your cook temperature for granted if you want the right rise—"

"It rises just fine!"

"—to your batter."

Brian paused, mouth opening and closing again. "Oh. Right."

"What did you think I was talking about?"

"What? Obviously, I knew what you were talking about! What else would you be talking about?"

"Okay…"

He ignored the sly smirk on their face as they set the second half of the batter into the fridge to chill.

He wasn't sure what to make of the awkwardness between them as they worked, largely because it stemmed from just how naturally Mia had fallen into place. They were obviously someone who knew their way around a kitchen, which Brian had already anticipated, but he hadn't expected that they'd fit so seamlessly into *his* kitchen, the two of them flowing around each other so instinctively that he had to wonder how he'd ever cooked a single thing without them.

Which just left him feeling even more humiliated.

Not just because they'd only known each other for half a summer, but because of everything they represented to him. If Anna was comfortable and homey, Mia was barreling down the freeway at a hundred with a busted headlight. They were always teasing him, pulling him in directions he wasn't sure he wanted to go in, and reminding him that he wasn't really the one steering, no matter how much control he wanted to believe he had.

And that was just the stuff Mia did intentionally. It didn't even scratch the surface of how hard it was for him to think straight just looking at them.

"So, what time should I come over for game night?" Mia

asked, slowly licking the wooden spoon.

Brian had to forcefully turn his face away long enough for the fog in his brain to clear so he could say, "Um, seven should be good. It might be better to pregame before you get here, though. I don't know how messy Pearl's friends will be."

Mia laughed. "I'll keep that in mind. So do you think you have enough to wow your girlfriend's parents?"

Brian winced. "I don't know. I'm not really sure how high they're setting their standards."

"I think you'll be okay. I mean, I think you did a pretty good job, and I've been making Japanese sweets since before I even learned how to spell them. Hope it's enough to keep your relationship intact, though."

"It's not like that," Brian said, a defensive edge in his voice.

"No?"

"We're not gonna break up over it, even if it sucks," he said. "Actually, it was my idea to bring something. I kept thinking about what you said the other day about things I like to do, and I realized I kind of wanted to get back into cooking again. Especially now that I have someone I can cook for again."

"Right. Because you only do things *other* people want you to do," Mia said.

Brian turned to them, an eyebrow raised. "That's kind of judgmental, don't you think?"

"Sorry, it's not supposed to be," Mia said, a blush rising in their cheeks. "I've just been thinking about the whole 'living through the lens of other people' thing. I guess I've kind of been doing that, too. Only I've been rebelling against what other people want for me, whereas it seems like maybe you've just been…settling."

"I'm not settling just because I'm okay with doing what other people like," Brian said. "I find a lot of things I like that way."

"Sure," Mia said, "but I have to wonder how often you miss out on other things you'd like, for the same reason. I mean, choosing not the worst option isn't the same as choosing the best one."

"There's more than one way to be happy."

"But settling isn't how you make yourself happy. That's how you placate yourself for now and then regret it once it's too late to fix it."

Brian rolled his eyes. "I'm not just settling, okay? I'm perfectly happy with my life. Did it ever occur to you that some of us like it when things are predictable? Some of us are okay with things going the way we expect them to without having to suddenly change our identities or alter our lifestyles on the fly."

"Yeah, I know," Mia said. "I just don't think you're one of those people."

"I don't think you know me well enough to argue that," Brian snapped.

"Okay, well, to be fair, I think you're the only one arguing," Mia said, voice soft. "But I'm sorry. I'll mind my own business."

And Brian wasn't sure why, but a hollow pit had formed in his stomach, only growing wider after Mia dismissed themself and headed home. Like maybe he'd been offered some sort of lifeline, but missing all the warning signs, he'd chosen instead to barrel right into the storm, full steam ahead.

Saturday morning, Pearl dragged Brian to the store to help stock up on booze and snacks.

"Why not just do a BYOB?" Brian suggested as he was forced to get dressed and stumble into the kitchen just before eight.

"Because I'm not an animal?" Pearl snapped.

Brian had been to plenty of BYOB parties, so that felt over-exaggerated, but then, most of those had been hosted by his frat brothers, so maybe that was the point Pearl was making. Either way, game night in a tiny New York apartment hardly felt like a real party worth stocking up for. Yet, instead of stopping at a bodega, Pearl insisted they go to a full-on grocer to make sure they had the best selection of half-empty bags of chips.

"How many people are even coming tonight?" Brian asked

as he staggered down the aisle behind her, a metal basket slung over his wrist since Pearl had insisted he be the one to carry it.

"Hmm, maybe eight?" she said. "Well, I guess it depends who's coming alone. I told everyone they can bring a guest."

Which wasn't news Pearl had relayed to Brian, but given he'd only invited Mia and Anna, it probably didn't matter.

"Can the apartment really handle that many people? We only have like three chairs."

Pearl shot him a pointed look. "Stop being so grumpy just because you're worried about your girlfriend and your mistress meeting each other."

"Okay, woah, Mia is not my mistress. We're not anything. We're friends."

Pearl rolled her eyes. "Yeah, yeah, I know. The whole 'friends' spiel."

"What the hell is that supposed to mean?" Brian snapped.

"It doesn't mean anything unless you want it to mean something. Let's go grab some nuts, too."

Brian really hated when Pearl did the whole "drop a fateful line and then bail" thing, especially when she'd already promised to stop meddling. But then, it wasn't like Pearl to ever actually stop meddling.

"Also, to be fair," Brian said, catching up to her, "you're the one who invited Anna, and you're the one who insisted I invite Mia, so any disaster that happens tonight is your fault. If you'd stayed out of it, neither of them would've been coming."

"Is that what you want?" Pearl said, turning to face him with a weirdly serious look. "Neither of them?"

Brian shook his head. "What are you even saying?"

"God, you're such a mess, you know that? It's Anna this or Mia that. You act like you're choosing between flannel shirts instead of people with actual feelings."

"I'm not choosing anything," Brian said. "I chose Anna. And there was never a choice anyway, because Mia and I were never anything to each other. So that's it."

"Then start acting like it!" Pearl shouted.

At the opening of the aisle, a mom with her toddler stared at them before quickly placing a hand into her son's dark curls and steering him toward the next aisle.

Brian just rolled his eyes. "What do I need to do to appease you, oh great, Pearl?"

"It's not about appeasing me," Pearl said. "You have no clue how miserable you make people. I mean, did you even notice how uncomfortable you're making Anna?"

Brian raised an eyebrow. "I'm not making her uncomfortable."

"Ah, so you haven't noticed. Of course not."

Brian groaned, turning and walking down the aisle away from her. He didn't need this right now. He just wanted to get whatever snacks Pearl needed and get home so he could take a shower.

Finally, he spun back around, locking eyes with her. "Okay, fine. Humor me. Why is she uncomfortable?"

Pearl shrugged. "Oh, please. Even when you're with Anna, you don't seem like you're all the way there, and I'm saying this as a third party. I can only imagine how much of that she's feeling. If Anna's your dream girl, then fine. I support you. But you need to start acting like it, because if you keep stringing her along by a thread, eventually that thread's gonna break, and not only are you gonna hurt her, but you're both gonna end up alone. And that's before we even get into Mia, who, by the way, you treat more like a side piece than a supposed friend."

"Okay, forget it," Brian said, taking a step back. "Can you handle your shopping alone?"

Pearl rolled her eyes. "Obviously."

"Good, then I'm going home."

He expected Pearl to call him back for another lecture, but she didn't say anything as he set the basket down on the ground at her feet before turning and stomping down the aisle.

24

Thomas considered canceling on game night at least once daily since he'd gone over to Brian's place, partially because of how things had ended, but even more so because the thought of being stuck in a small apartment with a bunch of strangers made Thomas's insides shrivel up.

He'd always felt a little out of place around new people, but having drag or Kris or some other buffer to kill some of the awkwardness had become a lifeline.

Now his falling out with Kris had only kicked Thomas's uncertainty into overdrive. Even barring the fear that Kris was right about him being manipulative, Thomas couldn't shake the fact that the one person who'd taken his side when everyone turned on him—the one person who hadn't twisted his intentions and made him into the enemy—clearly saw him as the enemy now.

So did that mean they were right?

And by overthinking all of this and making it about himself again, was Thomas just further proving Kris's point?

He somehow made it to Saturday without canceling, and that meant he had no choice but to get dressed and go.

A half hour passed as he stood in front of his closet, going back and forth on how feminine would be too feminine for an apartment full of strangers. Even if he opted to dress "comfortably," he ran the risk of looking like a slob, and if he opted to dress "nicely," he might run straight into attention-grabbing territory, which was the last thing he wanted.

Finally, he settled on jeans and a *Stars Wars* t-shirt, hoping it was generic enough that no one would stop to ask if he was actually in the fandom. His nerves were so tense that a single personal question might be enough to make him self-destruct, and he knew he'd never get over the humiliation of dying in someone else's living room.

Unfortunately, his fashion crisis ate all his preparation time, so instead of pre-gaming like Brian suggested, he raced out of his apartment totally sober but wishing he wasn't, already regretting his decision to go out when he probably should've just stayed in.

It didn't help that even as Brian opened the front door and said, "Ah, you made it," Thomas could already sense the tension in the air. Had Brian held a grudge against him for his comments the other day? Thomas felt his stomach plummet as Brian closed the door behind him and led him into the living room. He definitely should've stayed in tonight.

"Everyone, this is Mia," Brian said, motioning in Thomas's direction. He gestured around the room saying, "That's Dan, Terry, Vero, Shanae, Dustin, and—" His lip curled a bit, his voice taking on a little too much venom as he said, "—*Pearl*."

A bolt of anxiety shocked Thomas's system at the tone of Brian's voice. Could Brian really be so frustrated with him that even introducing Thomas to his friends had become this loaded?

But before Thomas could utter an apology for the other day, Pearl looked up with thinly veiled annoyance on her face saying, "What?"

"What?" Brian snapped back at her. "You have a problem with me introducing our friends now?"

Something about the defensive way Brian said the word "friends" made Thomas think that maybe the venom in his voice had nothing to do with Thomas at all.

"Um, anybody want drinks?" Dustin said, cutting through whatever charged tension shot between Brian and Pearl. He stood up, turning and heading toward the kitchen.

Even without any context, Thomas figured Dustin had the right idea. Maybe if everyone got wasted enough, some of the tension in the air would dissolve.

"Let's just get to this game," Pearl said, reaching for a box with an illustrated growling wolf with red eyes. "We've got a good group here, so this should be fun."

Dustin stepped back into the room, placing some beers down on the corner of the long table before setting a carrier of sodas and a bottle of vodka down on the floor. He passed everyone some red solo cups before taking his seat next to Pearl.

Thomas reached for the vodka, tempted to just fill the cup without a mixer, but opting instead to be civil and just take a shot.

"So how does this work, exactly?" Shanae asked, as she popped open a can of beer.

"It's like a witch hunt," Pearl said. "We hand out cards so everyone gets their roles, and then one person is a werewolf who chooses a player to kill off every night, and everyone else has to vote who they think the werewolf is. If the majority guesses the werewolf, the townspeople win. If not, whoever they voted for dies, and the werewolf gets to kill again the next night. I can be the moderator, so everyone can learn how it works."

"No," Brian said, "the moderator should be someone a little less biased, don't you think?"

"*Biased?*" Pearl snapped. "You know, just because some people have a complete and total lack of self-awareness doesn't mean I'm biased."

Brian scoffed. "Oh, yes, very subtle."

"Okay, it's fine," Dustin said, grabbing the box from Pearl. "I'll moderate. Let's just pass out the cards."

He shuffled the cards for a moment before passing them out to everyone, face down. Thomas scooted slightly away from Brian long enough to glance at the card without any roaming eyes, revealing the face of a dorky villager carrying a pitchfork.

Turning back toward the group, Thomas's leg accidentally brushed against Brian's, and Thomas's face went red. But as Brian jerked back, quickly sliding closer to the arm of the couch to get away from him, a jolt shot through Thomas's gut. Even if Kris had been right about Thomas twisting things to make them about him, he couldn't think of any reality in which Brian's reaction wasn't at least a little personal.

"Sorry," he mumbled, but Brian didn't acknowledge him.

"Okay, so everyone close your eyes and pretend to sleep," Dustin said.

Thomas closed his eyes, leaning back against the couch cushions. As awkward as it was being surrounded by so many strangers, the temporary darkness provided a nice reprieve from all the scrutinizing eyes and awkwardness. But it didn't last long, Dustin calling for the werewolf team to wake up and pick their kills only for him to tell everyone to open their eyes a moment later.

Dustin heaved a sigh that seemed almost too heavy to carry before saying, "Sorry, Pearl, you're dead."

"Wait, *what*?" Pearl screamed, jumping to her feet. "Who's side are you on?"

"I'm literally the moderator."

"Well, you're *about* to be single!"

Dustin spluttered. "It's just a game, Pearl!"

"Whatever," Pearl huffed, whirling around to cast her gaze down on the rest of the guests. "You all know who the werewolf is, then, because of course Brian would kill me first. Fucking rude."

Brian's eyes widened. "What the hell? Why would I do that? It would be too obvious. Besides, I'm sure there are tons of people who want you to shut up besides me."

"Think I'm gonna have to agree with Pearl on this one,"

Shanae said. "What do you guys think?

Dan and Vero just nodded along, but Terry's brow scrunched in deep thought as he mumbled, "I think Brian's right. It's too easy."

A knock on the door cut through the tension for a moment, and Thomas bit down his offer to answer it just to be able to escape the circle.

"Okay, pause," Brian said, standing up and heading for the door. When he pulled it open, his tone of voice changed entirely in a way that immediately sent a jolt down Thomas's spine, his back going rigid. "Hey!"

"Hello!"

And Thomas didn't need to recognize her voice to know who'd arrived. No one other than Brian's girlfriend would sound like *that* having a door opened for them.

Thomas's stomach knotted as disappointment settled over him. He hadn't even realized how presumptuous he'd been, but when he'd joined the group only to find she wasn't there, a part of him had gotten his hopes up that she wouldn't be coming at all.

But that was such a silly thing to hope for. Her arrival didn't actually change anything, except giving Brian a little more pep to his step as he led her into the living room and walked her over to the couch. He had an arm slung over her shoulders, and she leaned against his side like his whole physique had been carved out perfectly just to fit her.

"Everyone, this is Anna," he said before turning back to her. "We're playing Werewolf, and everyone's about to crucify me because they think I murdered Pearl."

"Oh?" Anna said, shooting a quick glance over to where Pearl sat, seething, across the room. "Seems too easy, doesn't it?"

Pearl rolled her eyes. "Great, so who do you think it was?"

Anna shrugged. "I'd say someone who knows Brian well enough to frame him, but obviously not me, because I just got here."

"Well, Dustin's moderating, so that's pretty much everyone," Pearl said. "Well, unless you count Mia."

Suddenly every pair of eyes in the room homed in on Thomas, and the knot in his stomach tightened.

"Care to defend yourself, Mia?" Shanae said.

"I-I don't really know what to say." Which was a bit of an understatement, because the bombardment of prying eyes made taking in enough air to speak more difficult.

"You can't defend yourself if you already know you're guilty," Anna said, and Thomas could've imagined it, but the edge in her voice only made him shrivel up further. Then she laughed. "I'm just kidding. I don't know who really did it."

But even as she laughed the accusation away, it still hung heavy in the air. Not the declaration that Thomas was the werewolf, but the proclamation of his guilt. Like no matter how hard he'd tried to play things off as normal, she could see right through him, prying back his layers to reveal every sin underneath.

Did she know about his drunken kiss with Brian? Or was Thomas just overthinking everything again, centering himself in a scandal that no one else even knew or cared about?

"No, you're right," Terry said, scratching his chin. It almost felt like further indictment against Thomas, until he added, "That would make perfect sense," and Thomas remembered they were all still talking about the game.

"I mean, it doesn't take a rocket scientist to figure out Pearl and I aren't on great terms right now," Brian said, stepping in to Thomas's defense. "It's not like you'd have to know us especially well to read into that."

"Oh, really?" Anna asked. "What happened?"

Brian just waved her off. "We can talk later."

Thomas sighed, shaking his head. "Brian, you don't have to sacrifice yourself for me."

Brian turned to him with a softness in his eyes that made Thomas's heart ache. "I'm not just gonna let you take the fall for something you didn't do."

And there was a soft fluttering in Thomas's chest as a smile tugged at his lips. "Really?"

"Sounds to me like Brian's just being a manipulator and trying to look like the hero," Pearl said. "Are we really gonna let someone like that corrupt the whole town?"

"I don't know, Pearl," Shanae said. "It sounds like Brian might actually be innocent."

Vero nodded. "Sounds like maybe Brian's the one getting played."

Thomas's heart sank.

"It's just a game, y'all!" Dustin said.

Thomas winced. Right. It was just a game. Even if everyone seemed about ready to go grab actual pitchforks, none of it really mattered.

Even what Brian had said.

Finally, Dustin heaved a sigh. "Okay, let's just take a vote. Brian or Mia?"

Three votes Mia, two votes Brian, with Brian and Thomas abstaining.

Thomas flipped over his card to show the little villager face, and Pearl screamed, pounding her fist down on the coffee table. "See, I told you it was that lying scumbag! This is what you get for not listening to me!"

"Jeez, Pearl, calm down," Dustin said, but Pearl just shot him a glare sharp enough to cut glass.

"Well, since I'm out, I'm just gonna go to the bathroom," Thomas said, getting up and dismissing himself from the circle without bothering to ask which way it was. He'd rather waste ten minutes looking for it than spend another ten minutes caught in everyone's bickering.

The shouts started up again before he even had the bathroom door closed behind him, but once he was alone, the knot in his stomach eased a bit.

He pulled out his phone, checking for any missed notifications but finding none. Part of him had hoped there'd be some sort of dire emergency to summon him away, but considering neither Kris nor Theo wanted anything to do with him, he probably should've realized that wouldn't happen.

He already regretted not just staying home tonight. Even without the loaded game of Werewolf starting to feel like a real life witch hunt, he should've known better than to waste an evening in Brian's living room with people around.

With *Anna* around.

But maybe Anna wasn't really the problem. Sure, he was struggling with the "happy for them" feeling he should probably feel watching his friend get fawned over by a girl who obviously had it bad for him. And then there was the pointed comment, the side glances, like maybe Anna already had it out for him despite them only having known each other a few minutes.

But all of that paled in comparison to the awkwardness Thomas had bred himself. Between the drunken kiss and then their conversation the other day when he'd implied Brian was just settling with Anna, of course Brian would feel uncomfortable around him. He'd all but told Brian to dump his girlfriend—a girlfriend he obviously loved a lot—and for what? To chase after Thomas even after he'd said that he wanted to keep things platonic? And even after Brian had made it clear that he was only into women?

Thomas sighed, stepping over to the counter. Maybe he should just make up an excuse to head home before things got worse. He could pretend Kris got into a car accident or something and rush off to go be the hero instead of sitting around here feeling humiliated.

He turned the faucet on, splashing some cool water onto his face before toweling off with the hand towel.

Was he being too dramatic? After all, it seemed like Brian's biggest adversary tonight was Pearl, so maybe he'd completely gotten over everything Thomas had said the other day. And maybe Anna's hostility was all in his head, too. Maybe he was just doing what Kris said and twisting everything to make it all about him.

Or maybe this was his remaining self-preservation kicking in before things could implode in his face.

Thomas sucked down a deep breath, trying to work out a compromise.

He could just stick around until the end of this round and try to be civil. Then, he could fake an emergency or something if things didn't get better, but, hopefully having spent more than twenty minutes at the party before running off would keep him from offending Brian further.

Thomas slipped his phone back into his pocket before meandering out into the living room. Baby steps. Since he'd been killed off in the game, he should be able to navigate the next round without drawing too much attention, so as long as he could keep his cool—

Then he froze as his eyes landed on Brian and Anna sitting on the couch, Anna half in his lap and her head against his shoulder.

And suddenly, he felt sick all over again.

"Maybe we should just restart so Anna can play," Brian said.

Pearl rolled her eyes. "You would say that now that you're on the top of everyone's hit list."

Brian groaned. "God, Pearl, it's a *game*. I'm just trying to be inclusive of our guests."

"Sounds good to me," Terry said.

"Okay, good, then I don't want to be the moderator anymore," Dustin said.

Pearl narrowed her eyes at him. "Coward."

"More like trying to save our six-year relationship, but okay."

"I can moderate," Brian said.

"Oh, so we're letting the *werewolf* moderate?" Pearl snapped.

"Okay, first of all, I wasn't the werewolf."

"A likely story!"

Shanae raised her hand. "I was the werewolf. I just killed Pearl 'cause I figured y'all would blame Brian."

Pearl turned to her like she was seeing her for the first time. "Shanae?!"

Thomas sucked in another breath as he tried to force his legs to carry him back to the couch, but there was no way he was getting through another round of this. Just the sight of Anna wrapped up in Brian was making his head spin, and mustering up enough of a voice to speak was becoming a nearly insurmountable task as his heart thudded painfully in his chest.

"Um, I'm gonna go," he said, his voice far lower than he'd intended it to be, but all eyes immediately shot to him, so he could only assume that meant he'd gotten the point across.

"Wait, you're leaving already?" Brian said, half tossing Anna out of his lap as he stood up and raced over to Thomas. The unceremonious gesture left Anna watching them with narrowed eyes, which made Thomas take an involuntary step back.

"Um, yeah, sorry," Thomas said. "Kris needs me so—"

"Aw, Anna, this is all your fault for framing her," Pearl said.

And whatever negative energy had charged the air around Anna when Brian stood up had festered into a full storm cloud, her whole body rigid as she said, "*Excuse me?* I didn't frame her. It was just a joke!"

"It's really not that serious," Dustin said, but his voice carried the defeated tone of someone who knew no one was listening.

"Yeah, I'm just gonna go—"

"Wait," Brian said, reaching out to grab Thomas's wrist. "Do you really have to go? Can't you stay a little longer?"

Anna rolled her eyes, jumping to her feet. "No, no, let her go."

"Anna—" Brian started, but Anna clearly wasn't having it.

"What? If she can't handle a little game, let her go. Why are you acting like the world is gonna end if she leaves?"

"I'm not acting like the world is gonna end. I just feel bad since she came all the way out here and—"

"It's okay. Really," Thomas said, his voice barely above a whisper. "It's fine."

"See, it's fine," Anna said, but Thomas couldn't even bring himself to look at her face and see what kind of vitriol was written there. "Now get over it and let her go."

Brian's eyes widened. "What the hell does that mean?"

"What do you *think* it means?" Anna snapped.

"Okay, bye!"

Thomas turned, rushing out of the apartment before Brian could try to draw him back again. His face burned, but it was his chest that ached, like the pounding of his heart had caved in his chest cavity enough that he could barely suck in a breath as he stumbled down the hallway.

"Mia!"

Thomas froze, the sound of Brian's voice at his back stopping him in his tracks, even as he desperately wished that it wouldn't. Despite his better judgment, he turned back, half expecting to explode into a pillar of salt right there in the hallway.

Brian jogged up to him, a devastating look on his face. "Are you okay?" he asked. "I'm so sorry about that. I don't even know what happened back there."

"I do," Thomas said, trying to keep his voice from cracking as he spoke. "Obviously, your girlfriend is jealous."

"I—yeah, I guess so," Brian admitted. "I'm sorry. I told her we were friends, but I guess—I don't know. I'm really sorry she snapped at you like that."

Thomas shook his head. "It's my fault. I'm the one who overstayed my welcome."

"I invited you to come tonight—"

"Not the party. Everything," Thomas said, the reality of the words settling in heavily around them. "The second you got back with Anna, I should've left you alone, but here I am making everything worse, and obviously that's starting to affect your relationship, and that's my fault."

Brian shook his head. "It's not your fault that she got so jealous over nothing."

And there it was. The confirmation.

Jealous over nothing.

Thomas really wished he'd just stayed home or at least that he'd refused to stop when Brian had called out to him. But maybe this was exactly what Thomas needed—to turn back and find the person he'd thought was following him wasn't what he'd expected at all. Maybe this was the sort of finality their story needed for him to finally accept what he'd lost and move on.

It was time he stopped dragging this out and finally let him go.

Thomas sighed, forcing back his own tears as he said, "This is my fault. I fucked everything up, and I'm sorry."

"You didn't. If this is about the other day—"

"It's about every day!" Thomas snapped, his eyes stinging. "Every day that we keep pretending we can be friends when we can't because you have a girlfriend, and I promised no strings, but I failed, okay? I can't just keep standing here pretending I don't have feelings for you when I'm drowning in them, and obviously Anna sees that, too, so I'm just…I'm just ruining everything."

"Mia—" Brian started, but he didn't continue, like his voice had been stolen from him mid-sentence. He just stood there, mouth agape, but maybe it was better that way.

If Thomas gave him a chance to explain things away, he might actually start to believe him. He might actually start to believe that they could really be friends and that this whole relationship wasn't slowly killing him, and then he'd be right back where he started.

No, the only thing Thomas could do now was leave, and he needed to do it before Brian could try to change his mind.

"I'm sorry," Thomas said, "but we have to stop seeing each other. We can't be friends." Then he turned on his heel, taking off down the hallway.

And even as Brian shouted out for him again, this time, he kept his face forward, refusing to look back.

25

Brian felt numb as he stepped back into the apartment. Everyone seemed to be fighting about something, but while he couldn't process if it was the game or something else, he wasn't sure he cared to.

We have to stop seeing each other. We can't be friends.

"Brian?"

Brian looked up to find Anna standing just a few feet in front of him. The rest of the party didn't even seem to notice that they weren't there, which only added to the feeling of detachment overtaking him. Did anything at this party even matter anymore?

Anna took his hand, leading him back out into the hallway, and Brian tried to focus on the warmth of her grip. *She* should matter. He knew that without question. But for some reason, at that moment, he barely felt anything toward her at all.

The hallway was empty, and Brian felt a bubble of hope pop seeing that Mia really was gone, not just waiting for him to come back out so they could talk.

"I'm sorry," Anna said, her voice low. "I mean, about causing a scene and everything. I went way too far, and it was completely uncalled for, and I'm sorry."

Brian shook his head, but he didn't know what to say. He

could tell her it wasn't her fault, that he understood why she'd gotten so defensive, but would that just make things worse? Confirm her fears that Brian really had been pulling away from her and just make her more upset at Mia?

But as much as Brian wanted to be open and honest with Anna to help assuage her fears, he wasn't entirely sure what the truth *was* anymore. He'd thought he'd done an okay job of pushing down any feelings he'd once had for Mia, but now it looked like everyone else had seen the truth except for him.

And then there was what she'd said before she left.

I promised no strings, but I failed, okay? I can't just keep standing here pretending I don't have feelings for you when I'm drowning in them.

All this time, Brian had convinced himself that any feelings he had were one-sided, that Mia had been the one who'd decided to keep things platonic, so there was no way she could feel anything other than friendly toward him. That was the single thing that had made everything in his line of sight clear as day.

So how was he supposed to ignore her saying something like that to him now?

"Brian?" Anna asked.

He looked up at her, quickly shaking his head. "I—don't be sorry."

"Jealousy isn't cute," Anna said. "I shouldn't have taken it out on you. Or Mia. I just got a little insecure after everything."

But Brian couldn't blame her for that now that the rose tint had shattered, and he was staring the past few weeks in the face. They'd only just gotten back together, and yet, here he was, inviting Mia everywhere and ignoring Anna's texts to hang out with Mia and her friends. And then there was the fact that even when he was trying to make a special dinner for Anna's parents, he'd invited Mia over to help.

None of it was supposed to mean anything. He'd just been hanging out with a friend.

But Mia had feelings for him, and as far as his own feelings for Mia went—well, he'd been all but running from that since his sexy Totoro dreams, and now it was exactly like Pearl had said.

If you keep stringing her along by a thread, eventually that thread's gonna break, and not only are you gonna hurt her, but you're both gonna end up alone.

Finally, Brian sighed. "Anna, what we have—I'm really happy with you. I'm sorry I haven't been making you feel like my dream girl because you deserve a lot better than that, and I really do want things to work out for us."

She flashed him a sad smile. "It's okay. I think we've both been a little off recently, but we can work things out, right?"

He nodded. They'd figure out a way to make things work.

He'd figure out a way to make things work.

Because no matter what Mia felt for him, it didn't change the fact that any future with her was nebulous at best, but Anna? He couldn't just throw away the life they could build together.

Brian took Anna's hand, and she laced her fingers through his as they headed back into the party to find Pearl chugging the vodka straight from the bottle.

"Um, everything okay?" Brian asked.

Dustin just sighed, draped over the chair back. "Maybe we should just play a different game. Like Tic Tac Toe or something."

Shanae rolled her eyes. "Please, you think Pearl can't get competitive over Tic Tac Toe?"

Dustin sighed again. "I'll grab more drinks."

Anna led Brian back over to the couch, cuddling up against his side as they got settled in.

He couldn't help looking over at Pearl, who sat half-draped over the coffee table now. She was definitely too wasted to have a real discussion, but he made a mental note to apologize to her later, considering she'd pretty much been right about everything.

But right now, he didn't want to waste any more energy thinking about Pearl or how wrong he'd been. Right now was just about him and Anna. The official start of the rest of their lives together.

Sunday morning, Brian woke up to a text from Anna reminding him about dinner with her parents the next day. He texted back a quick, *Can't wait!*, before rolling over in bed and considering staying there for good.

He hadn't gotten nearly drunk enough to forget the night before, but he had to wonder if maybe he should have. Not because of Anna, but just because of things with Mia. He still couldn't erase the look on her face when she'd confessed her feelings to him before taking off down the hall.

And then there were all the things he hadn't been able to say. To tell her that he knew exactly what she meant. That he'd felt those same things. To tell her that he'd rather have her in his life as a friend than not at all, that he could barely remember who he'd been before he met her, and he wasn't ready to have to figure that all out again.

But none of those things would've been fair to her or to Anna—not when Brian already had his future mapped out, and he didn't know how to fit them both into it.

Finally convincing himself to get out of bed, he threw some clothes on and stumbled out into the living room in search of Pearl. He figured she should be up by now, even with the massive hangover she was bound to be sporting after last night, and he should probably get that apology over and done with before he lost his nerve.

But when he reached the kitchen, instead of Pearl, he found Dustin, looking vaguely miserable as he stared blankly at a mug of black coffee.

"Um, morning?" Brian said.

Dustin looked up, startled, before flashing him a small smile. "Oh, hey. I figured you weren't home when you stayed in your room all morning."

Brian glanced over at the clock on the microwave to find that it was just after noon, which was a bit later than he'd expected. Even so, it was weird not seeing Pearl in the kitchen like she was just about every morning.

"Did Pearl go out?" Brian asked, starting to make his own coffee.

"She's probably at a hotel. I don't know. I haven't spoken to her since last night."

Brian froze, gears shifting into place in his mind as he struggled to make sense of what Dustin was saying. "*What?* What happened?"

Dustin stepped around the counter, taking a seat at the island. "So, you saw how competitive and stuff she was getting last night, right? Which is kind of typical Pearl, I guess, but then after you and Anna left, she went off on Shanae. She's just been really unreasonable lately. Like the other day, we went out with Shanae and Terry, and she just kept trying to outdo them. Terry's going to school for Dentistry, and Shanae's a legal aid, so I guess she felt threatened that they have more prestigious careers than we do, because she dropped how much I made at my last art show like four times in one night. It was humiliating."

"Wait, I thought you said she was trying to brag," Brian said. "Why was it humiliating?"

"Because they're our friends, and I don't want to compete with them!" Dustin said. "I mean, God, do you know how awkward it is to hear, 'Do you guys want to split an appetizer? Actually, don't worry about it! Dustin made thirty grand at his last art show!' Like what am I supposed to do with that?"

"Bro, you made *thirty grand* at your last art show? That's fucking amazing!"

Dustin winced. "I maintain that it was a fluke. Don't tell anyone."

"Oh, yeah, no worries."

"Anyway, last night after everybody left, I told her that I can't stand to be around her when she's like that and that I was at my limit. Then I offered to go stay at a hotel for a while, but she volunteered to go instead, since it was her fault."

"I-I can't believe it," Brian said.

"Why? She was being insufferable."

"No, I just meant, I didn't think you were physically capable of getting into a fight with anyone."

Dustin winced. "I mean, it's not really fight. It's just a…" He trailed off.

Brian sighed. "You two literally separated. That's kind of a fight."

Dustin rolled his eyes. "Okay, you know what, maybe it is. But it's also not the first time we've fought, and it won't be the last. She has a tendency to just go way too far sometimes."

"That's kind of disappointing," Brian said, and Dustin just raised an eyebrow. "Well, you and Pearl always seem so white-picket-fence perfect. It kinda sucks, pulling back the curtain and finding out she manages to fight with even you. It's like learning Santa Claus isn't real."

Dustin laughed. "Sorry to kill the magic. To be honest, I don't know if I believe in the whole white picket fence thing. I grew up in a house like that, and I'm kind of proud to say that my relationship looks nothing like that."

Brian smirked. "Even if you're separated?"

"We're not—" Dustin sagged. "Okay, you know what? I'll say this—Pearl and I, we're very different people, and our relationship isn't perfect. It's taken a lot of work to keep us together this long. Especially because her parents hate me."

"Woah, woah, woah," Brian said. "How can they hate you? You're literally the chillest person I know."

Dustin nodded. "And Pearl's parents are the micro-managing, abusive type. They had her on track to be their perfect little lawyer daughter until we started going out, and I told her that if she hated law so much, she should just give up on school, and I'd support her by selling furry porn. Hence, they hate me. And she hasn't spoken to them in years."

"Okay, but did you actually sell the furry porn?"

"How do you think we paid for this apartment? Anyway, the point is, I know why Pearl is the way she is. She's still learning how to shake off her parents' expectations and that deeply ingrained need to be the best at everything, and I think a part of her wishes she could rub it in her parents' faces that the artist they didn't want her to date is now earning as much as her tax accountant dad. But I already told her that it was a fluke, and I don't want to be dragged into it. So, sometimes it really frustrates me when she goes around picking fights with people, but—" Dustin shrugged. "—I love her, so it's just all kind of a package deal, I guess."

"It's nice how you can feel so confident that you'll just work things out," Brian said morosely. "I wish I had something like that."

"With Anna?"

Brian paused because, as much as he wanted to say yes, there was a part of him that just didn't feel ready to answer at all. Then he said, "You know, I think this is the longest conversation we've had since I moved in."

"Ah, yes. Sometimes I forget how quiet the room can be when Pearl isn't around."

"You miss her, don't you?"

"Absolutely," Dustin said. "But don't tell her I said that. I need some sort of power in this relationship."

Brian just laughed.

With no other plans for his Sunday, Brian decided he needed a distraction, so despite the inevitable dragging it would garner him, he decided to call Noah.

"Sup, bro!" Noah said. "Living your best life?"

"I mean, I just woke up, so—"

"*What?*" Noah said.

Brian sighed. Let the dragging ensue.

"Dude, it's literally the afternoon. What, d'you catch Covid or something?"

Brian just rolled his eyes. "Since when do you even wake up before lunchtime, anyway?"

He could practically hear the scowl in Noah's voice as he

said, "Since I got stuck with a nine a.m. class, and I promised Devin I'd stop skipping."

"Ah, that makes more sense."

"Whatever. What do you want? I find it hard to believe that you just woke up, this fine Sunday, desperately wanting to hear my voice."

It'd only been two years since Noah had told the family he was trans, but in that time, he'd changed his name, his style, started T, and become almost an entirely new person. Well, except his bad attitude, which he'd always had. But Brian couldn't help but acknowledge how much deeper his voice was compared to a couple of years before, like he'd aged a decade in just twenty-four months.

And it was funny that, when Noah had first come to stay with him for a summer in Denver, Brian had had to explain to him that even though he'd changed by going to college, he was still the same person, because now the whole thing was happening in reverse. With Noah living in California, they didn't see each other nearly as much as they had before Brian had gone off to college, and suddenly, it was like every time he saw his little brother again, he'd leveled up to a new stage that was hardly recognizable compared to the last.

It didn't make him feel uncomfortable, exactly, but it did fill him with a certain kind of longing. A sense of nostalgia for his childhood, back when his family was so much closer physically and emotionally, and the thought of starting his own family was just a distant dream he didn't need to worry about yet. It made him think about Mia, and all the fears she carried about letting her parents down. He'd never had to live with that sort of uncertainty, but ever since Maggie had gone off on a whole transphobic spiel about Noah, dating had felt so fraught. He wouldn't just surrender his first family to try to build a new one, but since his parents sold the house and moved across the country, he didn't really have a home to go back to. So if he couldn't forge a new one here, what did he even have left to hold onto?

"*Brain*," Noah said, his shitty childhood nickname shocking him out of his thoughts, "you good? If you're dying—well, I don't have your roommate's number, but I can Google every Pearl in New York and see if one picks up and actually knows you."

Brian laughed. "I'm fine. I was just...thinking, I guess."

"Oh ho ho!" The conniving eagerness in Noah's voice made Brian facepalm. He was like a harpy, digging his claws into the nearest drama and refusing to let go. "Well, don't hold back on me now, brother! What happened?"

Brian rolled his eyes. "It's just girlfriend stuff. You wouldn't understand."

"What? Because my partner's nonbinary? Gender's a construct! Tell me what happened!"

"No, because..." Brian sighed, carefully choosing his words. "How'd you see through Maggie?"

"I—*what*? What does that have to do with—ew, you're not back together with her, are you?"

"What?" Brian reared back in his seat, shocked. "*No.* I haven't spoken to her in years."

Noah breathed a sigh of relief, then said, "Okay, well, next time lead with that. Also, I don't know. She just had bad vibes."

"That's the least helpful thing you've ever said, which says a lot because—"

"Yeah, yeah, I know," Noah said. "But look, if this is about Anna, her vibes are fine. I mean, I wouldn't have suggested a white girl, but she passes the vibe check. She's still white, though, so make sure you season your food before she poisons you."

Brian rolled his eyes. It should've felt reassuring that Noah didn't think Anna was anything like Maggie, but it just left him feeling more confused. She got along fine with his family; she was sweet and pretty, and the sex was good. She basically had no flaws, so why was it so hard to just commit to her like he was supposed to?

"Okay, look," Noah said after a moment, "let me be real

with you. I don't know what's going on, but if you're calling me on a Sunday to vibe check your girlfriend, I have to assume either things aren't great, or you're just not that into her."

"It's not—"

"Bro, *please*, you've been with her for what? A year? That's literally the easy part. If she's not your everything right now, she won't be your anything when all the butterflies and sparkles and novelty go away. Like, I'm not gonna sit here and pretend I know shit about forever, because obviously, I don't, but I can promise you, I would not be calling up my brother to ask if I should still be with Devin. I just *know*."

Brian winced. "That's not—that's kind of presumptuous of you, don't you think? I wasn't calling to ask if we should break up. I was just...I don't know. Thinking about the future, I guess."

"Okay, well, try thinking about this—if you married her and started a family and ten years down the line, you met a hotter girl at a bar, then what? Because if that would just change everything, what do you think that'd do to her? To both of you? I just don't get why you're even considering a future with a girl you obviously feel lukewarm about."

"I don't feel lukewarm about her, okay!" Brian snapped. "I love her! I don't need relationship advice from my little brother."

"Yeah, okay," Noah said, but Brian could hear the smirk in his voice. "Just do both of you a favor, and before you go laying down roots or anything, make sure you're not just settling. I know how you work. You'll go along with anything if you think it makes other people happy. I mean, I still literally never paid you back for that time I borrowed your credit card. But you're talking about a life partner here. You owe yourself better than just settling for the easiest one."

Brian winced. The words had been a lot easier to reject coming from Mia than they were coming from Noah. And not just because they insisted on holding a mirror up to his past and exposing all the corners he'd done his best to ignore.

Noah really *had* matured a lot in the past two years, and while Brian could attribute a sizeable chunk of it to transitioning, he also knew a good part of it came from Devin.

And it wasn't because of how much chemistry they had or how well their families melded or how perfectly their future plans lined up, but simply because Devin was the type of person who never let Noah go unchecked. E always pointed out when his jokes went too far or when he'd ignored someone else's needs or when he just really needed to stop forcing his opinions on people. They complimented each other—Devin keeping Noah from getting lost in the clouds, and Noah pulling Devin out of eir shell, making em more confident and ambitious.

It kind of reminded him of Dustin and Pearl. And actually, the dynamic between his own parents, the more he thought on it.

So maybe that's what he should've been focused on from the beginning.

Maybe he just needed to focus on finding the perfect foil, and then he could let all the other stuff fall into place on its own.

26

Thomas truly believed that the right look could elevate a person from a mere peasant to royalty status, or take them from near desolation to at least some level of confidence.

But after the weekend she'd had, makeup wasn't doing shit.

It didn't help that while she'd thought she'd poured out all the tears she could manage during her constant cycle of on-again, off-again crying sessions, she'd apparently had enough to start bawling on the train to work when she caught sight of a couple meeting up on the platform. She'd had just enough time after arriving at the office to rush to the bathroom and clean up the messy black streaks down her cheeks, but as she stepped out of the bathroom, she couldn't find any work energy left in her.

It was a shame that Day had just told her they might actually have the funds to keep her on when she was about to get fired for failing to do her job.

But as she stepped down the hallway, the sound of shouting stopped her dead in her tracks. She didn't even recognize the voice doing the screaming, but the animalistic rage in their tone was enough to make her shrivel up as she stood frozen in the hallway.

The door to Day's office flew open, slamming into the wall with a loud clang. Felix stormed out, a look of disgust on his face. He shot a glare back toward the office door, but a second later, Day appeared in the doorway, and Felix quickly turned, taking off running toward the exit.

"GET FUCKED, FELIX!" Day shouted before catching sight of Thomas, the unchecked fury on their face melting away to their usual, timid demeanor. "Oh, hello."

Thomas stood frozen, mouth open, as she tried to process the situation. "Um, hi. What happened?"

Day winced. "Oh, well, um, Felix won't be working here anymore."

"That much I could figure out."

Day flashed her a smile and waved her into the office

Shaking off the initial shock, Thomas stepped into Day's office, taking a quick look around. Everything looked normal—no smashed office supplies or holes in the wall—but she still felt a little off after Day's outburst. Actually, not only had she never heard Day scream before, she wasn't sure she'd even ever seen them *angry* before. But the vitriol they'd launched at Felix didn't seem to be pulling any punches.

"Um, so what—"

"Sit," Day said before going behind the desk and opening a mini fridge. They pulled out a bottle of rosé and set it on the desk. "Bubbly?"

"At work?"

Day just rolled their eyes. "I can see the mascara stains, Thomas. I think we've earned this."

Thomas wasn't sure how to refute a claim like that, nor was she sure she wanted to, so she just shrugged, waiting for Day to fill a glass with wine before passing it over to her.

"So, *Felix*," Day said before taking a sip of wine. "I guess this one's kind of been a long time coming. I just didn't realize how bad things had gotten. I mean, I *knew* he was jealous, right? Like, that much was obvious. But to go so far—"

Thomas awkwardly raised her hand. "I still have no idea what happened."

"Oh, right," Day said with a half-hearted laugh. "I guess

Felix has been poisoning the well."

"Meaning?"

"Meaning, he sabotaged our app launch. That's why we were struggling to hold onto users. He was apparently sending mass spam to people that Kris recruited, hoping to frame him for it and get him dropped. I only found out because it accidentally got sent to one of the other temps who reported him."

"Woah," Thomas said. "Why would he do that?"

"I told you, he's a jealous bitch."

"Jealous of Kris?"

"Oh, you don't know," Day said, like it was the most obvious thing in the world, but Thomas was pretty sure that she, in fact, didn't know. "So, Felix and I dated in college. It wasn't a long thing, but I broke up with him, and he never entirely got over it. But we were still friends, so I didn't think it would be a big deal working together, you know? I don't get people who make drama. It's so exhausting."

"Okay, but I still don't get why that would make him jealous of Kris."

Day stared back at Thomas blankly for a moment. "Kris didn't tell you?"

"I think it's safe to assume that I just don't know anything."

Day sighed, leaning back in their seat and reaching for their phone. They scrolled along the screen for a moment before passing it over to Thomas, who looked down at the screen but couldn't process what she was seeing.

It was a picture of two kids dressed like Tiana and Lottie from *The Princess and the Frog*, the two of them probably only about six or seven, with their arms wrapped around each other.

Then Thomas looked up slowly, eyes shooting wide. "Wait, is this—"

"Kris and me? Yeah," Day said, a small smile tugging at their lips. "I never show people pictures of me pre-transition, but I can't bring myself to delete that one. Look how cute we are! Anyway, Kris and I go way back. Our town used to speculate that we were gonna get married one day. The not-racist folk, anyway. At least until I came out as trans."

Day held their hand out for their phone, and Thomas passed it back to them, the image of Day and Kris still vivid in her mind. It really was a cute picture, but the thing that had it seared in Thomas's brain was the sudden realization that he actually hadn't had any idea what Kris's childhood was like until that moment. He'd mentioned having two moms and growing up in Tennessee, but that was about it. He certainly hadn't mentioned Day before.

"But yeah," Day continued, "when Felix found out, he got super jealous about it. He started saying all this shit about how I shouldn't be hanging out with a white guy and how Kris was toxic, and I just thought he was being insecure because Felix has always been a little ashamed of being mixed, you know? But I think I really started to *see* it the other day. He just kept saying all this shit about how Kris is totally crazy, and we shouldn't trust a bitch like that to work in the company, and it just ticked me off, you know? I mean, Kris is psychotic, but he's a good guy. And he's brilliant when you give him the room to be." Day's tone shifted slightly on that last line, making way for something like pride. Then they scowled. "*Felix*, on the other hand, is a desperate, pathetic, good for nothing, mediocre, self-loathing—"

Thomas grimaced, and Day frowned.

"You okay?" Day asked. "Don't worry, I would never say anything like that about you. I guess I'm just kind of protective of Kris. He's been through a lot."

"And apparently I'm part of that," Thomas said.

Day raised an eyebrow.

But Thomas wasn't even sure where to begin explaining what happened. She definitely didn't want to get fired when she admitted to Day that she'd been just as shitty to their childhood friend as Felix had.

I don't even know what you're accusing me of, but it sounds to me like you need to up your meds because you're downright delusional. It'd been such a shitty thing to say, even before what Day had told her about Felix. Hell, if Kris had thought Thomas was shit-talking him with Felix, it was probably because Felix had planted the idea, and Thomas had probably just made it worse by getting so defensive. But that was always the problem, wasn't it? Whether it was Kris or Brian or Theo—she just couldn't stop hurting people she cared about in some useless attempt to protect herself.

Finally, Thomas sighed and said, "I fucked up, and I think Kris hates me now."

Day stared back at Thomas for a moment before laughing. "I'm sure you're fine. Kris doesn't really hate anyone. He just pretends he does because he sucks at being vulnerable."

And, now, Thomas felt worse.

"Look, I know he's giving you the runaround right now," Day said, "but it'll blow over, so just apologize when it does. He's a very forgiving person, even if he tries to pretend he isn't."

Thomas sniffled, reaching up to wipe the tears building in her eyes. She'd thought she'd finally run dry, but before she could stop herself, the tears overflowed again along with words she knew she probably shouldn't be confessing in Day's office. "I got kicked out of the drag community back in Vermont because I dated one queen's sister, and after I broke up with her, she spread all these rumors about me, and no one wanted anything to do with me after that. Kris was the only person who still talked to me, and I was so worried that he was gonna drop me, too, so I treated him like shit, and I called him delusional, and he probably hates me, and I deserve it."

She couldn't even bring herself to look up at Day as tears poured down her face with reckless abandon. Finally, Day held a tissue box out to her, and Thomas paused, slowly taking a tissue to wipe some of the smeared makeup off her face.

"Thomas," Day said with a voice so gentle, it made Thomas's heart hurt, "Kris cares about you a lot, okay? You don't have to ask how I know. I know that bitch, and I'm telling you. Just talk to him, okay?"

Thomas nodded, blotting her eyes again. She lacked Day's confidence, but their words were helping her feel better. "Thank you."

"Of course," Day said. "And hear me when I say this—if there's one thing I know about Kris, it's that he knows what it feels like to be unfairly judged. He would never just cut you off without giving you a chance to explain yourself, okay? Just give him some time."

Thomas nodded, some of the weight lifting from her chest. Then another thought bubbled up in her mind. "Um, so, the other day you said signups were way up, right?"

"Right?"

"I had a friend who works at an LGBTQ org spread the word at work, but now they're supposed to be putting on this big masquerade, but they need a sponsor to fund it, so I was wondering if we might be able to…lend a hand? You know, return the favor for all the help."

"You want to do some sort of partnership with them?"

It was probably a ridiculous request to make, given she'd already told Brian that they shouldn't even be friends anymore, but after everything she'd done to ruin his relationship with Anna, she at least wanted to give him something in return.

Day thought it over for a moment before saying, "I'd have to get approval from my stepfather, but it might work. It'd certainly be a good way to get the app around to more queer people, so if I posit it as a marketing opportunity, I could see that working out."

"Thank you," Thomas said again, a small smile spreading across her face. "Really, for everything. Hiring me, and your advice about Kris, and—"

"But, of course," Day said. "After all, we queers gotta stick together. But also, Thomas?"

"Yeah?"

"Be careful with Kris. If you do any damage to him, I'll make you regret it."

Day flashed Thomas a smile, and Thomas cringed. Contrary to a few hours before, she now felt pretty confident that Day not only meant it but could very much make it happen.

"I'll keep that in mind."

27

In anticipation of Monday's dinner, Brian set out to make the dessert Sunday night so he wouldn't have to try to rush home and cook after work. Trying to put all the pieces together without Mia there felt like trying to throw together an alternative for baking powder, but he shoved the bad memory and his discomfort aside. Having the full expanse of the kitchen to himself gave him some time to think, and after his call with Noah, he was grateful to have it.

Monday, Brian reported to work as usual before heading back to his apartment just long enough to change into something he hoped wouldn't scare Anna's parents off and grab the food he'd made the night before.

The trip to her parents' place was only three stops, but he spent all of it deep in thought and mired in worries. While his initial perception of New York had been fully filtered through his experiences with Anna, his vision was now colored by Mia, and while the whole plan had been to help him redefine the city for himself, he now felt all the more broken when he thought about trying to start over if things didn't work out with Anna.

A pit settled in his stomach as the train lurched to a stop at his destination. He took a quick survey of the other passengers getting ready to exit, but he felt painfully separate from all of them. The city was intimidating enough as it was, but he felt entirely hopeless, thinking about navigating it alone.

But no. It wasn't just the city.

If he lost Anna here, he'd be going back to Denver alone, too. He'd be back to starting over, trying to find someone else he could see himself rebuilding with. Could he really afford to do that?

Settling isn't how you make yourself happy. That's how you placate yourself for now and then regret it once it's too late to fix it.

He shook the thought out of his head as he stepped out of the train car. He needed to focus on keeping Anna's parents from turning against him a second time.

Arriving at the loft, he expected Anna to be waiting for him, but instead, he got her mother, hair tied up in a messy bun and lipstick as dark as red wine on her lips.

"Brian," she said with a smile, the same smile Anna had, "we're so glad you're here. Please come in."

He stepped inside as she closed the door behind him, humbly resisting the urge to kick off his shoes before following her toward the dining room.

An ambitious display of food was already laid out on the table, and he had to wonder if maybe the tray in his hands would end up being an insult in comparison. Anna circled the long stretch of mahogany, laying out silverware and cloth napkins. She looked almost radiant in the midnight blue dress that flowed like water down her legs.

She looked up as Brian entered, a huge smile lighting her face up even brighter.

"Hey, babe," she said, coming over to give him a quick kiss. She dropped her voice low to say, "I have more for you, but we can save that for when we're alone."

He smiled. "I appreciate that."

"Brian," her mom said, stepping up next to him, "let me take that to the kitchen."

He looked down at the tray in his hands, the weight of it suddenly heavier than he cared to tote.

"Right, sure," he said as he passed it over to her. "It's mochi and dorayaki."

She blinked back at him blankly.

"Uh, sorry. Japanese pastries. You can store them in the fridge, Mrs. Hastings."

"Oh, please, honey, call me Marge," she said before disappearing into the kitchen with the tray.

Brian turned back to Anna, a wince already forming on his face. "Am I really supposed to call your mom, Marge? It feels disrespectful."

Anna laughed. "Oh, come on, she's trying. This is at least better than before, right?"

"Guess I can't argue with that."

Marge returned from the kitchen, Anna's father just a step behind her. She motioned for everyone to take a seat at the table, so Brian slid into the seat next to Anna, following her lead in taking the cloth napkin and placing it in his lap.

"Brian," Anna's father started, "we really do want to apologize for last time. We know things were a bit uncomfortable, and we want to make it clear that it had nothing to do with our feelings toward you personally. We're glad that Anna's happy with you, and that's all that really matters to us."

With three pairs of eyes staring expectantly back at him, all he could manage to say was, "Thank you, Mr. Hastings."

Marge laughed. "So formal, huh?"

"You can call me Pete," Anna's father said. "Now, let's get to the food, shall we? Marge, do you want to say grace?"

Marge nodded, and she and her husband bowed their heads, clasping their hands together in front of them. Brian glanced at Anna, her head bowed over the table, before following suit.

It'd been years since he'd prayed before meals, something his parents had stopped enforcing a few years before he'd gone off to college. It'd always been more of a reflex than something he'd genuinely believed in, so when his parents dropped the routine, he hadn't missed it. But listening to the soft sound of

Marge's voice as she prayed felt almost nostalgic, like he was back in the home he'd grown up in.

Finally, she ended the prayer, spreading her arms out as she said, "Please, eat. I hope you're hungry because we made a lot."

"Oh, don't worry," Anna said. "Brian, you're gonna love my mom's cooking. She actually trained with a professional chef in Paris a couple decades ago."

"Oh, wow," Brian said. "That's really impressive."

Marge smiled. "Oh, it's alright. Anna, careful what you go around telling people."

Anna raised an eyebrow. "That you trained with a chef?"

"No, that it was a couple of decades ago! You're making me sound old."

"Now, Marge, don't worry about that," Pete said. "Age is just a number. You're still just as beautiful now as you were then."

As he leaned in to kiss his wife, Brian imagined him and Anna in the same position a couple decades into the future, seated around a table with their kids and their kids' significant others, still speaking sweetly to each other even after twenty-some years of marriage. And maybe they wouldn't have all the wealth Anna's parents had, but it'd be a sweet, simple suburban bliss, a picture-perfect nuclear family just like his own parents had.

If you married her and started a family and ten years down the line, you met a hotter girl at a bar, what do you think that'd do to her? To both of you? I just don't get why you're even considering a future with a girl you obviously feel lukewarm about.

Brian turned his face down to the plate in front of him, hoping the motion would be enough to shake Noah's words loose from his head.

"So, what do you do for work, Brian?" Marge asked.

Brian looked up. "Oh, um, I work for a nonprofit. Well, I'm interning right now. I don't know what I'm going to do after graduation, exactly."

"Oh, what kind of nonprofit?" Marge asked.

"Um—"

"It's an LGBTQ organization," Anna said. "You know, working to build community and provide support and stuff."

"Oh, that must be quite the experience," Pete said. "Is it uncomfortable being there?"

Brian raised an eyebrow. "Uncomfortable?"

"Well, I just mean being surrounded by all those people living alternative lifestyles. Do you feel out of place?"

The question wasn't even that odd, but Brian was caught off guard by how difficult it was to answer. Maybe he should say that he did feel out of place, that he never fit in there, and he knew he never could, but none of that felt like an authentic answer, because the truth was that as much as he'd *expected* to feel out of place, he'd only ever felt welcome. Even spending that night with Mia's friends, surrounded by a group of out and proud queer people, they'd made him feel like they were all part of one big happy family.

Even in a way that Anna's family distinctly hadn't.

"Oh my God, Dad," Anna said, "it's not like all the employees are queer. Straight people work there, too."

"Right, right," Pete said, closing the door on his unanswered question. "Of course. So what do you do for them? I imagine working for a nonprofit doesn't pay well."

"I mostly help plan events and stuff," he said.

Marge's eyes shot wide. "You're an event planner? That's an interesting career path."

"He's a marketing major," Anna clarified. "He just went into a PR and marketing internship that focuses largely on events."

"Ah, a marketing major," Pete said. "So you'll be moving on to something more lucrative once you graduate."

"Um, I'm not sure yet, honestly," Brian said. "I mean, I've really enjoyed the internship, and I like the idea of working somewhere that benefits people."

"Oh, there are many benefits to working corporate," Pete said. "If you need some contacts and connections, I can help you out."

"*Dad*," Anna said.

"What?"

"Stop putting so much pressure on him," Anna said, voice taut.

"Right, right, sorry." Pete waved her off. "Anyway, Brian, let me know if you want help. Especially after you graduate, it can be hard to find a good job, but I know people. I'm sure they can help."

"Um, thank you," Brian said.

It wasn't every day that someone you barely knew offered to hook you up with a well-paying job right out of school with no other qualifications or real experience, but he guessed that was what happened when you had a wealthy white girlfriend.

"What do you think of the food, Brian?" Marge asked.

The main dish consisted of some kind of dry, white meat chicken, a side of buttered vegetables, and some rice. A bit lackluster, given she'd apparently flown across the Atlantic to learn how to make it, but it was fine. Nothing inedible.

Brian smiled. "It's great."

But as he looked down at his plate again, Noah's words played over and over again in his head.

Settling.

How would he feel, eating chicken and vegetables every night for the rest of his life? Talking business with Pete and showering Marge with empty compliments because that was the way things were supposed to be?

How long before some random girl at a bar started to look more beautiful than his own wife just because she was something different?

He looked up at Anna, at the way she wore her hair messily around her face. It looked beautiful, if not exactly like her mother's. In thirty years, would they still be in the exact same place, making the same small talk, while she wore her hair the exact same way?

If she's not your everything right now, she won't be your anything when all the butterflies and sparkles and novelty go away.

And maybe that was the whole problem, the thing that Pearl had been trying to get at from the jump.

Because in the time he'd known Mia, his perspectives had changed so much more than they had in the year he'd been with Anna. Mia was an ever-changing art exhibit, but each piece was just as beautiful as the last. And while things between them hadn't been easy—and they'd sure as hell never been simple— he couldn't help but replay the ache in his chest that he'd felt as they retreated down the hallway, the urgency with which he wanted to reach out and pull them back.

To fight for them.

Because no matter how much it hurt, no matter how hard it was, they were someone who made it all feel worthwhile.

And maybe it'd taken Brian too long to realize that. Maybe things between them were long over, and no amount of begging and pleading would be enough to get Mia back. And maybe, even if he did, their time would end too fast, their futures pulling them in opposite directions that would inevitably wrench them apart.

But even if the only thing that could possibly exist for them was a summer fling that was already over, that couldn't justify what he was doing to Anna.

"Brian?" Anna said, placing a hand on his arm. "Are you okay?"

He shook his head, quickly standing up from the table. "I'm sorry. I can't do this."

Her eyes shot wide, and he couldn't even bring himself to glance at her parents as he turned and headed for the door.

"Brian!" Anna called out as she followed behind him.

And, God, he wished he could just turn around and go right back to dinner with her, but that wouldn't be fair to her. Not that any of this was. But at the very least, he owed her an explanation.

He turned back before he could reach the door to find her just a few steps behind him, tears in her eyes.

"I'm sorry, Anna," he said. "I really am. I just—I don't think this is gonna work out."

"Why?" she asked, her voice cracking. "What did I do? I can fix it. I can do better."

He just shook his head, resisting the urge to reach out to her. "Anna, you're great. You really are. But I—you deserve somebody who can make you their world. And that just isn't me."

She stared back at him, mouth opening and closing like she had something she needed to say, something that would change everything. But then she just closed it one more time, brushing the tears away from her face. "It's Mia, isn't it? You're in love with her."

But Brian just shook his head again. Regardless of how he felt about Mia, it didn't change the fact that he didn't love Anna as much as he wanted to. He was settling for her, and that wasn't fair to either of them.

"I don't know how I feel about Mia, but this isn't about her," he said. "It's about us. I just think we deserve more than what we have here."

Anna laughed humorlessly. "Yeah, okay. Honestly, Brian, you can lie to me if it makes you feel better, but at least don't lie to yourself."

"I'm not—"

She waved him off. "I believe you're doing this because you think it's best. I even believe you're breaking up with me only because of me. But we both know how you feel about Mia. Lying to yourself isn't going to help anyone, and it's definitely not going to help you move on."

He didn't even know what to say to that, but before he could even try, Anna stepped past him, opening the door and motioning for him to leave. "I hope you don't mind if we keep the dessert."

And Brian spared her a sad smile. "Of course not. I hope you like it."

28

After leaving Day's office, Thomas had stopped by Kris's to find that he hadn't come into work today. She'd then proceeded to try his phone every other hour for the rest of the day, but even as she stepped back into her apartment and kicked off her shoes for the evening, all she could get was a full voicemail.

Day had seemed pretty confident that they could patch things up, but Thomas's confidence waned further with every call that went unconnected. And while Thomas knew there were easily a few different reasons he might not be answering that really had nothing to do with her, old habits died hard, and her fear of abandonment died harder.

With the rosé from earlier long since worn off, she opted to retreat into a bottle of vodka, working her way through most of it over the next hour and a half. She stared down at the dwindling liquid, but she didn't have nearly enough energy or balance to go buy more, so she opted to just lean back against the couch, staring up at the ceiling and regretting her life choices.

At least until a knock on the door startled her out of her drunken stupor.

"Kinda busy!" she shouted. "Come back later."

Then, the pounding just echoed louder, the resounding

booms vibrating the wall, and Thomas's skull by extension. She sighed, throwing herself off the couch and grumbling as she staggered into an upright position. She couldn't imagine anyone but a landlord or a police officer would ever knock so aggressively, but she was too drunk to feel the usual terror at that thought.

Once she'd dragged herself over to the door, she pulled it open and froze.

"*Theo?*" she said. "What are you doing here?"

Theo half-shoved her inside as he pushed into the apartment, a glare knitted between his eyebrows. "Do you just not answer your phone anymore?"

Thomas stared back at him for a moment before tossing the door closed. "I could say the same to you."

"I called you like six times," Theo snapped. "I thought you died."

Thomas glanced over to the bed where he'd left his phone just after getting home and getting too drunk to remember that he'd done that. "Whoops. So, what *are* you doing here?"

"Well, I *was* trying to invite you to dinner with Gabi and me, but then you didn't answer, so I got worried," Theo said, casually staring in the opposite direction.

Thomas smiled. "You were worried about me?"

"Don't sound so happy about that."

"I guess I figured you hated me, after the other day." Theo turned to face her, eyes narrowed. "If I was gonna hate you, I would've done it back in third grade when you *shaved my hair while I was sleeping.*"

Thomas laughed. "Oh, right. I forgot about that."

"Yeah, *you* would."

But some of the uneasiness Thomas had felt for the past few days had finally started to ebb, and he pulled Theo into a hug.

Theo went rigid. "Why are you touching me? Are you sick?"

Thomas pulled away, shaking his head. "No, just a little

tipsy."

Theo stared back at her like he barely recognized her, and Thomas supposed that was to be expected. Even given their family's general allergy to physical affection, Thomas had always been particularly distant in that respect. Part of it was the way that men weren't supposed to do that sort of thing, and she'd always felt like she needed to prove her manliness to keep from being discovered, and part of it was just guilt. Guilt that she'd never really been the brother that Theo needed, the kind of brother who'd stand up for him against their family and keep him from getting hurt. She'd always just been a coward who was too afraid to make noise or be seen.

But somehow, she didn't feel so afraid anymore.

With a deep sigh, Thomas said, "Theo, I'm sorry. Really sorry. About everything, but especially about the way I've treated Gabi. I—I really am happy for you, and he seems like a great guy, and I'm sorry I haven't been more supportive."

Theo blinked back at him before saying, "Yeah, I know."

"You know?"

"I mean, I knew you didn't have a personal vendetta against Gabi or anything," Theo said. "I figured it was something else. I just feel really protective of him, so I'm sorry for losing it on you."

"No, you didn't. I mean, it's not like you said anything out of line. I deserved it."

"Comparing you to ā mā?" Theo said. "You're nothing like that. I never would've even had the guts to date Gabi if you hadn't been so supportive of me back then."

Thomas sat down on the couch, head in her hands. "Theo?"

"What?"

Thomas looked up, but her eyes burned, and humiliation washed over her at the realization that she was literally crying in front of her little brother. But she also didn't want to waste what might be her last chance to clear the air between them.

"When you mentioned that you were thinking about

marrying Gabi—I'm sorry about the way I reacted. It really had nothing to do with him, so I just—I'm sorry."

"So…what *does* it have to do with?"

Thomas shook her head. "Don't worry about it. It's not your problem."

"The hell it isn't," Theo snapped. "In case your time in the big city made you forget, you realize I'm still your brother, right? You can talk to me. I want to help."

He said it with so much matter-of-fact conviction that it basically slapped Thomas across the face as she realized she hadn't actually looked at it that way before. *She* was the older brother. It was her job to make sure that Theo was taken care of, that his life was together, that he was building up to a bright future. It never occurred to Thomas that it could work the other way around.

Before she could stop it, tears spilled down her face as she raced to wipe them away.

"Thomas?" Theo said, his voice soft as he sat down next to her. "What is it? Are you okay?"

Laughing, Thomas wiped the rest of the tears away. "You're right. I *had* forgotten. Thank you for reminding me."

She looked over at Theo to find him staring back at her for a moment before frowning and saying, "So are you gonna tell me what happened, or…?"

"Let's just say, a friend made me realize that I was just jealous, and I was taking that out on you and Gabi."

"Jealous?"

Thomas sighed. "Just promise me that no matter who you add to the family, you're not gonna forget about me, okay?"

Theo rolled his eyes. "Obviously not. There are very few people in the world nearly as annoying as you."

Thomas smiled. "Thank you."

Leaning back against the couch, Theo said, "So, about this friend… Is this like…a special kind of friend?"

Thomas groaned. "I wanted him to be, but that was never gonna happen."

"Why not?"

"He's with the love of his life, and to be clear, that's not me."

Theo just shook his head. "Well, obviously he has shit taste and doesn't deserve you. You'll find someone who appreciates you."

And Thomas wanted to believe that, but it was pretty hard to internalize when she could barely appreciate herself.

"Anyway," Theo said, getting to his feet, "do you want to get dinner with Gabi and me tonight? Beats drinking alone, I think."

Thomas smiled. "You would be right. Just let me go change."

She went rifling through her clothes to find something that had less of a "getting drunk alone" vibe and more of a "night out" vibe. Considering she and Theo were still working their way up to being fully open and honest with each other, she didn't want to hit him with something too jarring, but she also wanted to wear something comfortable and something that made her feel alive. Considering all the time she'd spent moping around, it only seemed fair that she should get to throw on something that made her feel a little more vibrant.

She settled on a pair of fitted black and blue color-block jeans and a loose black blouse. She felt queer enough to be hot but not get hate-crimed on the subway, and that felt like a pretty good compromise.

Theo waited for her by the door, looking bored as he scrolled through his phone. He looked up as Thomas headed for him, but he didn't make any weird comments or stare at her awkwardly, so she took that as a good sign.

Then a loud knock cut through Thomas's thoughts.

"Who's that?" Theo asked.

Thomas shrugged. "I don't know. I don't really have a lot of friends."

Theo laughed as Thomas headed for the door. She pulled it open to find the last person she expected to see on the other side.

"Brian?" Thomas said. "I-I thought I told you we shouldn't see each other anymore."

He looked a little sloppy, his hair windswept and his breathing uneven, like he'd just been out for a jog, but the sight of him was still enough to get Thomas's heartbeat racing, and God, she hated that.

"I'm sorry," Brian said. "Mia, I know—the last thing I want is to make you uncomfortable, but we really need to talk."

"Who is it?" Theo asked, half-peeking over Thomas's shoulder.

Thomas rolled his eyes, turning back to Theo just long enough to say, "*The friend.*"

"The friend?" Brian repeated.

But Theo just said, "Ooooohhhh, the *friend,*" forcing Thomas to resist the urge to slap him.

"I'm sorry, Brian," Thomas said, "but now's a bad time. You see, my brother's in town, and we were just about to go out, so—"

"No, no!" Theo said. "Actually, Gabi and I would love a night alone. I mean, God, inviting yourself to your little brother's date night? So inconsiderate of you."

Thomas scowled. "You can't be seri—"

"Anyway, I should be going!" Theo said, dramatically sliding over the threshold and out into the hallway. "Good luck!"

And then he disappeared down the hall at a leopard's pace.

Thomas turned back to Brian, his heart in his throat.

"If you're busy," Brian started, "I can come back later, but—"

"No, it's fine," Thomas said, holding the door open. Any excuses he could've made would only be insulting at this point. "Come in."

Brian flashed her a quick smile as he stepped inside.

But once Thomas closed the door, she just stood there like a misplaced mannequin. She couldn't figure out what to do with her hands, and she was far too antsy to sit. Finally, she just crossed her arms over her chest and said, "So what did you want to talk about?"

Thomas turned to find Brian looking just as nauseous as she felt, any confidence from earlier gone without a trace. The way he fidgeted as he awkwardly shifted from one foot to the other, hands drifting behind his back before moving up to his hair and down again, actually eased Thomas's nerves a little. If Brian looked this out of his depth, at least Thomas didn't have to feel so alone in her awkwardness.

Finally, Brian looked at her and said, "I'm really sorry. I mean, about making things so awkward for you, and not realizing what I was putting you through. When you said you wanted to keep things platonic, I really thought you meant it, and—"

Thomas waved him off. "I *did* mean it when I said it, so it's really not your fault, and you don't have to apologize. I didn't ask for space because I was mad at you. I just—I just need to be able to move on, you know?"

"I know, but I don't want that."

Thomas's jaw dropped. "You don't *want* me to be able to live my life?"

Brian winced, quickly shaking his head. "Sorry, wait, that came out wrong. I meant—look, Anna's wonderful. Like really, truly wonderful. And she's beautiful, and smart—"

"Brian, I don't need you to tell me how much better your girlfriend is than me."

"What? No! That's not—" Brian groaned, running a hand through his hair. "I'm sorry. I'm doing this all wrong."

"Look, I get it. I really do. And for what it's worth, I really did value our friendship, and I'm sorry to end it this way. I really am."

Brian took a step closer, and Thomas resisted the urge to step back. What was she even doing? Why had she even let him in? Because now, standing this close, Thomas could barely catch her breath.

Then Brian said, "I could be happy with Anna. Really

happy, even. Maybe for a year, or a few years, but that would be all there was for us. In ten years, I'd wake up and realize I'd settled for dry chicken and business talk and shoe prints all over our floors."

Thomas stared back at him blankly. "You've lost me."

Brian just laughed, shaking his head again. "What I mean is, you made me realize that I don't want what my parents have. I mean, they're happy, sure, and maybe I'd learn to be okay with all of that, too. But I don't want easy. I don't want to be with someone just because I know we can make it work. I want to be with someone who challenges me and makes me think about things I'd never think about and see meaning in colors that just look like colors. Someone who isn't just gonna drag me along with them wherever they're going but who wants to go somewhere together, wherever the hell we end up. And I don't know about forever, or twenty years from now, but I want someone who makes me feel...well, who makes me *feel*, and who makes me want to keep feeling and growing and changing so we can keep growing together, not get stuck in some pasty suburban house with two-point-five kids, wondering where we lost ourselves. And I'm not gonna find any of that with Anna, but if you'll let me, I'd want to try to find it with you."

The room fell into silence, the two of them locked in a standstill, but neither of them making a move.

Then Brian said, "Please say something."

Thomas shook her head, but all that she could manage to say was, "You know I'm not a woman, right?"

Brian just laughed. "Yeah, you know, the whole 'ally' thing just never really worked for me. I might need to try a new label."

Thomas smiled. "Well, lucky for you, you already keep very queer company. And, I mean, if you really want to try some things out, see what you like, we can always get creative or—"

Then Brian closed the space separating them, pulling Thomas's face to his and letting their lips meet. And everything about it felt natural, the way their bodies melded together, the warmth of Brian's skin.

Then Thomas pulled away, a small smile tugging at her lips. "Thomas," she said. "My name is Thomas. I figured you should probably know that."

"Oh!" Brian said, his smile growing. "Is that your final form?"

Thomas pressed her lips together. "I don't know yet. But you can call me that for now, and I'll let you know if it changes."

Brian smiled. "Well, then, I'm looking forward to it, Thomas."

So Thomas kissed him again.

29

Brian had never quite hated the existence of Mondays as much as he did when Thomas finally shoved him away and said, "It's getting late. You should probably go."

"It's not that late," Brian said, but he already knew how weak of an excuse that was when it was nearly midnight on a worknight.

So he let himself savor a few more kisses before disentangling himself from Thomas and heading home, no matter how much it pained him to do it. It probably wouldn't even be that long before he got to see her again, but the thought was still agonizing, and as he slipped into bed for the night, he found himself dreaming of her again, only this time, she'd traded the sexy Totoro costume for form-fitting jeans. Not that it really mattered when he tore through them all the same.

After getting home late, he woke up even later, quickly leaping out of bed and getting dressed so he could stand a chance of making it to work on time. As he stopped to brush his teeth, he noticed that his lips were still a little pink, a holdover stain from the lipstick Thomas had been wearing the night before. He licked his lower lip, savoring the sweetness of Thomas's kiss a moment longer before finishing his morning ritual.

Just before he could blow out of the apartment, he found Pearl in the kitchen making coffee, and given he hadn't seen her since game night, he let himself put work on the backburner for a moment.

"Morning," he said, and she looked up and flashed him a smile. "I take it you and Dustin made up."

Pearl rolled her eyes. "Obviously. He's a saint. I told you, bi guys are the best."

"Oh, well, then do I have good news for you."

Pearl raised an eyebrow, and Brian just laughed.

"So, Mia and I talked last night," Brian said, "and we maybe came to the conclusion that I am bisexual, and also that we're into each other, which is no longer a problem since I broke up with Anna—"

"Woah, woah, woah," Pearl said, waving a hand through the air. "I spend two nights at a hotel and missed an entire telenovela playing out?"

Brian rolled his eyes. "Whatever. The point is, Mia and I are together now. Well, we didn't officially label anything, but you know, you get the point. Also, her name is Thomas."

Pearl just stared back at him blankly, and Brian couldn't help but smile.

"Also, I owe you an apology," Brian continued. "I probably should've just listened to you from the jump and saved us all a boatload of problems."

Pearl sighed, casually waving him off. "Please, if I can piss off even Dustin, it's probably better you don't listen to me."

Brian laughed. "Well, the point still stands. I really appreciate you trying to steer me straight—or bi, I guess?"

"Oh great, you've already reached bi pun level."

"I just want to say thanks for being such a good friend," Brian said. "I'm really lucky to have you."

Pearl rolled her eyes, even as a small smile tugged at her lips. "Yeah, well, you're not bad to have around either, Ramirez. Also, I'm looking forward to getting to know your new boyfriend." Pearl paused. "...girlfriend?"

"I guess I will let you know when we actually make things official," Brian said. "So everything's fine with you and Dustin, right? I'm not gonna come home to the apartment on fire or anything?"

"Shut up. You know Dustin doesn't really *fight*," Pearl said, but a slight blush rose in her cheeks as she raised her coffee mug to cover it. "Anyway, things are fine. I mean, I was the problem, so I just had to swallow my pride and apologize, and everything's all good now."

Brian smiled. "You're not a *problem*, Pearl. You could stand to be a little less competitive, though."

Pearl smirked. "Yeah, Dustin said the same thing. Must be a bi thing."

Brian rolled his eyes.

"Aren't you late?"

Brian winced. "Uh, yeah, talk later!"

"You *found* a sponsor?" Ella exclaimed, her eyes wide and practically bursting with stars.

"I mean, it's still tentative," Brian said, but he doubted Ella was even listening anymore.

Thomas had mentioned that his company might be able to sponsor the ball somewhere between makeout sessions the night before, so when Brian saw Ella stressing about how to find a discount DJ on Bluesky, he figured he should mention it before she got lost in her spiral.

Her voice came out in a small whisper, like her disbelief had sucked the volume right out of her words. "This changes everything…"

"I mean, it definitely will once it's confirmed…"

He felt a little bad laying on the false hope if everything fell through, but considering the overwhelming stress Ella had been under for a while now, and the way she seemed about ready to break down crying when he showed up late, he figured he owed her something, at the very least. Thomas seemed pretty confident they could make this work, though, so hopefully there wouldn't be any bad news on the horizon.

"Okay, I need you to put me in contact with these people,"

Ella said. "If we start reworking the plans now, we can probably salvage this whole thing. And then we have to work on getting the word out."

"Yeah, okay," Brian said, pulling out his phone and sending a text to Thomas asking for Day's contact. Then he followed it up with, *Also, do you want to do lunch later?*

He knew he should probably keep his mind on work, but he figured he'd only be more distracted if he didn't get his fix now. At least if he got to spend an hour with Thomas, that should hold him over until he got off work.

"Also, Brian," Ella said, drawing his attention back up from his phone, "I know this internship is a little outside of your comfort zone, but I appreciate all the time you've put into it this summer. I know it doesn't seem like much, but there are a lot of people who use our services to find community and find themselves, and you've really done a lot to help them get there, so thank you."

Brian couldn't help the smile spreading across his face. As far removed as this internship was from his original career goals, he had to admit that he didn't regret taking it. At the very least, he felt a lot better about this decision than he could've ever felt talking corporate interests with Pete.

"Thanks for having me on," Brian said.

His phone vibrated, and he glanced down at the screen to find a text from Thomas.

I'd love to do lunch! Also, here's Day's info.

Another text came in with Day's contact attached, so he forwarded it to Ella. If there was any hesitance on their side, as far as whether or not the company was interested in sponsoring the ball, he was confident Ella could persuade them.

After Ella released him for lunch, Brian decided to make a quick phone call before meeting up with Thomas.

Noah answered on the second ring, voice far too enthusiastic as he said, "Soooo, how'd it go?"

"How did what go?"

"Your girlfriend problems, obviously."

And Brian should've known once Noah answered on the second ring that he should be bracing himself for nosy prying, but he was in too good of a mood to let that drag him down.

"Fine. Don't worry about it."

"Boo, you're boring," Noah jeered.

"Anyway, I just wanted to call and ask if you've ever wanted to go to a masquerade ball? Seems like the kind of thing you'd like. Plus, it's in New York, so you'd get a chance to see the city if you want."

The line went quiet for a moment. Then Noah said, "What'd you do? Sell your soul to the Devil?"

"*What*? No! It's just an event I'm putting together with my internship. The ticket money goes to helping the queer community, so I just thought I'd let you know in case you wanted to come."

"Oh, I see. Yup, that sounds aesthetic as fuck. I'm in. I gotta tell Devin," Noah said. Then his voice turned vaguely diabolical as he said, "Are *you* bringing anyone?"

"Okay, bye, Noah."

"YOU'RE NO FUN!"

Brian hung up the phone, a feeling of satisfaction washing over him. Yeah, he could definitely get used to that. He looked down at his screen to find a new text from Thomas.

I'm so sorry, but I'm gonna have to take a raincheck on lunch. I think Kris wants to talk.

A little pit of disappointment settled in Brian's stomach, but he pushed it away. The future ahead of him was infinite, and he'd get more than enough chances to see Thomas, wherever life chose to take them.

He texted back a quick, *Good luck*! Then he messaged Ella to ask if she wanted anything from the deli. Even if he couldn't have lunch with the love of his life, this was New York City, and he didn't have to go particularly far to find good company.

30

Five minutes after Brian texted asking to have lunch, Thomas mentally checked out of the office.

With things going well with the app, he'd finally been cleared to actually do some coding. They were just working on setting up a desktop landing space for the time being, with all the bells and whistles coming later, but even laying out the basics beat coffee runs and sitting in pitch meetings where he never felt like his ideas actually contributed anything.

But the work did little to draw his attention when Brian came into the mix. The night before had been pretty much perfect, and getting to see him again today had Thomas's heart picking up speed every time he thought about it.

So when he put his computer to sleep and turned to leave his cubicle only to find Kris standing a few yards away waiting for him, his brain took a moment to recalibrate.

"Got a minute?" Kris said.

And a part of Thomas wanted to say no, just so he could stay on his current planned track without the disruption throwing everything off, but if Kris actually wanted to talk to him, the last thing he was gonna do was throw that away.

"Yeah, just a second," he said, quickly pulling out his phone to let Brian know he wouldn't be able to make it.

"Day told me you were looking for me," Kris said, voice low. "Also, that you have a boyfriend now or something."

Word traveled fast, since Thomas had only brought that up to Day a couple hours before, when he'd checked in about sponsoring Brian's ball. But now that he knew how close Day and Kris were, he should probably be more aware of what he said to them.

"My trillion calls didn't tell you I was looking for you?" Thomas said, hoping to inject some levity into the stale air.

Kris just stared back at him with the sort of lifeless stare that Thomas would never have associated with Kris before.

"Are you okay?" Thomas asked.

Kris rolled his eyes, motioning for Thomas to follow him to his office, so Thomas obliged, quietly closing the door behind him as Kris sat down at his desk. His movements lacked the usual flourish, and Thomas couldn't help but notice that his nails weren't even painted.

"I considered texting you, but I needed a vacation from you for a while," Kris said. Then he winced. "Also, I was waiting to come down from my manic episode, so I wouldn't say more things I'd regret."

Thomas smiled, relief bubbling up in his chest. "I'm just glad you're talking to me again. Kris, I'm so, so—"

Kris just waved him off. "Yeah, I know. Don't worry about it."

"What I said about the whole Felix thing—that was so out of line. I never meant to—"

"Yeah, I *know*. It's fine, okay? I'm sorry, too. Don't worry about it."

Thomas just stared blankly back at him for a moment, a knot forming in his stomach. As long as Thomas had known him, Kris was definitely the firecracker anger type. For him to be this dismissive of Thomas's fuck-up felt almost worse than if he'd slammed the door in Thomas's face and told him to go fuck himself.

"If you're mad at me, please just say that," Thomas said.

Kris raised an eyebrow at him. "I just said I'm not."

"Then why are you being so weird?"

Kris stared at him blankly for a moment before frowning. "Sorry. Depression brain fog, I guess."

The knot in Thomas's stomach only grew larger. "Kris, I'm really sorry—"

"Yes, I got that. You said some bitchy things. It's fine, Thomas."

"Not about that," Thomas said. "I mean, I *am* sorry about that, but also for being such a shitty friend. It's just like you said. I make everything about me, and—"

"Oh my God, relax," Kris said. "You don't make *everything* about you, okay? I was just on a bitchy tirade because mania fucks with my head. I mean, you can be a little melodramatic sometimes, but we're in an office full of queers. It's kind of par for the course."

"I just meant, I'm sorry for not checking in with you. I mean, you're my best friend, and I should've been there if you needed me, and I haven't been. I'm sorry."

Kris stared back at him for a moment, but something about his gaze felt less sharp than usual. In fact, if Thomas didn't know better, he'd almost say it looked vulnerable.

Finally, Thomas said, "Are you okay?"

And Kris offered him a small smile in return. "I'll be fine, now that that bitch Felix is gone."

Thomas smiled back. "You should've heard Day. They went *off*. I didn't even know they could get mad like that."

"Oh, you'd be surprised," Kris said. "I'm a little impressed they actually snapped at Felix, though. Kinda seemed like they thought that boy could do no wrong."

"I think they were just being protective of you."

Kris paused, mouth pressing into a thin line. "What did you say?"

Thomas felt a dangerous charged energy waft through the air, like maybe he should backtrack and pretend he'd said something totally different, but finally, he just said, "I mean, they sounded really pissed about the shit he said to you. Is that...a bad thing?"

Kris paused for a moment. Then he said, "I'm gonna tell you something, but if you tell another soul, you're dead to me, you hear that? I'm not giving you a second chance for something like this."

Thomas just raised his hands in surrender. "I mean, if you'd rather nobody knew, maybe you just shouldn't tell—"

"Fine, I'll say it. You don't have to pry it out of me," Kris said with a dramatic sigh, and Thomas just rolled his eyes. "Anyway, I'm in love with Day. I thought it would go away, but it hasn't."

"I—wait," Thomas said, "I thought you were aromantic."

"I *am*. I'm just on the part of the spectrum where there's this much romantic attraction." He held his forefinger and thumb up to show a sliver of space between them. "And unfortunately, it's for Day. It's humiliating, I know."

Thomas laughed. "It's not humiliating. It's sweet. You two have known each other forever, right? They showed me the Tiana and Lottie photo."

Kris's face fell into abject misery. "Yeah, but that's the thing, right? If there was any hope for us, it would've happened by now. Instead, they dated Felix."

Kris's voice broke on Felix's name, and Thomas's heart broke with it. He'd never seen Kris so messed up before, and he'd definitely never seen Kris messed up over a romantic prospect. He was the type of person who bounced from one person's bed to the next like breathing. Or, at least, Thomas had thought he was.

"Anyway," Kris said, idly waving him off, "that's why I've been so, well, awful lately. I mean, Felix was obviously a *problem*, but it's also Day. It's hard for me not to be...*weird* around them, I guess. Sorry for taking that out on you."

Thomas shook his head. "It's okay. Thank you for telling me."

Kris gave him a forced smile. "Yeah, well, I'm kind of shit

at opening up to people, and I hate the vulnerability thing, but my therapist seems to think it's good for me. Go figure."

Thomas smiled. "Well, if you ever want to talk, I'm here. We can even just shit on Felix all day if you want. He did always have bad vibes, and you know his eyeliner? Always uneven."

Kris laughed, which at least sounded a little more genuine. "Thanks, Thomas. You're a good friend. I love you, bitch."

"I love you, too."

By the time he finished talking to Kris, Thomas only had about twenty minutes to grab lunch and get back to work, but he made sure to squeeze in a quick call to Brian to apologize for canceling and invite him out for dinner later.

He was surprised by how much easier it was to sit at his desk and get work done, now that the office felt a little less hostile. Actually, between Felix's departure and the fact that Lola and Damien ultimately left right after "in solidarity," the office was pretty quiet, but Thomas didn't mind it. At least he didn't have to worry about competing for the limited hiring budget at the end of the summer.

At first, he'd been a little worried about what came next, between his job and Brian and drag, but he had to admit that he didn't totally hate a little spontaneity. As long as he had his people with him, he was sure they could figure it out.

EPILOGUE

BRIAN

"You can just improvise if you get bored," Thomas said, sprinkling some sugar into the pot.

Brian leaned over their shoulder, watching as they slowly stirred the red bean paste. Inviting Thomas over to make breakfast for Pearl, Dustin, and him was probably the single greatest idea he'd ever had. Not just because it meant their kitchen now smelled heavenly at just after nine in the morning, but also because it meant he got to enjoy two of his favorite things at the very start of his day.

Sliding his arms around Thomas's waist, he leaned his head against their shoulder, gently tracing kisses along their neck.

Thomas laughed. "What are you doing?"

"Improvising."

"You know what I meant."

Summer was just about over, and Brian would be heading back to Denver next week to start his final semester, so he knew he needed to cherish these moments while he had them. Of course, once the semester ended, he'd have to figure out where he wanted to go, and New York might be a viable option if he could pin down a decent job. As much fun as it was living with

Pearl and Dustin, he felt bad mooching off them long term.

"Do *not* distract the chef," Pearl snapped, stepping into the kitchen. "We are *hungry*."

Thomas turned the stove off, pushing the pot to one of the back burners. "I'm almost done, though it'd probably be easier if Brian was actually helping like he said he would."

Brian winced, letting go of Thomas. "Okay, okay, what do you need me to do."

"Go grab a pan and the batter," Thomas said.

"Yeah, okay."

Pearl smirked. "Yeah, I like him better when you're around."

Brian turned toward her, a bowl of pancake batter in his hands. "Watch me dump this on your head."

Thomas's eyes widened. "Don't waste my food!"

Brian grinned at them. "Sorry, babe."

"So," Pearl said, leaning against the counter and flashing Thomas a smile, "will you be staying for dinner?"

Brian rolled his eyes. "No, we're going out."

Pearl pouted. "Really?"

Thomas accepted the bowl of batter from Brian, quickly pouring some out into the new pan. "My brother's in town, so we're getting dinner with him and his boyfriend. But don't worry, I'll come back and cook for you again."

Pearl grinned widely, throwing her arms around Thomas and squeezing tight. "Ah! I knew you were the better choice!"

"*Pearl*," Brian hissed, "Thomas doesn't do hugs. Back off."

Thomas smiled. "It's okay. I think they're actually starting to grow on me."

Pearl turned to Brian, flipping him off. "See? You're the only one who doesn't appreciate me."

"I appreciate you!" Brian snapped before adding under his breath, "You know, usually."

He slipped up next to Thomas, draping an arm around their waist. "So, need any more distractions while you work?"

Thomas grinned at him. "Nope. I'm good. Go set the

table."

Ordinarily, the idea of meeting his significant other's family would probably be enough to have Brian running for the hills, but Thomas assured him he had nothing to worry about.

"It's just my brother and his boyfriend," she said. "We'll work out a plan before you meet my parents."

Still, despite the reassurances, he was a little anxious. Not so much that things would end disastrously, but considering they'd only been together about a month, the thought of family awkwardness throwing a wrench in their relationship had his nerves worked up. Especially with the impending long distance between them, the last thing he needed was to sour things before they could even really get started.

But as they stepped off the train, Thomas slipped her hand into Brian's, and he felt some of his nerves settle.

Approaching the restaurant, he immediately recognized Theo from the night he'd confessed his feelings for Thomas, and that meant the brown kid next to him must be Gabi. Even from a distance, Brian could see what Thomas meant about them complimenting each other. Despite having totally opposite energy, they looked like they flowed cleanly around each other, like they were pushing and pulling each other like the tides, just enough to keep both of them upright.

"Theo!" Thomas said as she and Brian joined them in front of the shop. "This is Brian. Brian, this is my brother, Theo."

Theo turned to Brian with a scrutinizing look before holding out his hand like he wasn't sure he wanted to talk to Brian at all.

Brian shook it apprehensively, saying, "Um, hi."

"If you're just stringing Thomas along, I'll kill you."

"Theo," Thomas said, sounding disappointed but not surprised. She turned to Brian. "He's joking. You know, mostly."

Brian just smiled. "It's okay."

Thomas turned to Gabi and paused, her mouth opening

and closing again. Finally, she said, "Hi, Gabi. It's good to see you."

Gabi smiled. "Yeah, you, too."

"Okay," Theo said, "let's go."

Theo and Gabi picked the restaurant—a little ramen shop with a lucky cat waving its paw from the window—but Brian couldn't complain.

"So, wait, let me get this straight," Theo said as they all slid into their booths. "You two have only been going out for a month, and he already has you cooking breakfast for his roommates? What are you, some glorified housewife?"

Thomas shook her head. "No, no, I volunteered. I've been kind of out of practice, so I figured I should get back to it before Mom and Dad kill me."

"I'll cook for you next time," Brian said. "I have a few recipes I've been meaning to revisit."

"Oh, you cook?" Gabi said. Then he turned a knowing smirk toward Theo. "Your parents'll love that."

Theo just playfully shoved Gabi's shoulder. "Shush. Don't give him any ammo."

"It's fine," Thomas said. "Brian'll grow on you."

Theo scoffed. "We'll see about that."

But there wasn't nearly as much animosity there as Brian had first expected, so maybe Thomas was right. Either way, he felt pretty confident Thomas's family wasn't about to let his life get boring, so maybe he should count that as a win. And as far as drawbacks went, an over-protective little brother wasn't anything he couldn't handle.

After all, if Brian had his way, he'd make sure no harm ever came to Thomas, too, but maybe he could just share that responsibility with Theo. That way he'd know there was someone on this coast to look out for her, even while they were apart.

As dinner came to an end, Thomas watched Gabi slip something to Theo, who immediately stood up and said, "I'm going to the bathroom. Bye!"

Thomas shook Brian's arm. "*Brian!*"

"What?" Brian said, taking a sip of his water. Then he caught sight of Theo rushing away from the booth, and his eyes widened. "He's gonna pay the check, isn't he?"

"Go!" Thomas squealed, pushing Brian out of the booth.

Brian let out a string of curses as he raced toward the register.

Gabi winced, watching them go. "It's like an Olympic sport."

Thomas smiled. "Oh, you'd better believe it. And the injuries involved can be much worse."

"Um, Thomas?" Gabi said.

Thomas tilted his head. "What?"

"Um, nothing."

Ah, and there it was. The all but lethal awkwardness. He'd managed to spend a little bit of time with Gabi the last time he and Theo were in town, but Theo had been extra cautious not to leave them alone together, so this was the first time Thomas was experiencing it in full force.

Gabi looked down at the table before saying, "I guess I just wanted to say that I'm sorry if I did anything to make things weird between us."

Thomas shook his head. "No, you're fine."

Gabi looked up. "I—well, it's just that Theo cares about you a lot, and I hated seeing how much it messed him up when you two weren't talking, so if I did something—"

Thomas smiled. "It's not your fault, Gabi. Really. And you don't have to worry about Theo and me. I'm happy for you both, and I'm glad you have each other."

Gabi smiled back. "Thank you."

Brian and Theo came back to the booth, Brian grinning

while a scowl spread across Theo's face.

Thomas smirked at Theo and said, "I take it you lost."

Theo just shot him a glare in reply.

"You'll just have to be quicker next time," Brian said.

"Oh, no, Brian, don't declare war," Thomas said.

But Theo shook his head. "Too late, bitch. You better watch yourself next time, 'cause you're going *down*."

"Mia, honey, you're testing my patience and not in a good way."

"What's the *good* way?"

"What, you never try to see how long you can hold out? That's basic self-care."

Thomas rolled his eyes as he stepped out of the bathroom to find Kris and Day sitting on the couch waiting for him. The plan was to finish getting ready for the show once they got to the comedy club, but Thomas still wanted to make sure everything was fitting properly and whatnot before they left.

Considering the last time Thomas had worn his sexy Howl costume, it had only stayed on for maybe thirty minutes before Brian was ready to rip it off, he figured everything should fit fine. But given this would be the last show Brian got to come to before returning to Denver, he'd rather be safe than sorry.

"Brian's not even here yet," Thomas said, plopping down on the couch. "No need to rush me."

"Oh, definite need," Kris said, passing him a shot. "It's against my religion to drink without the whole team ready."

"Since when?" Day said.

"Since like five minutes ago."

Day rolled their eyes, but the gesture read pretty affectionately. Thomas wasn't the best at reading people, but he couldn't help but notice that the dynamic between Kris and Day had become a lot more organic once Felix was out of the picture, like whatever walls had formed between them had completely shattered. Day still hadn't come around to the Tiana and Lottie performance Kris kept insisting on, but it seemed like maybe he was wearing them down.

Kris raised his shot glass. "To our show, to our company, and to Thomas's new boo thang. May you get the goods in more ways than one."

Day chuckled, and Thomas just rolled his eyes as they all clinked glasses.

"Why do you have to keep making this weird?" Thomas asked before downing his shot.

"I'm just happy for you, baby."

"Mhm."

A knock sounded at the door, and Thomas wasted no time getting up to answer it. Brian's eyes widened as the door swung open, a smile creeping across his face.

"See something you like?" Thomas asked, doing a quick twirl so Brian could get a better look.

"Like you even need to ask that."

Kris shouted from the couch, "Put your money where your mouth is, sweetie! Or, you know, your mouth where your eyes are. Whatever."

"You are insufferable, you know that?" Day said without the slightest hint of animosity to their tone.

Thomas just turned back to Brian and said, "Okay, ignore them. You ready to go? Or do you need a drink first? I know this isn't exactly your scene."

Though, Thomas had to admit that Brian definitely seemed to be growing into it.

"I don't mind. I like stepping out of my comfort zone," Brian said. "Besides, I'm always comfortable when I'm with you."

Thomas grinned. "Well, don't get too comfortable. I have some surprises waiting for you later."

Brian just smiled, leaning in to kiss him. "Can't wait."

EMERY LEE

is the award-winning author of MEET CUTE DIARY and CAFÉ CON LYCHEE. E's the founder of #Transbooks365, a community hashtag made to celebrate books by and about trans people. Coming from a university background of creative writing, e's gone on to write entertainment news, edit literary magazines, and work as a trade book reviewer. Outside of novels, e's written interactive fiction, short stories, and webcomics. Eir books have received starred reviews, been featured in ALA's rainbow booklist, and been translated into multiple languages. Drawing inspiration from anime, pop punk music, and eir own cultures and identities, e seeks to tell multi-layered stories about complex characters that challenge conventional power structures and make room for marginalized readers across fandom spaces.

Find em online at emeryleebooks.com.

The team who helped make **DON'T DRAG THIS OUT** possible are:

Edited by Alex Abraham
Copy edited by Gabriel Hargrave
Proofread by Lion's Tooth Editing
Cover design by M. Ishii Arts
Cover illustration by M. Ishii Arts
Interior Layout by Kai Wen

And a special thanks to the Kickstarter backers who helped get this project fully funded ahead of release. This book would not exist without you!

Next by Emery Lee:

Be Gay, Organize Crime

A [killer] found family romcom

Shoot your shot 2026